D0881675

10 00

by John Fante

The Saga of Arturo Bandini:
Wait Until Spring, Bandini (1938, 1983)
Ask the Dust (1939, 1980)
Full of Life (1952)
Dreams from Bunker Hill (1982)

Dago Red (1940)
Brotherhood of the Grape (1977)
The Wine of Youth: Selected Stories
    of John Fante (1985)

JOHN FANTE

THE WINE OF YOUTH

SELECTED STORIES

BLACK SPARROW PRESS
SANTA BARBARA—1985

THE WINE OF YOUTH: SELECTED STORIES OF JOHN FANTE.
Copyright © 1940 by John Fante. Copyright © 1985 by Joyce Fante.

All rights reserved. Printed in the United States of America. No part
of this book may be used or reproduced in any manner whatsoever
without written permission except in the case of brief quotations
embodied in critical articles and reviews. For information address
Black Sparrow Press, P.O. Box 3993, Santa Barbara, CA 93130.

LIBRARY OF CONGRESS CATALOGING IN PUBLICATION DATA

Fante, John, 1909-
    The wine of youth.

    I. Title.
PS3511.A594W5   1985   813'.52   84-20454
ISBN 0-87685-583-4
ISBN 0-87685-584-2 (signed hard)
ISBN 0-87685-582-6 (pbk.)

For Carey McWilliams and Ross Wills —

good friends, evil companions

Contents

Dago Red

Later Stories

Dago Red

A Kidnaping in the Family

THERE WAS AN OLD TRUNK in my mother's bedroom. It was the oldest trunk I ever saw. It was one of those trunks with a round lid like a fat man's belly. Away down in this trunk, beneath wedding linen that was never used because it was wedding linen, and silverware that was never used because it was a wedding present, and beneath all kinds of fancy ribbons, buttons, birth certificates, beneath all this was a box containing family pictures. My mother wouldn't permit anyone to open this trunk, and she hid the key. But one day I found the key. I found it hidden under a corner of the rug.

On spring afternoons that year I would come home from school and find my mother working in the kitchen. Her arms would be limp and white like dry clay from toil, her hair thin and dry against her head, and her eyes sunken and large and sad in their sockets.

The picture! I would think. Oh, that picture in the trunk!

When my mother wasn't looking I would steal into her bedroom, lock the door, and open the trunk. There were many pictures down there, and I loved all of them, but there was one alone which my fingers ached to clutch and my eyes longed to see when I found my mother that way — it was a picture of her taken a week before she married my father.

Such a picture!

She sat on the arm of a plush chair in a white dress spilling down to her toes. The sleeves were puffy and frothy: they were very elegant sleeves. There was scarcely any neck to the dress, and at her throat was a cameo on a thin gold chain. Her hat was the biggest hat I ever saw in my life. It went entirely around her

11

shoulders like a white parasol, the brim dipping slightly, and covering most of her hair except a dark mound in back. But I could see the green, heavy eyes, so big that not even that hat could hide them.

I would stare at that strange picture, kissing it and crying over it, happy because once it had been true. And I remember an afternoon when I took it down to the creek bank, set it upon a stone, and prayed to it. And in the kitchen was my mother, imprisoned behind pots and pans: a woman no longer the lovely woman in the picture.

And so it was with me, a kid home from school.

Other times I did other things. I would stand at the dresser mirror with the picture at my ear, facing the round mirror. A sheepishness, a shivering delight would possess me. How unbelievable this grand lady, this queen! And I remember that I would be speechless.

My mother in the kitchen at that moment was not my mother. I wouldn't have it. Here was my mother, the lady in the big hat. Why couldn't I remember anything about her? Why did I have to be so young when I was born? Why couldn't I have been born at the age of fourteen? I couldn't remember a thing. When had my mother changed? What caused the change? How did she grow old? I made up my mind that if I ever saw my mother as beautiful as she was in the picture I would immediately ask her to marry me. She had never refused me anything, and I felt she would not refuse me as a husband. I elaborated on this determination, even discovering a way to dispose of my father: my mother could divorce him. If the Church would not grant a divorce, we could wait and be married as soon as my father died. I searched my catechism and prayer book for a law which stated that mothers could not marry their sons. I was satisfied to find nothing on the subject.

One evening I slipped the picture under my waist and took it to my father. He sat reading the paper on the front porch.

"Look," I said. "Guess who?"

He looked at it through a haze of cigar smoke. His indifference annoyed me. He examined it as though it were a bug, or something; a piece of stale cake, or something. His eyes slid up

12

and down the picture three times, then crosswise three times. Turning it over, he examined the back. The composition interested him more than the subject, and I had hoped his eyes would pop and that he would shout with excitement.

"It's Mamma!" I said. "Don't you recognize her?"

He looked at me wearily. "Put it back where you found it," he said, picking up his newspaper.

"But it's Mamma!"

"Good God!" he said. "I know who it is! I'm the man who married her."

"But look!"

"Go away," he said.

"But, Papa! Look!"

"Go away. I'm reading."

I wanted to hit him. I was embarrassed and sad. Something happened at that moment and the picture was never so wonderful again. It became another picture — just a picture. I seldom looked at it again, and after that evening I never opened my mother's trunk and burrowed for treasure at the bottom.

Before her marriage my mother was Maria Scarpi. She was the daughter of Giuseppe and Stella Scarpi. They were peasants from Naples. Giuseppe Scarpi — he was a shoemaker. He and his wife came to Denver from Italy. My mother, Maria Scarpi, was born there in Denver. She was the fourth child. With her brothers and sisters she went to the Sisters' school. Then she went to a public high school for three years. But this public high school wasn't like the Sisters' school, and she didn't like it. Her two brothers and four sisters married after completing high school.

But Maria Scarpi would not marry. She told her people marriage did not interest her. What she wanted was to become a nun. This shocked the whole family. Her brothers and sisters thought such an ambition didn't make sense. What about children? What about home, and a nice husband, a fine man like Paul Carnati? And to all these questions the woman who became my mother put her nose in the air and held to her monastic ambitions. She was a rebel, and her brothers and sisters brought all sorts of possible suitors to the house in an effort to persuade her to get over her foolishness. But Maria Scarpi was cold and mean, even

13

refusing to speak to them. Hearing voices downstairs, she would lock herself in the bedroom and stay there until they went away.

Paul Carnati owned a bakery. He made lots of money, he had a lot of good ideas, and he was crazy about my mother. One day he drove up to the Scarpi house in a brand-new buggy with rubber tires and a fine young horse pulling it. This Carnati had so much money that he was actually going to give the horse and buggy to my mother for nothing. My mother wouldn't look at it; she wouldn't even come downstairs, and Paul Carnati went away so angry and insulted he never came back again. He carried his grief further by charging the Scarpi family twice as much for bread, until they had to quit buying from him; and, to top it all off, he furiously married somebody else. Italians called this a spite marriage.

My mother told me of her first meeting with my father. It was in 1910. It was in August of that year, on the feast day of Saint Rocco, the powerful patron saint of all Italians. On that great day the Italians lined the streets of the North Side, and down the middle of the street passed the gaudy parade, with three complete bands and the Sons of Saint Rocco in their red uniforms with white plumes in their hats. The Knights of Columbus were there, and they had a band, and the Sons of Little Italy were there with their band. In fact, everybody who counted was there, including a lot of Americans who didn't count but who came down just to look and laugh, because they thought feast days on the North Side were amusing.

The parade moved down Osage Street to Belmont, and east on Belmont to St. Stephen's Church. My mother stood on the corner of Osage and Belmont, in front of the drugstore, which still stands there, and watched the parade.

She was alone, surrounded by young Italian fellows who had hurried away from the pool-tables in the Star Hall, cues in their hands, hats on the back of their heads. They knew my mother, the young fellows did, they knew all about her. Everybody on the North Side knew Maria Scarpi who wanted to become a nun instead of a wife. She stood with her back to them, detesting them; they were hoodlums, first of the gangster breed which later brought disgrace upon the good name of Italians in Denver.

14

They pretended they were interested in the parade. But they weren't. It was a bluff. What they were interested in was my mother. Here was a peculiar situation, foreign to hoodlums. What could a man say to a girl about to become a nun? They said nothing, not a word. They merely stood there applauding the parade.

There was a commotion in the rear. Somebody was shoving. Nudging this fellow and that, snarling with importance — he was not a big man, so he snarled twice as hard as necessary — he pushed his way through until, lo, who was this before him? This girl under the great hat? Guido Toscana was gay with white wine, but he saw beauty much clearer that way. Puffing a twisted cigar, he halted. The others ignored him. Who the hell did he think he was? They had never seen him before, although they were sure that like themselves he was an Italian.

My mother felt him near, the brim of her hat touching his shoulder. She moved forward. But not too far. The gutter was an inch from her toes.

"Good day!" said Guido Toscana.

"I don't know you," she said.

"Ho!" he said. "Ho ho! My name is Guido Toscana. What is your name?"

He turned and winked at the young men. Their faces froze. My mother's eyes raced along the faces across the street in search of one of her brothers. A drunken man. And she a girl who wanted to become a nun! O dear God, she prayed, please help me! But apparently even God was enjoying this, or He was too busy watching the parade in honor of His sainted Rocco, for He permitted Guido Toscana other liberties. Filling his cheeks with cigar smoke, my future father leaned over and — pouffff! — squirted smoke under the brim of my future mother's hat. The white pungency stung. She gagged, coughed into a small handkerchief. Toscana laughed uproariously, turning to the young men for approbation. They pretended they had not seen. Ah, thought Guido Toscana, so that's it: the Dagos!

My mother had had enough. Clutching her hat, she pushed him aside, broke through the crowd of Italians, and walked rapidly up the street. The Scarpi house was three blocks away. At

15

the end of the block she turned the corner, glancing over her shoulder.

Her breath leaped. He was following her! He had taken off his hat and, dodging through the crowd, he was waving to her, beckoning her to return. She ran then, those two remaining blocks. He too ran.

"Mamma!" screamed Maria Scarpi. "Mamma! Mamma!"

She ascended the six porch steps in one jump. Mamma Scarpi, big and wide as three ordinary mothers, opened the front door and Maria flew inside. The door slammed, the bolt clicked. Guido Toscana came puffing down the street. All was peaceful and quiet when he reached the house. The shades were down and no smoke came from the chimney. The place looked vacant. But he loitered. He would not go away. Up and down he walked like a sentinel before the Scarpi house. Up and down. Up and down. From behind a curtain upstairs peeped the head of Maria Scarpi. Up and down walked Guido Toscana. Up and down.

Fearless Mamma Scarpi opened the front door and stood behind the screen. In a shrill Italian she yelled: "What do you want, you drunken vagabond? Go away from here! Begone!"

"I wish to speak to the young lady," said Guido Toscana.

"Go away from this house, you drunken pig!"

"I am not drunk. I wish to speak to the young lady."

"On your way before I shout for the police, you drunken pig!"

He tried to smile away his fear of the police.

"A word with the young lady, and I will go."

"*Polizia!*" screamed Mamma Scarpi. "*Polizia!*"

Guido Toscana winced, closed his eyes, and made grimaces. He held his palms before his face, as though Mamma Scarpi's screams were bottles aimed at his head.

"*Polizia! Polizia! Polizia!*"

There was a movement at the window upstairs. The shade went up with a squeal and a succession of flappings. The window rose and Maria Scarpi's head appeared.

"Mamma!" she called. "Please don't yell. People will think we're crazy!"

To Guido Toscana her voice was that little girl in the throat of Enrico Caruso.

"Don't yell, Mamma! Let's see what he wants."

"Yes," said the great Mamma. "What do you want, you drunken pig?"

He stood under the window, looked up, and spoke in Italian.

"What is your name?"

A sigh.

"My name is Maria Scarpi."

"Will you marry me?"

Mamma Scarpi was too disgusted.

"Get out of this yard!" she yelled. "Back to the drunken pigs — you drunken pig!"

He was not listening. He opened his mouth and began to sing. There was no stopping him. People returning from the parade gaped in amazement. Mamma Scarpi slammed the door and went inside. My mother, not much for sharp wits, a soft-hearted girl who wanted to become a nun and pray for the sins of the world, was transfixed at the window.

She is still transfixed. She still wonders. And this used to annoy me, a kid home from school.

"I didn't know what to do," she would say. "All those people and all—I felt sorry for him."

"What did he sing?"

"That crazy song, the one he sings when he shaves."

I knew that song. Everybody for blocks around knew it. Every time he stood before a mirror lathering his face I thought of him under a window in Denver a year before I was born. The song was "Mena, Me!"

> Ah, lass, you've hurt me sadly. Oh, sadly.
> My heart is bleeding badly. Yes, badly.
> My life blood's ebbing slowly,
> And I cannot stop the flow.
> Mena, me! Let me be!
> Give a kiss. One kiss. You must do this!
> A little kiss is not amiss.
> Mind you, don't get coquettish,
> What's a little kiss to you?
> See the state you've got me into.
> Have a little pity, do!

17

"What happened after that, Mamma?"

She was sweeping the kitchen floor, stooping to reach the crumbs of coal behind the concave stove legs. I could hear the cracking of her joints as she bent down.

"My brother Joe came home, and he saw your father."

"What did Uncle Joe say?"

"I don't know. I don't remember."

"Yes, you do. What did Uncle Joe say?"

"He laughed."

"Didn't he get sore?"

"No. Not at all."

"I'll bet he was afraid of Papa, wasn't he?"

"Not at all."

"Just the same, I'll bet he was scared to death."

"Have it your own way, then."

"What did Uncle Joe do, if he wasn't sore?"

"He invited your father in."

"Didn't they have a fight, or anything? Didn't Papa lick him, or anything?"

"No. Not at all."

"Did Papa go in?"

"Yes."

"What did you do?"

"I don't remember."

"Yes, you do too."

"It's been so long—I've forgotten."

"No, you haven't. You just won't tell me."

She raised herself, gasping for breath.

"I stayed upstairs in my room for a while, and then Uncle Joe came up and told me to come down. So I did."

"And what happened?"

"Nothing."

"Something *did* happen! What happened?"

"Nothing happened!" she said in exasperation. "Your uncle told me who your father was, and we shook hands. And that's *all!*"

"Is that all?"

"That's all."

"Didn't anything else happen?"

"Your father courted me, and after a few months we were married. That's all."

But I didn't like it that way. I hated it. I wouldn't have it. I couldn't believe it. I wouldn't believe it.

"No sirree!" I said. "It didn't happen like that."

"But it did! Why should I lie to you? There's nothing to hide."

"Didn't he do anything to you? Didn't he kidnap you, or something?"

"I don't remember being kidnaped."

"But you *were* kidnaped!"

She sat down, the broom between her knees, her two hands clutching it, and her head resting on her hands. She was so tired, and yet the fatigue melted from her face and she smiled vaguely, the ghost-smile of the lady in the picture.

"Yes!" she said. "He did kidnap me! He came one night when I was asleep and took me away."

"Yes!" I said. "Yes!"

"He took me to an outlaw cabin in the mountains!"

"Sure! And he was carrying a gun, wasn't he?"

"Yes! A big gun! With a pearl handle."

"And he was riding a black horse."

"Oh," she said, "I shall never forget that horse. He was a beauty!"

"And you were scared to death, weren't you?"

"Petrified," she said. " Simply petrified."

"You screamed for help, didn't you?"

"I screamed and screamed."

"But he got away, didn't he?"

"Yes, he got away."

"He took you to the outlaw cabin."

"Yes, that's where he took me."

"You were scared, but you liked it, didn't you?"

"I loved it."

"He kept you a prisoner, didn't he?"

"Yes, but he was good to me."

"Were you wearing that white dress? The one in the picture?"

"I certainly was. Why?"

19

"I just wanted to know," I said. "How long did he keep you prisoner?"

"Three days and nights."

"And on the third night he proposed to you, didn't he?"

Her eyes closed reminiscently.

"I shall never forget it," she said. "He got down on his knees and begged me to marry him."

"You wouldn't marry him at first, would you?"

"Not at first. I should say not! It was a long time before I said yes."

"But finally you did, huh?"

"Yes," she said. "Finally."

This was too much for me. Too much. I threw my arms around her and kissed her, and on my lips was the sharp tang of tears.

Bricklayer in the Snow

THOSE COLORADO WINTERS were merciless. Every day snow fell from the sky, and in the evening the sun was a depressing red as it went down the other side of the Rockies. Fog laced the mountains, so low we reached it with snowballs. The white deluge gave the trees no rest. The wind rushed the snow into swollen and dead heaps against fences and coal sheds.

The water was too cold for drinking. It seized your teeth like electricity and you sucked it timidly. Unless we left our faucets running all night, we had to wait until noon for the pipes to thaw. We burned lots of coal, which was expensive and put my father in a bad temper.

My father was a bricklayer. Because of the snow he couldn't work. His mortar froze before it adhered, and his fingers were like clumsy sticks. But he was a man of ceaseless activity, he had to be doing something, and the long pull of white days exasperated him and made him a dangerous man around the house. He smoked one cigar after another, cracked his knuckles noisily, and paced from room to room like a man in an iron cage. When he paced that way we children were terrified and crept away as soon as his short, big-muscled body appeared on quiet feet. Everywhere we went was the strong aroma of his twisty Toscanelli cigars.

He tried to keep busy. He would spend time with his drawing. Huddled over a huge roll-top desk foreign to the rest of the dining-room furniture, he designed everything from ashpits to cathedrals. He forbade loud talking during these sessions. Sometimes he couldn't find his T-square or his compass; then, God help us! Under his breath he would begin a mumbo-jumbo

21

of horrible curses, and he would keep it up with increasing anger until my mother or one of the children found his T-square in the washing machine, or in the bath-tub, or in the ice-box, or wherever it is that children conceal T-squares and then forget about them. My mother always got the blame. If he did not accuse her outright of leaving the T-square in the bath-tub, he denounced her for bringing up children who would do such a thing. We kids, relieved of the blame, happily agreed with him, and frowned at Mother in silent accusation, as if to say:"See! That's just what you get!"

It was great fun for us when my father sat idly and improvised with his pencil, drawing according to his whims. Then he usually drew satires. His favorite subjects were his brothers-in-law, my mother's brothers. He would draw a donkey with the face of Uncle Carlo, or a pig that resembled Uncle Tony. These sketches made him laugh uproariously. He would hand them to us, and we would pass them around. We too would laugh. We didn't really think the sketches were funny, but we laughed because he laughed. Our hearts felt free at last when he laughed, and sometimes my little sister Clara would begin in laughter and end in tears. He would urge us to take the sketches to the kitchen.

"Show them to your mother," he would say.

My mother would look at them coldly, then hand them back, unimpressed.

"Shame on him," she would say. "Tell him I said: 'Shame on him.' " And we would troop back to him in the dining room.

"She said to tell you: 'Shame on you.' "

He would grunt in amusement.

He drew faces of the children, always with great seriousness. Little Clara was his favorite. He would wind a dish towel or a scarf around her hair while she knelt with her hands in prayer. Everyone had to be perfectly silent at times like these. He forbade my mother and us three boys to enter the room. My sister would kneel with eyes lifted. He would sit comfortably, a cigar in one hand, a pencil in the other. Always as he drew he mournfully mumbled the words of that tune "In the Shade of the Old Apple Tree." He knew only eight words of the song, and over and over he sang them:

In the shade of the old apple tree,
In the shade of the old apple tree,
In the shade of the old apple tree.

Pausing, he would smile at his daughter.

"Who's Papa's little Blessed Virgin?"

Tingling with happiness, Clara would point her forefinger at her own face and titter.

"That's the way to talk," he would say. "That's what I call *real* talking!"

She would scream with delight at the picture, and my mother and all of us would examine it excitedly. My mother was always pleased. In all seriousness she would ask my father: "Why don't you open a little shop and start a picture store?"

"Oh, God!" my father would despair. "That's a woman all over."

He never allowed his drawings to be kept, and my sister's tears had no effect upon him. After an hour or so he would grow tired abruptly and begin crushing paper into balls and throwing the balls into the kitchen stove. He kept an accurate account of his sketches, for when we tried to conceal one he instantly missed it and demanded it, threatening to beat the four of us indiscriminately. The missing picture was always returned.

II

Every winter my father was brimming with firm intentions and new resolutions to get out of debt and improve his home. He would come home in the middle of the afternoon with a bucket of paint and begin doing one of the rooms. For two hours he would whistle and hum at his work. He was happy, and the spirit of his heart gave a song to the house, and everyone in it was happy. Then weariness would steal upon him. He would cover the paint bucket and sit at the window, brooding over the snow and over the money it kept him from earning. He was dangerous again. We could not go near him. Tomorrow he would finish

23

the painting. But that tomorrow never arrived. In the end it was my mother who would complete the task, at odd moments from her usual work, a stroke at a time.

Conscience-stricken, he would protect himself from himself by criticizing her efforts.

"Look at it," he would say. "That's not the way to paint. Paint with the grain. Don't let all that paint drip off'n your brush."

"Then why don't you do it yourself?"

"Too late now. You ruined it."

He slept badly, with a body that demanded the exhaustion of the sun and the ache of quivering muscles. When idle his brain attacked him, breeding restlessness he could not master. Some mornings he would startle everyone by leaping from bed at four o'clock, dressing, and rushing outside. My mother knew his torment and made no effort to comfort him, for idleness and comfort were the very devils that tortured him. Upon arising later in the morning, she would see him through the window in the back yard, chugging on a cigar as he shoveled paths through the snow he hated so madly. His efforts were tremendous. Snow would be piled everywhere, the whole of the back yard stripped of it to the black frozen soil. Wearing gloves and a sweater, he would come to breakfast with a body exuberant and hot with perspiration and hands alive with the joy of pain.

He would wait patiently for my mother's praise of his early morning efforts, continually glancing out the window at the white mountains of snow on either side of the yard, all of it done by his arms. At first my mother would say nothing, for she was never sure of herself. Eating ravenously, he would be so famished for her comment that finally he would say:

"Take a look at the back yard."

Then she would pretend she saw it for the first time.

"Oh!" she would say. "Did you do that?"

A nod from him.

"All by yourself? All of that?"

"Of course."

"You must be all tired out."

"Me tired? I should say not!"

That day he would be happier, and that night he would be

24

gentler, sleeping with his arm around her, perhaps even saying something to make her laugh.

He was an inventor too. His workbench was the living room. He brought home a cigar box and a fruit carton. With hammer and saw he shaped his mysterious invention. My mother and we children were curious spectators. None of us could make out what it was. There was no use asking, because you couldn't make him talk. All that Saturday afternoon he worked on it. At last it was finished, whatever it was. It must have been finished, for he stopped working and held it up.

And what was it? Lord knows. Nobody knew. But what he said was this: he said it was a device for releasing automobiles when they became stuck in the snow. We thought differently.

"It looks like a violin," my brother said.

"I thought it was a guitar," I said.

My mother refused to become involved. Holding her breath, she retreated to the kitchen with an excuse about the potatoes burning. But he heard her laughing, and then all of us laughed except him. The thought that it might also be a guitar set him to scratching his head and wondering whether he had run into a double invention. Nothing ever came of the invention. It lay about the house, my mother moving it from one closet to another, but nothing was ever done about it.

III

One afternoon my mother asked him to carry in a bucket of coal. He took an empty bucket from behind the kitchen stove, and as he went out he told her to go easy with that coal.

"It costs money," he said. "Burn newspapers."

In a little while he returned with a loaded bucket and went out again. Presently he came back with a second bucketful. My mother watched him curiously. He said nothing as he went out again. Through the kitchen window she saw him almost running toward the coal shed. Now there were no more buckets. My mother saw him disappear into the shed and come out again, a big lump of coal in his hands. He brought it inside and placed it upon the two filled buckets. Then he went out again. He was in a kind of frenzy, and my mother was frightened. When he returned she protested.

"Don't bring any more," she said.

"I know what I'm doing," he answered, hurrying out again.

In a little while he had piled up a mountain of coal nearly five feet high behind the stove. There was not an inch of space between the stove and the wall. The great black column tottered precariously, leaning toward the stove. He had to stand on tiptoe to stack the last chunk. Then he was finished. He backed away and surveyed the work with satisfaction. My mother was spellbound. He turned to her, his hands black with coal dust.

"There," he said. "There's your coal."

"But why so much?" she complained.

He was deeply hurt, or pretended to be. "Now isn't that just like a woman?" he asked an imaginary audience. "She asked for coal, didn't she? And I brought her coal, didn't I? And now she's mad because I brought her coal!" He shook his head dismally, feigning hopeless puzzlement. Then he said: "Mother in Heaven, what can you do with a woman?"

My mother sighed. "Those lumps are too big," she said. "They won't fit in the firebox."

"Get a hammer," he said. "Chop them up."

She tried to lift the top lump. He watched her.

"Why don't you stand on a chair?" he said. "You might get hurt."

"Why don't you shut up?" she flared. "You've done enough foolishness, bringing all this coal into this small kitchen!"

He shrugged innocently. "I was only trying to help," he said.

Bent over the sink, he washed the coal dust from his hands. As always, his hat was cocked on the side of his head; he had to be reminded of its existence or he never took it from his head. He stood with legs apart, washing himself noisily. One of his prides was his toughness. He used to boast that he never used soft bath soap. The best thing in the world for a workingman's face, he said, was hard dish soap.

My mother struggled with the heavy clod of coal, drawing it carefully from the pile at the height of her head. The jagged surface made it almost impossible to grip firmly. The mountain crackled and creaked. It began to fall upon her. She leaped aside. The coal boomed against the floor, crumbling into a million pieces. The kitchen shook. The windows rattled. My mother was frightened and peevish.

"There!" she gasped. "There! What did I tell you?"

He was only mildly surprised, standing with his wet hands dripping soap suds. He clicked his tongue and shook his head at the mess.

"Don't just stand there!" my mother said. "What on earth am I going to *do* with all this coal?"

"Didn't I tell you to get a chair? Didn't I tell you to get a hammer?"

"You make me sick!"

He looked at the black jumble and chuckled. His idea was that this was a very witty situation.

"Well," he said. "You wanted coal, and there it is."

"Heaven's sakes, keep still!"

He was indignant. No woman could talk to him in that tone of voice. "Then keep still yourself!"

"But look at the mess. Look what you've done!"

"Me?" he gasped, shocked. "Me?" That hurt look came over his face. "I haven't done a thing. I was standing here washing my hands."

My mother closed her eyes wearily. Ah, well, there was nothing you could do with him. She took a long breath, token of resignation and forgiveness, and reached for the broom.

IV

It was mid-afternoon. We children were at school. My brother Mike came home. He tossed his cap some place and his books some place else and his coat some place else and came sniffing into the kitchen for something to eat. After school, if my father wasn't home to stop us, we ate stacks of bread and jam, thereby ruining our appetites for supper.

My mother was sweeping the scattered bits of coal.

"Good gosh!" Mike said. "Lookee all the coal! Whatcha gonna do with it?"

27

"Burn it," my father said. "What do you usually do with coal?"

"I know, but—"

"But shut up! Not a word!"

"Your father brought it in," my mother explained sarcastically as she straightened up. "He's so good that way."

"He didn't hafta bring it all in, did he?"

"Never mind," my father said.

They were silent for a moment. Then my father thought of something. He turned suddenly and looked at Mike, then at my mother.

"Say," he said thoughtfully. "Did this little devil get you a bucket of coal before he went to school this morning?"

Mike whitened. His eyes swelled. He hadn't. That always meant trouble. He backed out of the kitchen, his hands pressed against his seat. My father followed slowly, threateningly. At the door Mike started running. My father leaped forward and let fly with his foot. Close enough, and yet a miss. Howling with relief, Mike ran outside. My father let out a streak of curses as he shook his fist toward the slammed door. My mother touched his arm to quiet him.

"Please," she said. "Why say those shameful things?"

"Shameful!" he said. "What did I say that was shameful?"

He went to the closet and got his overcoat. She watched him as he fought his way into it.

"Where are you going?" she said. "It's nearly time for supper."

"How do I know where I'm going?" he shouted.

He always left the house so violently that it made her helpless and drained her strength. She would make excuses to try to keep him home. But he was so tempestuous they had no effect on him.

"Shall I cook spaghetti tonight?" she smiled.

"I don't care," he said. "Cook anything."

He was buttoning up the front of his overcoat. "Yes," he said. "Cook spaghetti tonight. With lots of cheese."

"I used all the cheese last time," she said.

"Buy some more, then."

She walked to him.

"I was going to ask you," she said. "Have you got a half a dollar?"

28

"Where would I get a half a dollar?"

He took her by the arm to the window, sweeping the curtains aside and pointing at the snow.

"Do you see it? Snow! Now will you tell me where I'm going to get a half a dollar?"

She straightened herself petulantly, her petulance a fear of him. "I only thought you had it," she said. "I don't see why you have to get so mad about it."

He slapped his fist into the palm of his other hand, shouting excitedly: "I haven't got it! Hear me! I haven't got it!"

"But don't get so excited! I understand."

"*Ach!* You women. You don't understand anything."

He took a cigar from his inside pocket and rammed it at his face, his mouth leaping for it. The cigar was his last. He lit up, extinguishing the flame by spluttering at it.

"When you go to the store," he said, "get me some cigars."

My mother sat down and covered her eyes. "I can't charge any more cigars," she said. "I just can't do it. I won't. If you only knew the way the grocer looks at me. I feel *so* embarrassed!"

My father never understood any hesitancy about adding to the already incredibly large charge account with the grocer, but he never went to the store himself. He always sent my mother or one of us kids.

"Tell that grocer he'll get his money when I get mine," he said.

My mother recalled something. She got up from the chair. "Wait a minute," she said.

She disappeared into the bedroom. My father's memory for discarded cigar butts was bad. He would leave them lying around in a score of different places. Everywhere: in the bedroom, in the bathroom, on the dresser, on window-sills, on the back porch, on chairs, atop pictures and mirrors; everywhere. Sometimes he would send the whole family on searching expeditions for a particular butt. We children always wondered how he knew the difference between one and another, for they all looked alike to us, but he would shake his head until the right one was brought to him.

And so my mother, knowing his peculiar habits, had gathered a great many of these butts into a cigar box. She returned from the bedroom and held the box out, the lid open, and he looked into it with a frown of inquisition and surprise.

"Where did you get these?"

She was quite proud of the feat. "They're yours!" she said.

"No they're not," he lied.

"But they are!"

"No they're not."

"But they are too! You don't suppose . . ."

"Humpf." He examined them closely. He put his hand into the box and pressed one of the butts. The leaf cracked dryly and fell apart in his fingers. He shook his head.

"I can't use them," he said. "They're too old."

"Look again," she coaxed. "Maybe you'll find a fresh one."

"Did you ever smoke a cigar?"

"Why, no," she said.

"All right, then. I want some more cigars. Throw those away."

"But I can't charge cigars at the store! They're an extravagance, and Mr. O'Neil gets so mad!"

"Never mind O'Neil. Tell him to wait. Ask him if he ever tried to lay brick in the snow. Just ask him that some time, and see what kind of an answer you get."

He left her standing there, the box of butts in her hands. She watched him at the window as he trudged down the street, his eyes to the heavens as he shook his head in hopeless bewilderment. It made her think of a puppy lost in the snow.

First Communion

HOW WELL I REMEMBER my first Confession and Communion! I was nine years old then. The day is high and clear in my mind. I remember that I had six sins to confess. I had to tell my confessor that I had used bad words six times. I didn't want to tell him. I didn't want to name the words. He was a holy man. I knelt in the pew and tried to find a way of language that would convey the essence of my sins. I thought of many devices. I thought I could say: "I used bad words six times," or: "I sinned against the Third Commandment six times," or: "I used wicked words six times," or: "I talked evil six times," or: "I said bad things six times."

For a month the nuns had taught us the solemnity and the liturgy of the confessional. Going to it for the first time would be the most important event of our lives, for thereafter we would have the consciences of sinners. We would know the good from the bad.

There were eight boys and eight girls in our first Confession class. We were seven or eight or nine years old. The girls knelt in two pews before the boys. An ugly little girl who grew up to become a nun knelt in front of me. She was Catherine. She was a little girl with thin white skin and shoulder blades that stuck out. She was crying pitifully. Her shoulders quivered and twitched as I leaned my chin on the pew before me and juggled my six sins. The old, cold church was empty except for the sixteen of us and a nun. The sobs of Catherine rose and filled it like timid puffs of smoke. Her dress danced to the jerk of them. The nun tiptoed in from the vestibule. She put a black-draped arm around the little girl's shoulder and gently stroked her curls.

"There, there!" she whispered. "Don't you take it so hard. I'm sure our Lord knows you're sorry for your sins."

We guys looked at one another and snickered. Sissy Catherine, sorry for her sins! Sissy Catherine, sorry for her sins!

Sorry for her sins? I looked at the dancing curls. Why should *she* be crying? If there was anybody in that class who had a right to cry, it was I. Catherine crying? Huh! Sissy, sissy, sissy! Wait until she had something really wicked to confess. Then she could cry, all right. Wait until she had to confess what *I* had to confess. Little sissy Catherine!

Straightway, I began a bad habit which lived with me for a long time thenceforth. I began to examine her conscience for her. I looked for faults in her as big as mine. She was a very good little girl. She got high marks. She knew by heart "Excelsior" and "Lead, Kindly Light." I went over the summertimes and days I had known her. I could think of nothing worth crying over. I imagined her in the act of committing a sin. I took her out of the church pew and transposed her to the filling-station grounds, my favorite hang-out. I leaned her against the filling-station wall, put a cigarette butt into her mouth, and made her swear, say the six wicked words. But it was hardly convincing. Sissy Catherine simply would not do that. She could not swear as I did. Nobody could swear like me. Nobody had the nerve to swear like me. Nobody was bad enough to swear like me. Nobody was dirty enough. Nobody . . . I sniffed.

Long before the priest came down from the sacristy I was out-bawling little Catherine. I was the dirtiest guy who ever was. I drew my forearm across my nose and snuggled my face into it. The boy on my left was crying softly. The fellow on my right cleared his throat. White handkerchiefs fluttered among the little girls in the two front pews. Everybody cried. The nun, moved to ecstatic tears herself, pronounced us her most edifying class.

II

The priest came out of the sacristy and knelt for a moment in prayer at the altar. Maybe, I thought, he is praying to our Lord, asking Him please not to send anybody into the confessional who has dirty words to confess. The statue of Christ, His toga opened to a red and bloody heart pierced by two stilettos, pleaded to us from the peak of the marble altar. I was sure I saw His eyes move. I was sure I saw Him breathing. I was sure blood dripped from His heart.

I burrowed into my elbow and howled: "O dear Jesus, I won't say it any more! I'll be good! I won't hang around the filling-station any more! Wait and see! Gimme another chance, and wait and see!"

The priest came down from the altar to the confessional. His feet buried themselves into the carpet like iron chains. He took a toothpick out of his mouth and spat a splinter of it to the floor. With breathless curiosity and anxiety the sixteen of us watched him. Then he blew his nose and patted it amiably with his handkerchief. He stared up at the choir-loft for a moment as if he had forgotten something. He smiled to the nun, counted us, sighed, and entered the confessional.

The Confessions began. The girls were first. Each rose from her pew and looked back timorously at the nun. She nodded kindly, and pointed to the confessional. The girls entered softly, one by one. Through the glazed door we could see each penitent in turn, kneeling in the booth. Came the click-clack, click-clack, at two-minute intervals, of the little slide grating that separates priest from penitent. One after another the girls went in and came out. Their eyes were still wrinkled from tears, but their lips turned meek smiles of relief.

The first boy who confessed came out with a lot of noise. He blustered, his chest in the air. The next had a little opinion in his eyes; a cinch! it said.

Suddenly I made up my mind to confess frankly. I began to get boldly sorry now. I wanted to go in and get it over with. I pitied the priest. My Confession would burn his insides.

When my turn came at last, I was greedy to enter. I jumped up and went in. I knelt and blessed myself. The booth was dark and cold, smelling like an ice-box. The sliding door clicked. There was the priest with his nose in his handkerchief. I drew a long breath. I began the prescribed ritual. At once my courage froze.

33

"Bless me, Father, I confess to Almighty God and to you, Father, that I have sinned. This is my first Confession."

Then: "I made six sins. I said something very bad, Father. I knew it was a sin, too. I said something you will not like, Father. I won't do it again, Father. I am awfully sorry, Father. And now I ask penance and absolution of you, Father."

"I can't give you penance and absolution until I know the sins you committed," the priest whispered.

"They were awful bad, Father. I think you will be mad when I tell you, Father."

"No, I will not be mad. You must tell me."

"Oh, Father! They were awful. You will not like it, Father."

The priest changed his position, moving his arm. I jumped. I thought he was going to hit me.

He said: "Did you take the name of the Lord?"

"Oh, it was a lot worse than that, Father. You don't know how bad it was, Father."

"Did you speak foully? You must tell me. You mustn't be afraid."

"Oh, I'm awfully sorry, Father."

"Tell me. The priest is your friend."

"Oh, I'm awfully sorry, Father."

The priest sighed.

"Did you say 'God damn'? "

"Oh, it was worse, Father."

"Did you say 'Jesus Christ'? "

"Oh, no, Father, I never say that."

"Did you say 'bastard'? "

"No, Father. It was almost that, though, Father."

"Was it 'son of a bitch'? "

"Yes, Father."

The priest sighed.

"Is that all?"

"Oh, yes, Father."

I recited the rest of the formula: "And I am sorry for these and all the sins of my past life, and I ask penance, pardon, and absolution of you, Father."

He gave me my penance — a few short prayers. He lifted his

34

hand in quiet absolution. I came out of the confessional. I was happy, very happy. I knelt at the altar and said my penance. I went out into the sunshine of a serene afternoon. I never felt so clean. I was a bar of soap. I was fresh water. I was bright tinfoil. I was a new suit of clothes. I was a haircut. I was Christmas Eve and a box of candy. I floated. I whistled. Some day I would be a priest. I had better run home now and feed the chickens, and mow the lawn, and get in the coal and wood, and go to the store.

III

The next morning the sixteen of us were to receive our first Holy Communion. The boys were to wear white shirt-waists and dark breeches. My mother was in the hospital, so my father asked my grandmother to take charge of me, to dress me. I didn't have a white waist, but my grandmother said she would fix that, all right. You bet she fixed it! She went to the bureau for one of my father's white shirts. She snipped the sleeves off at the elbows. I could wear it now, she said. I thought it was a grand shirt to wear, my father's. It covered me like a sheet. The pockets sank below my belt. The sleeves were still too long. The tail bagged like a pillow. My grandmother agreed: it certainly was a swell shirt. She blessed me, and I went to nine o'clock Mass. I was to offer my first Communion for the success of my mother's operation. They would wheel her into the operating room that morning.

But only my grandmother and I thought I wore a grand shirt. The Sister Superior screeched when she saw me standing in line with my partner. She ran to me. She seized my sleeve, long and dangling with unraveled thread. The cloth shrieked, ripping to my elbow.

"For heaven's sake! Go home and put something on."

It was hard to understand. I thought it was a swell shirt, my father's. The guys laughed and said things about tents and awnings and gunnysacks. Mass would start in five minutes.

My mother would fix my shirt. But I had to hurry. Pretty soon

35

they would begin to operate. I knew of such things, for it had happened twice before in the same year.

I ran across town — twenty blocks — to the hospital. I sprawled and crawled up the three flights of stairs to my mother's room. I opened the door to see them lifting her from the bed on posts to the bed on wheels. I saw my mother. She was too white to sew. She looked as if her face was covered with talcum; like a girl, she had her hair in a braid.

She saw me. She took my hand and smiled.

"He's an angel," my mother said to the nurse. "He went to Communion for me this morning. That's why I'm not afraid."

I blurted: "I never went yet, Ma."

She didn't hear. I half repeated it, but the nurse pasted a funny-smelling hand over my mouth. They pulled my mother away. I followed them down the rubbery, smelly corridor. The bed on wheels swung quietly into the operating room. My mother saw me in the hall. She asked the nurses to stop. She waved her fingers to me. I ran tiptoe to her side.

"Isn't that Papa's shirt?" she asked.

"Yeah," I said.

"Let me fix it."

"You can't now," the nurse said. "The doctor's waiting."

"Just a safety pin," my mother said.

The nurse gave her one. She pinned it at the elbow of the torn sleeve, to prevent any further ripping.

"Tell Grandma to fix it," my mother said. We kissed.

They pushed her inside, and I went down the hospital steps. I was too late for my first Communion. I went home slowly. Soon I forgot all about Communion. I was proud of this swell shirt, my father's. I pulled the collar down and let the breeze fill my waist. The shirt ballooned out.

I tried to explain to my grandmother. She spoke little English and understood less.

"No Communion," I said. "Shirt no good. Sister no like. Sleeve too long. Sister tear. Mamma say fix."

"Yah, yah," she said. "Me fix 'um."

She got the scissors and cut the sleeves off at the shoulders. Now the shirt drooped to my elbows.

36

IV

That evening my father sighed to see his fine shirt so amputated, and he made a noise with his teeth and tongue: Sssk, sssk, sssk.

"Thank God when your mother comes home," he said.

When he learned the why of it, he clattered the dishes with a wild fist. He was furious with the nun. I watched and listened with a great pride. He growled and pressed his temples.

"By Jesus Christ, tomorrow you go to Communion, and you wear a blue work shirt, understand? A work shirt. Not a white shirt, or a green shirt, but a *blue* shirt. A *blue* shirt. *Blue! Blue! Blue!* And I'm gonna take you out of the Catholic school. And I'll put you in the public school. I'm tired paying taxes, anyway."

"Shut up!" my grandmother said in Italian. "All the time you talk, talk, talk, and say nothing. All the time. Shut up!"

"Shut up yourself!" my father said. "Who's running this house? Me or you?"

"Blah!" my grandmother answered. "Pie-face!"

The next morning there were many surprises on my bed. There was a new pairs of breeches. And a new pair of shoes. And three new white waists. And a new pair of stockings. And two new pairs of B.V.D.'s. And a new cap. And two new neckties.

In the kitchen I heard my father humming over his breakfast. He had been with my mother most of the night, and her operation had been a success.

My grandmother said to my father: "Why did you buy him white shirts? They soil easily, and he will tear them. Blue is best."

My father said: "No son of mine will ever wear a blue shirt."

"You are crazy," my grandmother said.

"I know what I'm doing," my father said.

"You are crazy," my grandmother said.

"Some more bacon," my father said.

I went to church. After the bells rang at the Sanctus, I walked down the aisle to the Communion rail. There were a million singing crickets in my new shoes. People looked up from their prayers to see who made the noise. They bent their necks to see my new shoes.

Oh, boy!

Altar Boy

ONE TIME I SERVED MASS with Allie Saler, and Allie had the right side to serve. I mean he had to hand the priest wine and ring the bells and move the missal and pretty near all the important things that altar boys do. All of us guys in the altar boys used to like serving on the right side on account of it was so important. It is a lot more important than the left-side server. He hardly ever does anything. All he does is genuflect and hold the paten at Holy Communion.

We got to the sacristy about ten minutes before Mass started, and when it came time to figure out who got the right side, I said I did, and he said he did. We started in saying dirty things back and forth, and Father Andrew came in.

He said: "Here, here, what is going on here?"

We told him.

He said: "Oh, that is nothing. I will settle it by having Allie take it this morning."

I just hated that look on Allie's face. It was just like he had it all figured out with Father Andrew that I was going to get the left, and Father looked straight at Allie, just like I was not there, and it was just like saying: "I like you better than him, and your father owns the drug-store, and his father never does come to church, so that is why you get the right."

It says in the Catechism that to think evil things is the same as doing them, so right away I knew I was sinning to beat the band while I was standing there, and I knew my sins were awful ones, maybe mortal sins, because I was standing there wishing Father Andrew was a man instead of a priest, and more my size, so I could knock the hell out of him, and get even. I was not

39

wishing any such thing as that on Allie because it was a waste of wishes. I knew I would lay into him good and hard after Mass. He knew it too. I could tell, all right.

But it was all settled that he got the right side, so we started to get things ready for Mass. Father put on his vestments. Allie lit the candles and I got the wine and water ready.

The wine was not real wine at all. My father has swell red stuff in his cellar, but this was blackish-red grape juice, kind of bitter, and just as thick as ink. The guys used to swipe a mouthful every once in a while and pretend they were stewed, but I did not because it did not taste so good, and my father says you can down a whole barrel of it without it fazing you. Father Andrew likes his wine plain, without mixing it with water, and about an inch of it for every Mass. I mean the wine would be an inch deep in the pitcher.

While I was fixing the wine, all of a sudden I got a hunch on how to get even. It did not make much difference then about another sin, the sin of getting even, because I had already committed a mortal sin when I wished evil to a priest. One mortal sin is just as bad as twenty. I mean if you commit one, you go to Hell just as quick as if you had twenty against you. It says so in the Catechism. I knew there was a bottle of red ink in the supply drawer, so I went there and got it. Nobody was looking, and I poured it into the wine bottle, about one-fifth, then I filled the rest with grape juice.

Mass started, and while I was kneeling at the altar I got to thinking about what I did. Father Andrew was moving softly back and forth on the altar, saying prayers in Latin, with his eyes shut, and I could see how holy he looked. The organ was playing sad, sacred music. Then it came to me all at once what I did. I committed a horrid sin because the ink I put in the bottle would be consecrated and changed into the body and blood of our Lord. I felt terrible to think that Jesus had been crucified for my sins, and there I was, kneeling at this sacrifice without even feeling ashamed.

Gosh, I was scared to death. I did not know what to do next. I could see how ungrateful I was to our Lord. I could see Him up in Heaven, with blood oozing out of His feet, and crying tears of blood for what I did. I kept saying over and over: "Sweet Jesus, forgive me! Sweet Jesus, forgive me! Sweet Jesus, forgive me!" I knew I deserved to burn forever for my sin, but I kept on begging our Lord for forgiveness anyhow, because it says in the Catechism that true contrition is sufficient for salvation, and I wanted to prove how really sad I was for my sin.

At the Consecration Allie gave Father the wine, and he gobbled it up without so much as blinking, so I guess he did not catch on. But all this time, there I was kneeling on the green carpet that covers the altar steps, and praying to beat the band for our Lord to forgive me. I prayed for all I was worth, trying to feel perfect contrition. Perfect contrition is just as good as Confession if you can't go to Confession. If you get a tough grip on yourself, hold yourself real stiff, and think nothing but sorrow, sorrow, sorrow, pretty soon you do have real sorrow, and that is what I was wanting.

After Mass I made another Act of Contrition and said some Hail Marys to boot. Then I went into the sacristy, and Father Andrew smiled at me, because he likes to see holy guys, and when he smiled, his teeth were red like he had been eating cherries. I did not laugh or anything when I saw his red teeth. I was really scared, and if I did not know it was ink I would have swore it was our Lord's blood. Miracles like that happen every now and then.

Father patted my shoulder, and I went around to the other side of the church and took off my cassock and surplice. Allie Saler was gone already. I hurried and ran outside and saw him a block away. The snow was starting to melt, getting ready for spring, and Allie went along kicking up slush.

I ran up to him, put my hand on his chest and my right leg back of his knees, and pushed him, jujitsu fashion. The trick worked swell. Allie sat down in the wettest, muddiest slush. That is how I got even with him. Nobody knew about the red ink except Father Joseph. I told him in Confession. For penance, he made me promise not to do it again, and I did, and to say five Our Fathers and five Hail Marys. So all in all, I got off pretty easy.

41

On the first of May, because May is the month of our Mother, and by that I mean the Blessed Virgin, everybody in the altar boys had to line up two at a time in a great big long line and go to the Blessed Virgin's altar in the church to say the Rosary. We went in with our partners and knelt down in the aisle, and Harold Maguire, who was president of the altar boys, began to say the Rosary out loud. I mean like this. Here is what he said: "Hail Mary, full of grace, the Lord is with thee, blessed art thou among women and blessed is the fruit of thy womb, Jesus." He stopped there, and the rest of us guys took it up, only we prayed like this: "Holy Mary, mother of God, pray for us sinners now and at the hour of our death. Amen."

Worms Kelley was my partner. Worms hated Maguire like the dickens, and so did everybody else, but Worms hated him most because Maguire was a snitch baby, and he had a suck with the nuns. What I mean by suck is that when Maguire wanted something off the nuns, like going to the washroom every few minutes, he got to go, and nobody else did, except maybe two or three girls with sucks, too. I did not like Maguire to look at. He was sissified, with thick eye-glasses made out of black celluloid. His hands were little bitty things. He used to stay on the steps at noon with his *Bible Stories*, so Sister Prefect could see him. He carried his lunch in a blue bucket, and the sandwiches were wrapped in the white tissue paper that you buy, instead of good old bread wrapper. His dessert every day was a big apple, or cake or pie or something like that. His mother came for him after school in a Studebaker. She was very tall, and looked like she had strong muscles. She was president of the Ladies' Altar Society, and when she came after Harold she would lean out of the car door and talk awful courteous to Sister Marie, who was upstairs looking out the window, keeping an eye on us guys so we would not break ranks.

Harold got going good on the Rosary and everything was all right when all of a sudden Worms started to make noises with his mouth. Sister Cecilia was in the first pew. She did not look up right away, but every one of the guys except Harold kept turning around, looking straight at Worms and me because we were kneeling close together. We were all snickering to beat the band, so Worms got nervier and nervier. He made noises louder and louder. Sister Cecilia moved a little, like she was itching all over, so Worms stopped the noises. I was glad because Worms was my partner, and I might get the blame.

We got to the Fifth Joyful Mystery, that is the last part of the Rosary, when for no good reason Worms made a noise that was the funniest yet. You could hear it echo away up behind the organ-pipes. All of us except Maguire sat back on our heels and just busted out laughing. Maguire turned around to Sister like he was asking for help. It was awful. I wanted to stop laughing because it is a grievous sin to be disrespectful in church, but I could not, I just could not. I laughed and laughed, and so did Worms, and so did everybody else.

Sister Cecilia was redder than a beet. She put up her hand for silence, the way Mussolini does in *Pathé News*.

She said: "No one leaves this church until I find the pig who did that."

Nobody said anything. We were just as quiet as can be.

"Very well," she said. "You'll stay until I find out."

We had to kneel up straight and it got pretty tough on the knees. Away back in the vestibule you could hear a clock ticking. After a half-hour the ticking sounded like heavy rocks hitting a slate roof. The guys started to look at Worms as if to tell him to go ahead and admit it, but the longer he kept still the worse it got, until finally he did not dare to talk. Then old Maguire turned around and saw all the guys looking at us, and after a minute he got up and went to where Sister was. He was snitching, that is what he was doing. It was as plain as day.

We started to hiss: "Snitch baby! Snitch baby! Snitch baby!" And Maguire was sure in for a walloping from us guys.

Sister looked straight at me and Worms, and said: "Will you please follow me into the sacristy?"

I nearly keeled over. I held my breath and blinked my eyes and wondered what the heck. The only thing to do was to take it on the cheek for Worms. The guys whispered: "That's the boy!" and that was pretty good to hear, but it did not help much. I knew I was in for it. I gave Maguire a dirty look when I went by, and I bet he knew I was going to ruin him when I got him alone, because I sure was. Sister Cecilia was ready for me.

I was holding a rosary, fooling with it, standing in front of Sister Cecilia, waiting for her to do what she was going to do.

"Put the rosary away," she said. I did it.

She rolled up her black sleeves, sort of got her distance, made a moaning sound, and with all her might she let me have one smack on the cheek. The sting was something fierce and I started crying a little, but not much. The guys must have heard the smack, because it sounded just like when a cottonwood cracks and falls. I felt awful cheap. My cheek was very hot. I rubbed it. Sister Cecilia was crying too, and I thought she was sure nuts, because I was getting hit, not her. But I felt sorry for her and I did not know why, either.

She said: "Go back and kneel down, you little heathen. I'll see you later."

The guys saw my face, which was very red. It made me feel very cheap. I gave Maguire another dirty look. He was going to get it. The guys would get him tomorrow. Me and the guys would. We could not get him after Rosary because his mother would be there in her Studebaker to take the sissy home.

All the guys went home, and of course I had to go to our room, and of course I had to write "I must not be disrespectful in church" five hundred times. I did not get through until seven o'clock. After the sun went behind the peaks, there was no light except the street lamps. I was scared and lonesome. When I got through, I put the papers on Sister's desk and went home.

My old man was waiting when I got there. I should say he was waiting. He knew all about it. Sister Cecilia had snitched, just like Maguire. My father made a run for me as soon as I got in the house. What he did to me was more than what Sister did to me, but I did not cry or anything. I took it like a real guy. The reason is, I knew he was my father, and he would stop hitting before he hurt me too serious. He kept saying he was going to kill me, but he is my father, and he does not scare me with that stuff.

Next day at school the altar boys got out at noon so we could go up to the foothills to pick flowers for the Blessed Virgin's altar.

44

The main reason I pray to the Blessed Virgin is because we get out of a lot of school on account of her. We started out in a bunch, two at a time, and had to walk clear through town, with Sister Cecilia leading us like we were a bunch of convicts or something. Like we were dangerous. I do not like it at all. The Protestants stop every time to look at us as if we are freaks. And the Sisters look funny with their funny dresses.

We walked clear through town to the edge of the foothills. They were full of yellow anemones and wild daisies and violets. Anemones and daisies are easy to pick. Violets smell swell, but they are the nuts to pick. It takes a whole bushel to make a bouquet.

We broke ranks, and my partner Worms showed me a brand new package of Camels. Worms smoked all the time. He even inhaled. Sister Cecilia went looking for flowers, and me and Worms sneaked behind some sagebrush and crawled on our hands and knees into a gulch that used to be a creek. We lit up and took it easy.

Pretty soon we finished our snipes and crawled out of the gulch. We saw the guys scattered all over the hills. They were very far away from us. Some of them were in bunches, some were alone, carrying armloads of flowers. We could barely see who they were, they were so far off. We could see Sister Cecilia in black and white. She was walking crosswise from us, and taking it easy. The day was awfully pretty and calm. There was not a cloud or a breeze, and it was warm. Me and Worms wanted to go fishing.

All at once, who should walk into us from behind the sagebrush? No one else but Harold Maguire. He was carrying flowers in his cap. He was so surprised he was scared to death. We were surprised too, but we were not scared. We were just surprised.

This was our chance to get even, and we knew it, and so did he. It was just like our Lord had planned it out for him to meet us. But I do not know if our Lord had planned it out for us to get even, because that is a grievous sin. I do not think our Lord had anything to do with that. I guess that was the Devil.

"Let's ding-bump him," Worms said.

45

"Let's," I said.

It takes two to ding-bump a man. You get him on his back, and one of you grab his arms, and the other his legs, and you lift him up and down as hard as you can, so that his seat bumps the ground.

Harold was so scared he did not fight back. We told him to get on his back, and he did it. We told him to take off his specs, and he did it. We told him we would teach him not to snitch, and he said he would not any more. He started to cry. That made me want to hurry up.

After we bumped him the first time, he yelled as loud as he could. The guys and Sister heard him, because they came running from everywhere. It is too bad the guys were not closer. They would of got a big kick out of it. Sister Cecilia was nearly running. She was almost half a mile away.

I saw a cactus plant with short thorns, not even half an inch long.

"Let's sit him in that, and then beat it," I said.

We did it. We sat him in the cactus and ran away.

They nearly kicked us out of school for what we did. I mean the nuns.

We had to apologize to them and to Father Andrew and to the whole school. We got lickings at home and in school. We had to stay every night until five for a month. We did not get to go to the altar boy banquet.

But we did not care a bit. We got even. You can ask any of the guys about Harold Maguire now. They will tell you he used to be a snitch baby, but he is not one now. He is a swell guy now.

III

Bill Shafer is the worst altar boy in the bunch. He swipes stuff, and he chews gum before Communion. I do not see how he does it. I do not think his mother cares, because I saw him eat meat on Friday. It was a sandwich. His mother makes his lunch. If she cared, she would make him eat fish. Bill says it is not his sin if he eats meat. It is her sin. She put it in. Bill has four Sunday suits. He wears them to school a lot. His mother is sure keen-looking. If my mother was as keen-looking as she is, I would sure feel good. I do not mean that my mother is not good-looking. I mean that Bill's mother is sure good-looking.

Bill showed me how to swipe agates at the ten-cent store. You open your waist, and then you lean away over the counter. When the girl is not looking, you·roll the migs into your waist. It is a good way. It works every time. I do not think Bill told his in Confession, but I told Father Andrew mine.

Father Andrew said I had to return the migs or pay for them. He sure was sore. He almost hollered at me. Bill won all my migs, so I will have to pay for them with money sometime. I will do it when I get bigger. I bet Bill never does pay for his.

One time I was walking home from school with Bill. He had a dime, so we went to Drake's to get Eskimo pies.

When we were in there, he said: "Hey, do you want a fountain-pen?"

I said: "Sure."

He said: "Wait a minute."

He said to Mr. Drake: "Hey, Mr. Drake, can I use your phone?"

Mr. Drake said: "Sure."

So Bill went to the phone in back. At first I wondered what the heck. Then I knew he was going to swipe a pen for me. I did not snitch, though; I am not a snitch baby. I did not watch, because Old Man Drake might catch on. He was piling Eskimo pies, and I looked at his bald head. His neck was real little. I started to think maybe somebody would come into the store. Maybe somebody would, then we would get caught and get sent to Golden. The big reform school is in Golden. Sister says there is not a Catholic boy in there. There never has been. If we were caught, we would be the first Catholics. I did not want to get caught. I thought I better pray that we would not get caught.

I looked at old Drake's bald head and prayed to myself. In my head, I mean.

I said: "Hail Mary, please do not let anybody come in. Please do not let anybody come in."

The Blessed Virgin heard my prayer, because just then Bill came back.

47

When we got outside, he said: "Hey, come on. Run like hell."
Hell is not swearing. Hell is on every page of the Catechism. You
can say it.

We did not stop until we got to the Twelfth Street bridge. We
crawled under it.

Bill said: "Hey, that was sure easy as pie."

I said: "Gee, Bill, you sure swipe stuff!" He did not say anything.
We knew he committed a mortal sin, but we did not say anything.

He opened his waist and showed me. I thought he swiped one,
but he swiped fifteen. They were in a box made out of velvet.
They were pens that cost a whole lot. One of them had a ticket.
It said: "$18." I got scared to death.

Bill said: "Hey, which one do you want?"

I did not want Bill to think I was chicken or scared or yellow.

I said: "Oh, I will take this one." I took the cheapest. It was
five dollars.

He took the eighteen-dollar one and said: "Hey, what will we
do with the rest?"

I said: "I do not know."

He said: "Well, here goes." He threw them into the water. It
was a sandy bottom. You could see the pens.

I wanted to run. I am not goofy, and a fountain-pen does not
scare me, but I wanted to run away. I did not want to go to Confession, because the last time I confessed stealing migs, and Father
Andrew got sore. I mean he talked real loud. If I told him I swiped
a five-dollar pen, I bet he would yell. The holy people outside
would hear him.

Bill said: "Hey, we better beat it. Let me go first. You wait five
minutes."

He crawled away and left me all alone with the pens.

The pens did not scare me or anything, but I was scared about
something. I got some rocks and mud and covered up the pens.
It made the water muddy-looking. There was a long streak of
muddy water. It made me feel like a thief. But Bill did it.

All of a sudden I felt like running. I crawled out and started
in. I ran and ran. I forgot where I was going until I got right
in front of Drake's. I nearly keeled over when I saw where I was.
I was winded, but I started in again. I ran all the harder. Pretty

soon I was right in front of the church. The church and school are right next to each other. I thought it was funny as heck to be there again, because it was pretty near five o'clock, and a school is a punk place to be at five. I thought how come, and so I started for home.

I got a block away, and then I thought I better go back and say an Act of Contrition. Then I saw I was in a heck of a fix, because it says in the catechism that an Act of Contrition is good only if Confession cannot be had, and there I was only a block away from the priests' house. The priest would hear my Confession if I asked him. I thought I better go ahead and have it over with. Father Andrew would sure be sore.

Then I got a swell idea. I would ask for Father Joseph. He did not know about the migs, so he would not be hard on me. It was sure a good idea, because now I could go to Confession, and the fountain-pens would not scare me. I mean I would not be scared. Fountain-pens are nothing. It is nuts to be scared of them. I went back to the church. I ran all the way.

I asked the maid for Father Joseph, and he came down. Father Joseph has a great big belly and a double chin. He likes me. He says I am a keen pitcher. He knows a pitcher on the St. Louis Browns. He says I am the born image of this pitcher. I like Father Joseph very, very much.

I said: "Father, I want to go to Confession."

He said: "Why not? So does everybody."

We went into church, and Father got in the confessional.

I told him what I did. I did not snitch on Bill. I just said I was in bad company a little while ago, and I swiped a fountain-pen. I am not a snitch baby.

Father said I had to return the pen or what it was worth or he would not forgive me. I said I would. He gave me absolution. I went out to the altar and said my penance, which was five Our Fathers and five Hail Marys in honor of the Blessed Virgin. Father Joseph is sure a keen guy. He did not make me feel cheap at all. He hardly said anything.

I got outside and started for home. I felt just grand. I started whistling hymns like I always do after Confession. I had it all figured out about the five-dollar pen. I would keep it. I would tell my mother I found it. It was a lie, but a lie is only a venial sin. You do not go to Hell if you have a venial sin on your soul. You go to Purgatory. Then you go to Heaven. Some day I will pay old Drake for it. I will do it when I get bigger. I bet Bill Shafer never pays for his.

IV

Bill Shafer used to chew gum before Communion. He sure thought he was tough. He sure thought he was smart. When you go to Communion you cannot eat or drink anything that is food or drink after midnight. You must fast. Bill used to come around to us guys before Communion and pop gum in our ears. He sure thought he was smart.

Sister caught him doing it, and she made him spit it out. It sure was keen, the way she told him to spit. He spit, and all of us guys laughed right out loud. We were in church too, only we were in the vestibule. Bill sure thought he was tough. We did not laugh like it was real funny. We laughed different, so Bill would sort of feel cheap.

We laughed like this: "He he he he."

Bill said: "Hey, Sister, how come? Gum is not food or drink."

Sister said: "Gum has sugar in it."

We sure got a big kick out of it. Bill sure thought he was smart. He sure felt cheap.

The next day he did it again before Communion. I mean he popped his gum. He sure thought he was tough.

One of the guys snitched on him. I know who it was, but I am not going to snitch on him just because he snitched on Bill. I am not a snitch baby.

Sister pretty near ran to where Bill was standing. He was standing there popping. She got a hold of his hair and jerked him around and said: "Spit it out! Spit it out!"

Bill said: "Hey, Sister! No sugar in this gum. This is old gum. I been saving it."

Sister said: "Say, young man, I have had enough of this. You must not dare go to Holy Communion this morning. The very idea! Young man, I want you to see Father Andrew right after Mass."

In the afternoon, in Catechism class, Sister sat right up in front of Bill and told him right out, right in front of us guys. She said what she thought of a boy who chewed gum before Communion. Gosh, she sure sailed in! Old Bill was sure sore. Sister said a guy who will do that must come from a funny home. I guess Sister is right, because I saw Bill's mother chew gum a lot. She is sure keen-looking. I mean Bill's mother. Not Sister. Sister is goofy-looking.

Then Sister told us a whole gob of stories about smart guys like Bill. She told us how they tried to be smart aleck with our Lord, and how He fixed them. He sure got even good and proper.

Sister said there was once another smart aleck like Bill who used to go to Communion every day. He went so many times that he got used to it, and pretty soon he started to be disrespectful. One morning he thought he would do something. Oh, yes, he thought he was smart. He was going to do something real swell. He was going to take the Sacred Host out of his mouth after he received, and then take it home. So he went to Communion.

He did what he said he was going to do. When he came back from the altar, he put the Sacred Host in a dirty handkerchief. It was awful. I can hardly think about a guy who would do any such thing. But our Lord sure fixed him good and proper.

When this rotten guy got home, he took out his handkerchief, and for gosh sakes, was he scared! His handkerchief was all bloody. Our Lord's blood was all in it!

When the guy saw this, he fell on his knees and asked God to forgive him, for God's sake. Then he got up and went away and became a priest. He was so holy they made him a bishop. He is one now. He is back east some place.

Old Bill kept saying: "Bull! bull! bull!" He sure thought he was smart. He took out his handkerchief and played like he was looking for blood. He sure thought he was a wise guy.

After school, Bill said to me and Allie Saler: "Hey, I bet she made up that story about the bishop."

Allie said: "I bet she did not."

Bill said: "Hey, what you want to bet I can do it without getting my handkerchief all bloody?"

I said: "I bet you a million dollars."

Bill said: "Shake!"

We shook. I did not mean a real million dollars. I only have two dollars in my bank.

The next morning after Mass, Bill ran after me and Allie.

We were going home to breakfast. We go to Communion every morning in May.

He said: "Hey, you guys, come on! I want to show you."

We went to the washroom in the basement. There were some fourth-grade punks standing around.

Bill said: "Hey, you little kids, beat it."

We went into a washroom and locked the door. Bill took out his handkerchief. There was a Sacred Host in it. It was wrinkled and melty. You could see he took it out of his mouth.

I said: "Oh, my God!"

Allie made the sign of the cross. I thought it was a good thing to do, so I did too. Bill, he just laughed.

He said: "Hey, where is the blood?"

There was not a drop on it.

Allie said: "Come on, Jim. I have to go."

Bill said: "Hey, where is the blood?"

I said: "Bill, God will sure get even with you for this."

Bill said: "Hey, if you guys ever snitch, I sure will get even with you."

We said we would not snitch.

When we got outside the washroom, we heard the water running. I bet Bill threw the Host in. That is a sacrilege, and a big one, I bet. Bill will get his. Our Lord will punish him. He sure thinks he is tough. He sure thinks he is smart.

V

My favorite saint is Saint James. He is the one I was named after. Saint Joseph used to be my favorite, but since writing letters to him never has done much good, I have changed back to Saint

James, and Saint Joseph is not like he used to be. It is a funny thing to think, but every time I pray to Saint Joseph I think about Joe Kraut. I mean every time I pray to him and I am not in front of his statue, which is supposed to look like him, I think about Joe Kraut, and Joe Kraut is not so swell to think about. Joe is only eleven, and he has three or four whiskers on his chin already, and he has a squashy chin, and he is fat. I guess maybe that is why Saint Joseph is so hard to pray to, on account of I think of Joe Kraut, and that is not such a keen thought. But I like Joe Kraut. He always has a nickel or so, so we go to the bakery after school and buy day-old pies.

In a way, I think Saint Joseph played me kind of dirty, after all the letters I sent to him. We write to him every year on his feast day. I mean all the guys and girls have to write down on a little note what they want most, and they also write how many prayers they will say to get it, and then Sister Agnes gets all the notes together in a bunch and she burns them, with the stove-lid off, so Saint Joseph will read them in the smoke. Anyhow, that is what Sister says, but I do not think much of it any more, or maybe Saint Joseph never read my notes, or if he did, he does not like me very much.

His feast day comes once every year, and on that day for three straight times I asked for a bicycle. I asked for one of those swell Ranger bikes, brown frame, nickel-plated spokes, and vacuum-cup tires. I never did get what I wanted.

After I did not get my bike the first two times, I went to Sister Agnes and asked her how come. She said, well, seeing as how a saint only knows what is good for us, maybe he felt like a bike would do me hurt. I might get run over and get killed. And that is the reason he did not send any. She also said maybe I asked for too much, but a saint is a saint, and a bike is not too much for him to get for me, and, besides, I would not get run over, because I can ride a bike better than anybody. After he reads your note, Saint Joseph goes to God and tells Him what is what, and God cannot refuse very well, because Saint Joseph was the foster father of the Infant Jesus when He was down here.

The other guys did not ask for as much as I did, I guess, but still most of them got what they wanted. Reinhardt asked for a new football and, sure enough, next day his father brought him home a keen Spalding. I think I know how that came off, though. I think Sister Agnes read his note to Saint Joseph, and then she telephoned to Reinhardt's dad, who got the football right in his store, because he owns a clothing store and sells Spalding stuff right in it.

Right after this last time I wrote to Saint Joseph, I went to Sister Agnes and said: "Sister, this makes the third time I'm asking Saint Joseph for a bike."

I told her this because I kind of had a hunch she would telephone my old man, and then I would maybe get the bike. All the time, I also kept saying over and over in my head to Saint Joseph, I mean I was praying, like this: "O Saint Joseph, dear, sweet Saint Joseph, if you do not send the bike I will not pray to you again." When I prayed like that, I thought the bike would come for sure, because if Saint Joseph found out I would quit praying to him if he did not send the bike, then he would send it. He would not want me to quit him.

I wrote to him that I wanted this bike to be on our front porch when I woke up next morning. I thought it would be keen to wake up and find it there. I also thought if Sister telephoned the old man, he would have time to get the bike on the porch by next morning.

I went to bed real early that night, about eight or half after, and I prayed to Saint Joseph until I went to sleep. I also said my night prayers. I wanted to make sure I said enough prayers.

The next morning I piled out and ran to the porch. There was a bike there, all right. But it was not what I wanted. It was the second-hand one that used to be in Benson's window all the time. It was full of fly specks. The paint was chipped off. It had crazy, old-fashioned handlebars. I fixed it up, anyway, and put on new paint, but I was awfully disappointed, because I wanted a new Ranger.

My mother cried when I told her how bad I felt. But she cries about everything about God. She said the bike got ruined on the way down from Heaven. She must think I am dumb as heck.

Big Leaguer

A LONG TIME AGO, when I was a little second-grader, they were
building the new school. At noon hour we used to go to where
they were putting up the new building and swipe tar. We chewed
it.

It was on account of the tar that Sister Agnes did not like me
when I was a little second-grader. But it was not my fault if she
got messed up. The desks were so little in the second grade that
when she sat down beside me she took up all the room, and I
did not know the tar was on the seat.

We were supposed to recite, but I was chewing tar. Sister Agnes
saw me. She came down to my desk. When I saw her coming,
I got scared. I took out the tar and dropped it. I thought it
hit the floor. But it fell on the seat. Heck! I didn't know that. I
didn't know she would sit down at the little desk with me. But
she did.

She shook her finger and said: "How many times must I tell
you not to chew that stuff?" She was mad. I did not answer, and
she got up. I mean she almost got up. I mean she tried to get
up. I mean the tar hung on.

Her dress pulled. I tried to help. The dress started to tear. She
got very mad. She told me to take my hands away. She slapped
me. It was a hard sock. Then she told a girl to get the scissors.
She cut a little hole in her dress.

She said: "You are a dirty boy, and I have a notion to beat
you to death."

I had to stay after school and clean up. Sister Agnes was there
too. I had to scrape with a knife. Not all the tar came off. I was
awfully sorry, but I did not tell her. I do not like to tell people

55

I am sorry. I was not scared, though. Who ever heard of me being scared of Sisters?

I got the black piece of cloth scraped off, and I tossed it into the waste-basket. Sister Agnes was still mad. She did not even look at me. She knew I was there, but she did not look at me. It was funny to say good-night to her, but you have to say it.

So I said: "Good-night, Sister."

She said: "Go to the basket and get that piece of cloth."

The cloth was tarry and sticky. I felt cheap, giving it to her. I felt sorry for her. I thought she was going to sew up the hole with the tarry piece. Tar stuck to her fingers. I got scared. I felt goofy.

She said: "You are a bad boy."

She said: "You are a very bad boy."

She said: "You are a very, very bad boy."

I played as if I did not hear. I looked at the door. I played as if I were rolling tar with my fingers. I was thinking I had better tell her I was sorry. But it would be sissified. I did not.

She said: "Are you listening to me?"

I was thinking about sissies.

I said: "What?"

You are not supposed to say "What?" to Sisters. You are supposed to say: "What did you say, Sister?" So I did wrong again. I was in for it again.

I knew it was coming, but I did not duck. I did pretty well for a little second-grader. It did not hurt at all. It would have hurt some other guy, but I was tough.

She said: "That's all. Go home."

I should have said: "I am sorry," then. I should have said it, but I didn't.

After that, Sister Agnes did not like me. Once she hollered in front of the whole room that my hands were dirty. I had to go out and wash them. Once I spilled ink, and I did not have a blotter.

Sister Agnes came down the aisle.

"Hurry!" she said. "Blot it up! Hurry!"

You are supposed to have blotters. I did not have any. I borrowed one from a girl.

In front of everybody, Sister Agnes hollered: "After this, bring you own. Good heavens, they only cost a penny!" I felt cheap. The kids thought I was poor.

II

Sister Agnes was not the second-grade teacher when we came back the next year to start the third grade. The second-graders had another teacher. I went to her and asked about Sister Agnes. She said Sister Agnes was in Philadelphia, which is where the great ball players come from.

That year I was only a third-grader, but I was the best ball player in school. I pitched. I struck out forty men. I banged out twenty homers. Sister Agnes should have been here. She should have seen the game I pitched against Whitman. She should have seen me hit home runs when I was a fourth-grader. She should have seen me bust out sixty-nine homers and eighty-seven triples when I was a fifth-grader. She should have been here last year to see me strike them out, one . . . two . . . three. And every game, too! I am sure great.

Last September, who do you think was teaching the second-graders again? Sister Agnes! I met her in the hall. Gee! When she came toward me, I felt just like the time she came down the aisle and sat on the tar. She did not talk about the tar, though. She said she had heard all about my great pitching. And that goes to show that when you are great, you are just great, and even when you do something bad, you are still great.

I liked her more and more every day. She helped me whenever I had to stay after school. That goofy Sister Justine, the principal, made me stay in. If the team had me pitching, we would have won the Emerson game. Now the Emerson kids think the Catholics are no good. That shows you. Do you think that goofy Sister Justine cared if the Emerson kids called us "red necks" and "popes"? Heck, no!

She said: "He has to be punished. I am going to show this boy that he can't do as he pleases around here." Blah, blah, blah.

But Sister Agnes was nice. She came into the room after school

57

and rooted for me by telling me to work faster. Nearly every day I had to write five hundred times: "I must not laugh during prayers." It took a long time to write that. The game was half over before I got done with "laugh."

I would look up, and Sister Agnes would be in front of me, watching me write. Oh, she was keen! Her hair was red, just red as bricks. And you could barely see tiny freckles on her face. Ho! Ho! That was funny. It made me laugh, because Sister Agnes used to say: "Hello, you red-headed, freckled-faced Italian scamp." Pretty good! What about *her* red hair? What about *her* freckles?

She would lean over and say: "Faster, faster, faster. Think of those homers! Think of those triples!"

I sure did think of them! I sure did! I wrote to beat the band. She counted every word. I thought I never would finish. When I did, I gave the pages to that goofy Sister Justine. Then I ran all the way up to Emerson. But all the guys were gone. I was late. Nobody was on the ball field, and the janitor told me how badly St. Catherine's was beaten. The team always gets the hell beaten out of them when I do not play.

Sister Agnes always asked about my house. She always said she was coming to my house to find out if I was mean to my mother. I am glad she did not come. My house is not a very good one. It is not really my house. I mean it belongs to my father. It is not so hot. The front window is busted open. My brother did it with a horseshoe. The hole makes the house look like poor people's. Our front porch used to be white, but when we play ball we keep score on the walls and posts. Now the porch looks crazy. Sister Agnes would think we were awfully poor if she saw it. In the front yard, where we have first base, second base, third base, shortstop, pitcher's box, and home plate, all the grass is worn off. Sister would see how poor we are if she saw it. I am glad she did not come.

My mother got excited when I told her Sister Agnes wanted to come. She told me to find out when she was coming. But I didn't. I lied. I told my mother that Sister Agnes would not come until summertime.

My mother was not polite to want Sister Agnes to come to

our house. Sisters do not eat out. They have a place. That is why they are Sisters. I would feel awfully cheap if Sister Agnes came. Our house is not much. She would think we were awfully poor when we started to eat. My mother would have macaroni. Sister would think that was crazy. We do not have a tablecloth. My mother spreads newspapers. She puts the funny pictures under my brother's plate and the box scores under mine. When I eat, I can see what the boys are doing up in the Big Time. It looks like the A's again this year.

III

One day my mother wrote to Sister Agnes. I went down to the creek and read the note. It was not a good note. It was blotted. My mother wrote it with that old pen. She made a mistake, too. She put her name down like this: "Maria Toscana." Which is wrong. When other mothers write notes to Sisters, they do it this way: "Mrs.———," and then they write their last names. They do not use the first name. My mother should have put her name down this way: "Mrs. Toscana." When she puts it this way, "Maria Toscana," people know we are poor.

My mother wrote:

Dear Sister Mary Agnes:
I am sorry indeed that you cannot come to see me. My boy tells me of you nearly every day, and I am eager to know you. May I send you a dish of my macaroni some time? Just a sentiment for the fine way you treat my boy.
Maria Toscana

I was in a heck of a fix. The note said my mother was sorry indeed, and Sister would think that was funny, because I did not ask her to come, so she could not say no, so why was my mother sorry?

I did not know what to do. I played hooky. I played hooky

59

all morning. I sat on the bench at the depot and watched the trains. The Athletics travel on big trains like those.

There is a guy they call Jumbo, and he came to the bench. He wanted to know if I was playing hooky. He is not a kid or anything. He is a man. He wanted to know why I was playing hooky. I showed him the note and told him.

"Oh," he said, "this is easy."

He tore the note into pieces. He said I should go to Sister Agnes and ask her, face to face, if she wanted some of my mother's macaroni. It was a very fine idea.

I went to school, and I told Sister Justine that the reason I was absent in the morning was that my mother had the pain in her side again, and I had to go to the drug-store for medicine. And do you know what? That dumb Sister Justine acted as if she did not believe me! Blah on her! Just because she is principal she thinks she can believe anything she wants. I fooled her, all right.

After school I went to Sister Agnes's room. Jumbo's idea was sure a swell one. I do not mind if I ask people face to face to eat my mother's macaroni, but I do mind if I have to give them notes. It is a lot different.

Sister Agnes was playing the organ. She was alone. The room, and the organ, and Sister Agnes, and everything made me think of the time when I was a kid. I looked around, and do you know what I was looking for? I was looking for the little desk with the tar stuck on the seat. And sure enough, there it was, in the back of the room. I sat at it. Gee, it was sad. There I was, the greatest pitcher this school ever had, and sitting at the same little desk I used when Sister Agnes was my teacher.

The organ stopped, and I heard her say: "Well, what on earth are you doing back there?"

I said: "Oh, nothing."

She said: "Come up here, and we will talk."

I started to get out of the little desk.

But she said: "Wait. I want to show you something." She walked down the aisle.

It was just like the time she came down the aisle and sat on the tar. I thought she did not remember the tar, but that was

60

what she wanted to show me. Gee, I got so red. I got freezy as ice when she found me at the same little desk.

But it was not so awful. She pulled my hair, and she told me about convicts who come back to the place they commit sin. I laughed and then she laughed and then we both laughed. Gee, she was pretty. I wish I could have said: "I am sorry" a long, long time ago. I should have said it just then, but I still do not like to say this to people.

Instead I said: "My mother wants you to eat some of her macaroni."

She said: "Sure! Thank your mother and tell her I'll be glad to eat a whole bucket of it."

I was sure surprised! I did not think Sisters ate macaroni. But I guess they do. Sister did not mean a real bucketful, though. She just meant a whole lot. But I guess my mother thought she really meant a whole bucketful.

Ye Gods! Next day I had to lug a bucket of macaroni to school. I hollered, but it did not help any. My father was home. I went up alleys so none of the boys could see me. I sneaked in the back door and gave it to Sister Cook and told her to give it to Sister Agnes.

Sister Agnes said it was the best macaroni she ever tasted. I bet she was fooling, though. I know about those things. I know that once my mother gave some macaroni to the Dows. They said it was good too. But Archer Dow said it tasted dirty, and I saw whole gobs of it in the chicken yard. I felt so cheap I beat up Archer. So I know people. I know what they do.

After I brought the macaroni, Sister Agnes liked me all the more. I used to ditch ball practice to talk to her. A swell player like me doesn't have to practice, anyhow. For a little while, Sister Agnes would talk to me about being a priest. Then she would figure my batting average. She knew how. She figured that I was hitting .599, which is a lot better than Rogers Hornsby. On the ball field I used to bust out homers just to see what Sister Agnes would say. I busted out eight homers, five triples, and three doubles in the Thoreau game. I pitched too. So that shows you. Sister Agnes did not believe I did so much in one game. I made the second-graders tell her all about it.

61

IV

Sister Agnes figured I would be thirty-five year old before I could become a priest.

I said: "Hey, Sister, how old are you?"

She said: "You must never ask a nun her age."

Then she lifted the blotter from her desk and showed me a picture. It was her mother and father and Sister Agnes when she was a girl. Sister Agnes wore a high hat with a feather in it. I looked at it for a long time.

She took it away from me and put it under the blotter.

"Now," she said, "how old do you think I am?"

I said: "I bet I can guess."

"Guess," she said.

'Twenty-five," I said. I was guessing any old number.

She laughed. That meant I guessed right. When people laugh that way, they mean you have guessed right.

Before she said good-night she told me to go to the sacristy and pray our Lord to make me a priest. I went. I prayed the way she said, but I did not pray very hard, because I did not really want to be a priest. I am going to be a big leaguer. I did not pray to get into the big leagues, though, because I pray for that on Sundays. I go to Communion for it. I am making a Novena for it, too. A Novena is when you go to Holy Communion nine straight times. If you make a perfect Novena you can ask our Lord for anything in the world. But I do not really need a Novena to make the big leagues. I am already a great player. A Novena cinches it for me.

Just when I got up to leave, I thought of a wonderful idea. I knelt down again and made up a prayer. A swell prayer. Here it is: "O dear, sweet Infant Jesus, if You will help me get Sister Agnes's picture, I will make my next Novena one about asking you to make a priest out of me." I prayed like the dickens. I was holy. I knelt up straight. I kept my hands togeather.

After praying, I went to Sister Agnes's classroom. I was going to ask her for the picture. I sure wanted it. Oh, you should see that Sister Agnes!

She was not there. But you could hear forks and knives in the convent. That meant the Sisters were eating supper. I sure wanted that picture.

So I stole it. I put it under my waist. I sneaked away and beat it for home. After supper I went up to the attic and hid the picture. I keep all my important stuff there, and nobody can see the picture. Nobody but me.

Next day I got to thinking, and I did not know what to do. It was awful, because Sister Agnes knew I did it. When I got to school, I did not go out on the field. I sneaked into the washroom and locked myself in until the bell rang. I stayed in the washroom at recess too. I stayed in there at twelve o'clock too.

After school, I broke ranks and ran behind the church. George McClure saw me, so I went into church to make an Act of Contrition, because stealing is a mortal sin. While I was kneeling there, up came George McClure.

He said: "Hey, Sister Agnes is looking for you."

I said: "What for?"

He said: "Search me."

I said: "Does she look sore or anything?"

He said: "Not that I know of."

Before I went to see her, I made up another prayer. It was a pretty good one. Here it is: "O dear, sweet Infant Jesus, if You ever helped anybody, please help me now."

Sister Agnes was playing the organ. She heard me come in. I was so scared I could not talk. I was all leery and freezy. It felt like the time she came down the aisle when I was a little second-grader.

She said: "Hello!" It was fishy. I can tell.

I said: "Hello."

She said: "You must never come here again."

She said: "You must never talk to me again."

Then she hollered: "You hear me?"

I said: "Yes, Sister."

She said: "Go home."

And after that she never liked me. I know she will never like me again. I can tell.

I did not go home, though. I went out on the ball field. I

thought I would practice hitting some long ones. I did. That night I hit six home runs and five triples.

My Mother's Goofy Song

MY MOTHER DOESN'T BELIEVE I got arrested for stealing carbide. I try to prove it and try to prove it, but she won't believe me. It doesn't do any good to talk to her.

This is how it happened. Me and Dibber got arrested on Sunday, right after church let out. We had paper sacks. We went behind the Colorado Miners' Supply Company. We hid in the high weeds in the alley. Nobody was looking, so I threw a brick through the back window. It made an awful racket, just like when a brick goes through a window. Me and Dibber got pretty scared. Nobody came, though.

Me and Dibber climbed through the busted window. Right there was the carbide in big black drums. The drums weighed five hundred pounds apiece, so we couldn't get away with one of them very well. Even if we could get away with one of them, we'd have to break down the door. Even if we did break down the door, we'd have to carry the drum home, and it was too heavy. Even if we did carry the drum home, we wouldn't know where to hide it. Even if we did know where to hide it, we'd have too much carbide. So we filled the paper sacks.

We didn't hear a sound. But just when we got through, Mr. Krasovich came into the back room from the front part of the store. He wasn't much to be scared of. Oh, no—not much! He only owns the store, that's all.

He said: "Just a minute, boys."

Dibber tried to jump through the window. Mr. Krasovich grabbed him by the pants. He had me by the necktie. I always wear a necktie on Sundays, darn it. But I wasn't trying to get away.

He said: "Come with me, boys."

He took us to his front office. He called on the telephone. He didn't call anybody very important. Oh, no — not very important! He only called the cops, that's all. He hung up. He swung around in his chair and looked at me and Dibber. He thought he was tough.

Dibber said: "If you'll leave us go, Mr. Krasovich, we'll promise never to steal from you again."

Mr. Krasovich said: "No, boys. I'm going to send you two to the state penitentiary." But he couldn't scare me and Dibber with that kind of talk. Me and Dibber are not so dumb as you think.

He sat there like he was the big cheese himself. We didn't want his old carbide, anyway. All we wanted was two little bitty sackfuls to blow the corks out of bottles.

Then Mr. Wagner, the speed cop, drove up with his motorcycle. Oh! Oh! The minute I saw him I knew I was in for it. He isn't very important. He doesn't know anybody very important. Oh, no! He only knows my father, that's all. Mr. Wagner and my father both belong to the Elks. After he found out what happened, Mr. Wagner said the cops would send us both to the penitentiary for fifteen years.

He took us out to his motorcycle and made us both get into the sidecar. I was crying a little, but not much. So was Dibber, and a whole lot. You would too. Mr. Wagner stepped on the starter, and the motorcycle started.

Mr. Krasovich hollered: "Well, good-by, boys. And lots of luck to you!" He is one of those wise guys. He thought he was funny.

Mr. Wagner drove us through town to the courthouse. People kept looking at us. I was glad I was on the bottom. Nobody saw me. Dibber was on my lap. The whole town saw him. He must have felt very cheap and freaky.

Mr. Wagner took us downstairs and put us in the jailhouse. We didn't try to escape or anything. It was a very fine jailhouse. Nobody ever did escape from it. Once, though, three crooks did. Mr. Wagner then went upstairs and telephoned our fathers. He told them to come over right away.

While me and Dibber were waiting for what was going to happen next, we took out our knives and cut our names in the wall. We copied from other names on the wall. If you're ever in that jailhouse, you'll see our names. Look over by the window.

You will see Dibber's cut this way: "Kansas City Lannon."

I cut mine: "Two-Gun Toscana, the Death Kid."

Pretty soon Dibber's father came to the courthouse. He was mad as everything. He was yelling when he came down the stairs.

He hollered: "Where is he! Where is he!"—meaning Dibber.

Mr. Wagner opened the jailhouse door, and Mr. Lannon ran in. He made a hard run for Dibber. He bent Dibber over the cot. And right there in front of me and Mr. Wagner he gave Dibber the worst licking I ever heard anybody get, except me. Old Dibber must have felt very cheap. I mean, you know how it is.

Then he quit licking Dibber, and took him home. He pulled him upstairs by the ear. I heard Dibber hollering away up in the corridor, and even when they got out in the yard, and even when they crossed the street. It was tough on Dibber, but he got off easy.

After a while, my father came down the stairs. He was not in the least bit of a hurry. Mr. Wagner opened the jailhouse door, and my father came in real slow.

He said: "So you're a thief, too, are you?"

I said: "No, Papa. I'm not a thief on purpose."

He said: "Purpose! By God, I'll show you some purpose!"

Oh, but that Dibber got off real easy to what I got. Oh, my father gave it to me with his belt. My father wears a belt because he likes to show off. I mean, what's the use to wear a belt if you're already wearing suspenders? I call that showing off. My father hurt me all the worse, because if you think bricklayer don't hurt, just feel their muscles. My pants hurt and hurt and hurt. What I mean is, they burned like a stove.

After my father got tired of licking me, he pushed me into the corner and put his belt on.

He said: "When you get home, tell your mother what you did, you twisted little snake. And if she doesn't knock the living hell out of you, then, by God, I will."

"You already did," I said.

"Then, by God, I'll do it again."

I went out of the jailhouse and up the stairs and down the corridor and out the door and down the front stairs and across the street. I started to run. I wanted to get home before my father, so my mother could give me my other licking, because if she didn't, my father would give it to me again, this time harder. That would be two straight for him, and I'd rather take a hundred and fifty million lickings from my mother than even half of one licking from my father.

Ho ho! You should see my mother when she gives me a licking. Ho ho! You should see her! Ho ho! She hits me like a little tiny sissified girl, and she thinks I'm dying from it. I make faces and groans, and before two or three hits she feels so sorry she has to stop, and before long *she's* the one who's crying, not me.

I was all out of breath when I got home. My mother was in the back yard, feeding the chickens. I told her what happened. I told her the honest-to-God truth. I told her and told her.

I said: "Mamma, I swiped carbide. I got arrested. I got put in jail. Papa got me out. He gave me a licking. He says for you to give me another one, too."

But she thought I was kidding. I told her and told her and told her, but she wouldn't believe me.

She said: "You mustn't talk like that."

I told her to hurry and lick me. I even got a stick. She wouldn't take it. We went into the house. I was scared about my father. He is a very fast walker. I knew he was coming.

But all my mother did was sit there and say: "You mustn't talk like that."

Then I figured out a swell way to prove it to her. I phoned Mr. Krasovich. I told him to hold the line a minute. But my mother wouldn't talk to him.

She said: "Hang up. I won't talk to him."

I said: "Honest, Ma."

I said: "Cross my heart, Ma."

I said: "Honest to God, Ma."

I said: "God strike me dead, Ma."

Then my father came home. I heard his shoes scrape on the front porch. I was out of luck. He came in without taking off his hat.

68

I said "Papa, Mamma doesn't believe I got pinched, and she won't lick me. You tell her."

He said: "Sure I will, later. Now you get in there" — meaning me. Also meaning the bedroom.

I went in there. I got it again. I got a hell of an awful licking. The worst I ever got in my whole life, except the time I broke Alloback's window and the time I kicked my brother in the head and the time I stole Mamma's purse. Anyhow, it was a plenty tough licking. It stung and stung and stung. Then my father threw me on the bed and went to talk to my mother.

He told my mother about it. I heard him. He told her and told her. But she would not believe him. She said I was too little to steal and get arrested; that made my father get mad.

He said: "By God, you don't know what a devil that kid is." And my father is right, because I am plenty tough.

He went out. My mother came into the bedroom. I was still crying from my licking. I had a right to cry, because it was the worst I got in my whole life. My mother got the menthol and pulled down my pants. She didn't believe me yet. The menthol felt like ice, cold ice. While she was rubbing me, she tried to tell me I didn't do it. But I said I did, all right.

She said: "I know you didn't do it."

I said: "I know I did."

She said: "Come on, say you didn't do it."

I said: "But I did, too, do it."

She said: "Oh, you did not."

I said: "I did!"

She said: "No you didn't. You can't fool your mother."

I said: "The heck I can't! If you don't believe me, go down to the jailhouse and see. You go there, and you'll see where me and Dibber cut our names on the wall."

But she shook her head, meaning she still thought I was fooling her.

She went away, and I could hear her in the kitchen. She was singing. My mother always sings the same old song, and it's not such a hot song, either. I learned it a long time ago, when I was a first-grade punk. It's "The Farmer in the Dell."

The right way to sing "The Farmer in the Dell" is like this:

> *The farmer in the dell,*
> *he farmer in the dell,*
> *Heigho, the merrio,*
> *The farmer in the dell.*

Which is plenty bad enough, but this is how my mother was singing it, which makes it a very goofy song:

> *Oh, I know he didn't do it,*
> *I know he didn't do it,*
> *Heigho, the merrio,*
> *I know he didn't do it.*

She meant me, she meant I didn't do it, which is nuts, because I did do it. And if she wants proof she can go down to the jailhouse and see mine and Dibber's names cut in the wall.

Dibber cut his: "Kansas City Lannon."

I cut mine: "Two-Gun Toscana, the Death Kid."

I like mine best.

A Wife for Dino Rossi

His name was Dino Rossi, and he was a barber down in North Denver, down there in the Italian quarter where we lived when we were kids. In the early days he had courted my mother. That was around 1909, before my father came upon the scene. Dino Rossi couldn't have been very ardent at courtship; he was too gentle for that; he was so thin, so soft-spoken, his hands and feet so small. He had been no match for my father, who was a bricklayer, no competition at all. Under Dino's very nose my father and mother had been married. Dino Rossi was one of my earliest memories. I can remember playing horseback on his knees, bouncing up and down on his bony knees.

Six or seven times a year Dino came to our house for dinner. Papa used to insist on his coming. Papa used to go out of his way to Dino's barber shop to invite him to dinner. To us kids, Mike and Tony and Clara and me, the reason was obvious: Papa liked Dino sitting there because Dino had failed in his efforts to marry Mamma, while Papa had succeeded. All the time, walking in and out of the room, hovering over the table and serving dinner, there was Mamma, one man's prize and another man's loss. Whenever Dino was there Papa developed a remarkable fondness for Mamma. From where he sat between Tony and me, Dino's soft eyes would watch Papa embrace Mamma every time she came from the kitchen with the roast, or the macaroni, or whatever it might be. Other times Papa would seize Mamma and kiss her violently.

This was extraordinary, as well as disgusting, because Papa never did such things when Dino wasn't around. Papa was inclined to fits of moodiness: he would sulk for days and make

71

scenes over trifles: if his eggs were too soft, or his handkerchiefs unironed, or a button was gone from his shirt, he would raise both fists to the ceiling, rip out tufts of his hair, and shout threats. If the bread or the salt and pepper were forgotten at table, he would generally warn us, Mamma in particular, that he was tiring of it all, and intended to strike out alone. We were used to these outbursts, and nobody paid any attention to them, not even Papa himself.

But if Dino was there, *mamma mia*, how different Papa was! I was fourteen in those days, but even my brother Tony, barely six, sensed the stiletto behind Papa's peculiar conduct. Papa was simply twisting it in, torturing Dino, who lived in two rooms behind the barber shop on Osage Street, and would probably never marry and have a wife take care of him. Papa would always bring up the subject of marriage — Dino's — in the presence of all of us, there at the table.

"What the devil's the matter with you, Dino? Are you a man, or what? Almost forty years old, your hair falling out, and still you live in that hole behind the barber shop. Get yourself a wife, Dino! *Madonna*, how can you stand it? How can you live without a woman?"

Then he would turn and grab Mamma by the waist, squeezing her with his heavy arms as Mamma smiled patiently, her gentle face begging Dino to understand, to forgive Papa.

"Look at me, now!" Papa would continue. "Look what I got. And look at the food on this table. Such cooking, so good for a man's stomach! Did you ever taste ravioli like this, Dino?"

Dino would smile his praises.

"Answer me, Dino! Don't be afraid. Don't be shy in front of my wife. You were once in love with her. Once you even tried to marry her."

Dino always spoke in Italian.

"The ravioli is delicious, Guido," he would answer. "Ambrosial!" And he would pluck a kiss from his lips and toss it toward the platter.

"Of course it is. Everything's ambrosial when your own wife cooks it. Ah, Dino, what a fool you are, living in that shack. You, with all your money saved, and what has it got you?

72

Nothing! Solitude, loneliness, gray hair, old age." Then his voice would change to a confidential tone. "Dino, you must have twenty-five, thirty thousand dollars in the bank, huh, Dino?"

Dino would lower his eyes, and all of us would suffer with him, for Dino was not a man who boasted of what he possessed; nor was he without generosity, Dino Rossi, who gave us free haircuts, and a quarter apiece every time he came to our house, and swell presents at Christmas time.

After dinner it was worse. Dino would help Mamma and Clara with the dishes, and then he would go into the front room, where Papa sat waiting impatiently for him, contemptuous of a full-grown man assisting in lowly female tasks. They would sip anisette and smoke cigars. It was our turn after dinner, our turn to become the tools of Papa's conceit.

We always sneaked away quietly to the back part of the house, out of his sight and out of his reach, but inevitably he would call us, his voice disgustingly affectionate, yet with a quality of command that we feared. We would drop our toys and march in, sullenly, with bitter mouths, unhappy for Dino, still more unhappy at what lay before us.

Papa would be sitting in the big rocker by the window, and Dino would be on the davenport near the bookcase. Like wooden soldiers we would march into the middle of the gray carpet, there to stand with our hands dangling foolishly, each of us aware that Papa's strong burgundy had by now reached its full effect upon him. There Papa sat, a Nero on his throne, his body deep in the rocker, his arms limp over the sides, his legs stretched before him. Mike and Tony and myself, we always felt like running deep into the night, there to hide our faces in shame. With Clara it was different; Papa didn't care much about her, because she was a girl.

"There they are, Dino," Papa would begin. "My sons. Flesh of my flesh, bone of my bone. My handiwork, Dino. I created these boys, I, and I alone. Ah, Dino! The joy of creating sons! Observe them; clear eyes, thick hair, strong bones, healthy skins. They carry my name, they immortalize me, they save me from the grave. When I am gone from this earth, my spirit goes on and on in the flesh of these boys, and their sons, and their sons' sons."

73

We three would look at one another, perplexed and feeling terribly naked, our eyes asking one another the same question: Why the heck does he *do* this? But in the end it was little Tony who got the worst of it, because he was the youngest and fairest, and it was he whom Papa called to him. Tony would frown as he walked with dragging toes toward Papa, and Papa would lift Tony up on his lap, holding him there and tightening his big arms every time Tony tried to squirm loose. Too bad for Tony! Mike and I would rush to the back of the house, gasping with relief, cursing: "Goddamn him, goddamn him." But Tony had to sit there and be bounced on Papa's knees, and even be kissed, which was pretty awful, because Papa smoked those powerful black Toscanelli cigars, and when Tony finally got away his mouth would stiffen, as though he were trying to push it away from his face.

"I have found a wife for Dino Rossi."

It was Papa talking. We were in bed, four of us in one bed, Tony and Hugo, our Airedale, in the middle, Mike and I on the outside. Clara slept on the davenport in the front room. Papa had just come home from the Little Italy Club, and we could hear him in the next room, talking to Mamma as he undressed, coins and nails jingling in his pockets as he took off his pants.

"You've found a wife?"

That was Mamma's voice, and the bed springs creaked, and we knew she had sat up at his words.

"A wife. Dino Rossi is going to get married, by God!"

"But when? Who?"

"Coletta Drigo," Papa said.

"And who's Coletta Drigo?"

"A woman," Papa said.

"But who? What kind of a woman?"

"A beautiful woman. From Chicago."

"Does Dino love her?"

"He ain't even met her yet."

Mamma gasped. Mike and I sat up, waiting to hear more. Hugo's ears stood out like funnels, and he began to growl. From the silence we knew Mamma was speechless. For a long time there wasn't a sound. One of Papa's shoes thumped to the floor, then

74

the other. Hugo began to lick Tony's face, and Tony sat up too. We heard Papa pad across the floor in his bare feet, heard the light switch click off, and the sound of his feet once more as he crossed to his side of the bed.

"You must be out of your head," Mamma said. "Dino doesn't want to get married. He's very happy."

"No he's not," Papa said.

"What kind of a woman is she?"

"Oh," Papa said, "she's not so bad." From the way he said it we knew that Coletta Drigo, whoever she was, must indeed be a pretty bad woman. Papa yawned. "Met her tonight," he said. "She's a stranger in town. She's coming to dinner tomorrow. So's Dino."

"You mean — coming here, to *this* house?"

"Sure," Papa said. "Where do you suppose?"

Mamma got out of bed, hurried across the room, and switched on the light. It leaped into our bedroom too, because the door was half open. "I won't have this woman in my house," Mamma said. "Do you hear me? I won't have her under my roof, eating at my table. I won't have anything to do with it."

"What do you mean, *your* house?" Papa said. "What do you mean, *your* roof? *Your* table? I'm the money maker in this family, and what I say goes."

"You heard me!" Mamma said. "Poor Dino, poor, innocent Dino. Well, I won't have it!" We heard the closet door rattle, the sound of Mamma slipping into her robe, then the soft sound of Mamma's feet pushing into bedroom slippers. The light in the front room flooded the rest of the house when Mamma left the bedroom. We could hear her walking around, as though walking furiously in a circle.

"A wife for Dino!" she gasped. "Why, the very idea!"

"Come to bed!" Papa shouted. "I'm a bricklayer, in case you don't remember. I got to be on the job at seven in the morning."

Mamma turned off the lights and went back to bed. We heard her talking unhappily to herself. Mike and I lay in the darkness, our ears alert. Tony was asleep now, Hugo's chin across his neck, Hugo's thick lips puffing in and out. After a while Mamma groaned and tossed. She was sitting up again. Papa gasped.

"What now?"

"She's not coming. I won't have it!"

"You heard me the first time. She's coming to dinner and so's Dino. It's about time he got married, and by God I'll see that he does."

"I won't cook dinner. I won't do it."

"Yes, you will."

Back and forth the argument went on, until Mike fell asleep and Hugo became so disgusted with the noise that he jumped from the bed and went to his place behind the kitchen stove. I listened to their voices in the darkness, but nothing more was said to clear up the mystery of Coletta Drigo. Mamma's voice was thick with bitterness. It was always "that woman," but never her name. Even as I fell asleep the argument went on, with Mamma insisting she wouldn't cook dinner for that woman, and Papa warning her that she'd better.

Papa won the argument. For that matter, Papa never lost an argument with Mamma, but I knew he had won again when I got home from school next afternoon and smelled the rich odor of ravioli sauce through the house. Ravioli meant one of two things at our house: either it was Easter Sunday or Christmas, or company was coming. It wasn't Christmas, and it wasn't Easter.

One look at Hugo's sad eyes and fallen ears, and I knew Mamma was dangerous. Hugo wouldn't even come into the house. I stepped into the kitchen and Mamma turned, her face hot and perspiring, and ordered me out of the room. Blobs of flour smeared her apron and she tried to blow a strand of hair from her eyes.

I just want some bread and peanut butter," I said.

She raised her arm and pointed toward the door. I didn't move. She stood there, pointing and blowing at the loose hair. I shrugged and walked away. Tony got the same treatment. He kicked and shrieked for his regular after-school bread and peanut butter, but it did no good. When Mike came home, he too walked empty-handed into the back yard. Clara was the only one who got anything. She stayed in the kitchen with Mama. We sat in silent

76

dejection under the apple tree. It was that woman, that Coletta Drigo person, who was the cause of it all.

Papa got home a few minutes before six. The back yard was pink in the sunset. We heard Papa in the house, his iron-cleated heels pounding the floor, and then the song he whistled as he shaved. Long shadows fell away from the back fence. We didn't say a word. After a while Papa stopped whistling, and Hugo whimpered uncomfortably. A strange calm came with darkness. We sat looking at the kitchen window, watching Mamma as she moved back and forth from the table to the stove. Pretty soon Papa came outside. He was shaved and powdered and we could smell him, and it was like sitting in a barber shop. He carried a small glass of wine. Seated on the back steps, he sipped it in the dangerous silence. Once he smacked his lips loudly, but that was bravado, for there was guilt in the way he looked about him; and when he snapped his fingers and called Hugo, the dog got up and slowly walked away.

Then Dino arrived. Mamma put her head out the door and told us to come in now. Papa jumped to his feet.

"Dino!" he said. "Is Dino here? Well, what do you know about that!"

It was as if he were trying to convince all of us that Dino's arrival was an extraordinary event, despite the fact that he had personally invited Dino to come. We went inside. Papa had rushed into the cellar to his wine barrels, and Dino stood over the stove, his eyes closed reverently as he inhaled the wonderful aroma of Mamma's tomato sauce. He had a way with him, that Dino. Mamma's cooking was so much better when he was there to praise it with small gesturing fingers and the worshipful sparkle in his cool eyes.

We stood against the kitchen wall, watching him from a different perspective than ever before. Hugo smelled his shoes suspiciously. We had always felt vaguely sorry for Dino, and now we pitied him and were ashamed that we knew in secret what was about to befall him. A woman was going to get Dino. It meant nothing to us, and yet it was catastrophic, but we didn't know why. When he saw our lugubrious faces he would not have it. With unexpected gusto he clapped his hands.

77

"Come, come!" he said. "Why so gloomy?"

He reached into his pockets and drew out all his silver and began dividing it among us. It wouldn't divide evenly. With an impatient smile he poured all the coins into Tony's hands. "Divide it among yourselves." We thanked him without enthusiasm. As we retreated to the front part of the house, he stood in the kitchen door and scratched his head, his face lined with amazement.

"What's the matter with them?"

"They are probably tired," Mamma said.

But what about the mysterious Coletta Drigo? Our eagerness to see her made us stiffen at the slightest sound on the front porch. Hugo put his nose against the crack at the base of the door and lay there waiting, now and then growling uncertainly.

In the kitchen Papa poured wine for himself and Dino. His voice had a wild, defensive tone. He seemed eager to distract Dino, and he went to absurd lengths to make Dino comfortable. He made foolish inquiries about Dino's health, his business, and how are you sleeping these nights, Dino, and is your wine cold enough, and how do you like the weather we're having? If Dino was suspicious, he concealed it, for he acted as always, his voice as gentle as his eyes.

"Dinner's ready," Mamma said. "Of course, that woman *would* be late."

"Someone else is coming?" Dino said.

Papa pretended to be astonished.

"Why, yes, Dino. Coletta Drigo is coming. Didn't you know? Didn't Maria tell you?"

"I was not told," Dino said.

Papa shouted at Mamma: "What's the idea, not telling Dino Coletta was coming? Didn't I tell you to tell him? What kind of a woman are you, anyway?"

Mamma's eyes were balls of ice.

"Now listen to me. I had nothing to do with this, understand? Absolutely nothing."

It quieted Papa, who purpled with a quiet rage. He walked out of the kitchen and came toward us in the front room, all ten fingers attacking his hair, his face like choppy water as he pulled back the curtain and looked into the street.

"She'll be here any minute now," he said to himself.

We knew why he had walked out of the kitchen: he was blundering, making a mess of the whole thing, and he had fled from Dino's calmness in order to get his bearings. There was sure to be a fight after Dino left tonight. Papa carried his grudges to the bitter end, and he would not forget that Mamma had failed to co-operate.

He was on his way back to the kitchen when Hugo began to bark and we heard a car stop in front of the house. Papa hurried back to the window and looked out. "She's come!" he shouted. "She's here!" It brought Mamma and Dino with frightened faces from the kitchen. Papa and Hugo ran outside, Hugo leaping joyfully. We got up and stood at the door in time to see Papa throw his arms around a woman taller than himself and kiss her on the cheek. Papa kissing another woman! Even Hugo looked amazed.

In the darkness we could not see her face, but her silhouette against the street lamp was round, soft, and stately. With arms locked, she and Papa entered. The sight of her, the sheer beauty of that woman, left us stunned, our mouths open as she looked down at us, her white teeth flashing.

Papa introduced us; I was first, then Tony, then Clara, and finally Mike. Hugo stood there laughing happily, his tongue hanging out, but he was only a dog, and everybody ignored him. We couldn't help feeling very proud of Papa, a mere bricklayer, but for all that a man who could be at ease in the presence of such beauty as we had never seen before. When she took my hand and pressed it with long, soft fingers, heavy gold bracelets at her wrists tinkling like bells, I was so upset that I giggled out loud.

I couldn't help envying Tony. Coletta put her arm around him and wove her fingers through his hair as she pressed him against her. He was overcome with delight, his face suffused with a smile I had never seen before. For a moment he seemed frightened, and then he raised his arms and gave himself languidly to her, his arms about her waist, his eyes closed as he pressed himself against her.

Mamma and Dino came from the kitchen. Mamma's face was hard, but Dino seemed ready for anything. Mamma wiped her hands on her apron and shook Coletta's hand. "How do you do?" Mamma said.

"Very well, thank you," Coletta said. "And you, Mrs. Toscana?" Mamma didn't answer.

They were about the same age, but thirty-five years might have been forty-five if Mamma's face had been a place for measuring time, while Coletta's might have been twenty-five. You saw four children in Mamma's face, you even saw Hugo there; you saw centuries of worry, ages of toil, aeons of work and distress. There was no record of children upon the face of Coletta Drigo, nor of worry, nor of distress; instead you saw a rare nuance of youth to maturity; you saw excitement; you saw great cities, happy times, the whole wonderful world; and, above all, her beauty, black hair, black eyes, the dark whitish skin. You were sure that if she had a pet it wasn't a dog but a cat, a Siamese cat.

Standing beside Mamma, Dino seemed more than ever like one of us, our brother or our uncle, and the beauty of Coletta Drigo made her lonely and unique among us. She gave Dino her hand, held it out like a limp white dove, and smiled as Dino rubbed the perspiration from his palm upon his thigh and took her hand with breathless hesitancy. He squeezed it faintly, his head bowed so that she saw the beginning of baldness at the crown of his head. Her black eyes opened wider with that look of recognition, as if marking him, as though to herself she were saying: "So *this* is the fellow!"

"It is an honor to know you," Dino said.

"Thank you," she said. "Thank you, Dino."

His name formed by her lips gave him strength. He looked at her bravely, a change coming over his face and body, happiness in his smile. Papa bustled around, nervous and grinning, and we could see that already he was beginning to feel that after all the dinner would be a success.

He pulled up a chair for Coletta, who peeled off her fur in a strange way that made me think she was naked beneath it. Mike and Tony and I held our breath, watched the tight black satin appear beneath the coat, and as one we rushed to take the coat from her. It ended in a tie, eight fists strangling the black and white fur. Hugo sank his teeth into a dangling sleeve and tugged

80

too, until Papa forced his jaws loose. We carried the fur into Mamma's room, and spread it lovingly upon the bed. Then Mike grabbed it between his arms and pushed his face into the deep collar.

"Holy Moses! Smell it — gee!"

"Perfume," Clara said.

Hugo sneezed.

It was a dinner to remember. Papa insisted that Dino sit next to Coletta, but Dino had already found a place for himself between Mike and me. Mamma came from the kitchen and stared coldly at Coletta.

"I'm not hungry tonight," Mamma said. "I couldn't possibly eat a thing." Since Mamma's place was always between Papa and Dino, that chair was now left vacant.

"Good!" Papa blurted out. "That's fine. Coletta, you sit in my wife's place, and, Dino, you come over here and sit beside Coletta."

Coletta arose and slid sensuously into Mamma's chair. Every time she moved it made me think she was naked. Dino was very polite, but he declined to move. He put his arms around Mike and me, his hands resting on our shoulders.

"I am content here," he said. "Between my two boys."

"You're my guest!" Papa said, banging the table with his fist. "You got to sit where I tell you."

Coletta dropped her eyes.

"Perhaps Dino doesn't wish to sit next to me," she murmured.

Dino leaped to his feet. He bowed grandly.

"Forgive me," he said in his polite Italian. "I meant no offense, Signorina Drigo. It would bring me great joy to sit next to you."

"Now you're talking!" Papa said. "Now we're getting some place. Sit down there, Dino, and let's eat. I'm hungry as hell. Maria!"

Mamma appeared from the kitchen.

"What do you want?"

"Food!" Papa yelled, his earlier gallantry gone. "What the hell do you think I want?"

Without a word Mamma served us. She filled the middle of that wide mahogany table with platters of chicken cacciatore and ravioli. She appeared with bowls of salad and vegetables. Her face was gray and stony; her eyes looked straight ahead. Not once did she speak. One word from her, one smile, and the dinner might have been saved. Instead it was a disaster. Her appearance from the kitchen brought a tenseness that forbade eating. The moment she was gone again Papa tried to lighten the silence with frantic stabs at conversation. It only increased the tension. The dinner was ruined and everyone knew it, especially Coletta.

But not Dino. He was the some old Dino, his ready smile and gentle eyes unmoved by the conflict about him. While the rest of us dabbled with our forks, he took two big helpings of everything, chewing and swallowing with the same slow, idolatrous reverence for Mamma's cooking.

Dessert was chocolate cake. Chocolate cake! The magic of Mamma's chocolate cake! We would have died for chocolate cake, we kids, but that night we just didn't want any chocolate cake. Nobody wanted any chocolate cake. Coffee, yes. Even Coletta agreed to a cup of black coffee, but no cake.

Except Dino. Impatiently we watched him eat one piece and then ask for another, his eyes full of adoration for each mouthful. Coletta sat with her chin high, a brave smile on her lips. Once she opened her purse, drew out a pack of cigarettes, considered them momentarily, and closed the purse with a resigned snap. We felt sorry for Coletta. Mamma's taciturn revolt was an attack upon her, and she seemed so alone, like an injured beautiful bird. We were ashamed of Mamma's cruelty. We pitied Papa, who kept breaking the silence with pathetic outbursts such as "Swell dinner!" and "Boy, what food!" and "Best meal I ever had." As for Dino, he ate with the appetite of a little pig.

As he finished the last of his cake, Mamma gathered the soiled dishes. Dino rose to help her.

"Please, Dino," Mamma said, "don't trouble yourself."

"Ah, Maria," Dino said, "to do this is little enough after such exquisite food."

Papa winked at Coletta.

"So! It's not enough that you refuse to sit next to the guest of honor. Now you want to leave her with me while you help my wife with a pile of dirty dishes!"

"Perhaps we could all help,"Dino said.

"Of course!" Coletta agreed, standing up.

But Mamma wouldn't have it. Plainly, she wanted no part of Coletta Drigo in her kitchen. The argument ended with Mamma and Clara doing the work, the rest of us gathering in the front room. Coletta slid her hands beneath her hips, smoothing back her dress as she sat in the middle of the divan. Leaning back, she sighed. Papa thumped himself down beside her. We sprawled on the carpet in the middle of the room, lying on our stomachs and gazing at the beautiful woman. She had crossed her legs, and her silken knees were like golden oranges. We stared in wonder and delight. Hugo cocked his head and lifted his ears. On the other side of the room, over in the corner, Dino had found a rocker. Lighting a cigar, he sent the smoke thinly from the corner of his mouth.

"What you doing 'way over there, Dino?" Papa said. "Why can't you be a gentleman and sit on the other side of Coletta?"

Dino looked at the cigar, uncertain of himself.

"I just know Dino doesn't like me," Coletta said. "I've felt it all evening long."

It stabbed Dino deeply. He rose, his two hands clutched at his chest, and said: "Forgive me, Signorina. I am so rude. I am not aware of these social niceties. You see, I am not often in the presence of one so lovely as yourself. It will be an honor to sit beside you, if you allow it."

She nodded sweetly and he sat down, frightened and ready for anything.

"He's right, Coletta," Papa said. "He's telling you the truth. He doesn't know a damn thing about women."

All at once Papa grew very friendly. He spread himself full length, crossed his feet, and raised both arms to the back of the divan. As if by accident his right arm fell across Coletta's smooth shoulders, but he didn't take it away, and his palm covered the rounded softness and he squeezed gently.

"Did you ever hear the one about the iceman and the woman who was taking a bath?"

"No," Coletta said. "Please tell it."

Papa shifted his cigar. "Well, this woman was taking a bath.

'Course she was all undressed, and she heard the ice truck, and she remembered she didn't put out the ice card. So she ran downstairs, naked, to put the card in the window, and when she got there she heard somebody coming, and she thought it was the iceman. So she jumped in the closet, and she didn't have a thing on. But it wasn't the iceman at all. It was the meterman to read the meter, and he opened the door, and there she was, stark naked, and she said: 'Oh! I thought you was the iceman.' "

Coletta laughed, hiding her face. Dino sat with his arms folded, smiling; it was plain he didn't understand the story, and neither did we. Papa thought of another one.

"Ever hear the one about the farmer who wanted to get married?"

"No," Coletta said. "Please tell it."

"Well, this farmer wanted to get married." Papa paused, looked around, as if he suspected eavesdropping. He saw us there on the floor. It was as though he didn't know we'd been there all the time.

"What the hell you kids doing here?"

We had been making a feast of the beauty of Coletta. We were not ready for his question. We could not answer him. "Beat it," he said. "Go outside and play."

We retreated heels first to the dining room, where Mamma's fretful hands snatched at the soiled dishes, the blood sucked from her pale lips. We stood there, content to listen to the melody of Coletta's voice.

"You too, Hugo," Papa said. "Beat it."

Hugo went reluctantly, looking over his shoulder a couple of times. Then from behind us we felt it, each of us at the same time, and before we turned and looked at her we knew that agony coming from behind us, flowing into us, and we all turned at once, and she stood there looking at us, and she seemed a million years old, Mamma, our mother, and we her children had felt her broken heart, she there in the kitchen door, an apron hiding the tumbled misery of her churning hands, little rivers of vanished beauty wandering vainly down the wasteland of her cheeks.

Once I too was like Coletta, said the speechless lips, but all that I ever was has gone into the four of you, and into him, and there you stand, my burden and my reward. We felt her message, but we could not understand it, for it confused and terrified us; and rather than suffer with her we fled past her and through the back door, while tears tumbled down her cheeks as Papa's laughter rattled through the house. But Clara stood there holding Mamma's hand.

We tiptoed around the house, through the strawberry and mint beds, until we were at the front-room window. I was tall enough and so were Mike and Hugo, but even when he was on tiptoe Tony's eyes didn't reach the top of the sill. We shushed him to be quiet, but he gasped and clawed to lemme see, lemme see, tearing at our shirts and raging with tears, and then he began to kick us, and he knocked Hugo down, bawling hysterically, screaming for us to get him a box to stand on, or else he'd spoil everything. It scared me: he pulled his hair and bit his fingers like a boy gone insane. I ran to the coal shed and hurried back with a box. He climbed up on it, and immediately he was quiet as he gazed and gazed at the beauty of Coletta Drigo, the last of his sobs trailing off into a kind of crooning contentment.

I shuddered at what I saw. Coletta was still seated between Papa and Dino, with her knees crossed, and I could see even more of the knees from the window. A paroxysm of sensual shocks staggered me as I devoured their roundness incased in golden silk. It was murkily sinful, and I wanted to enjoy it in secret; the presence of Mike and Tony and Hugo irritated me. It made me angry that perhaps Mike too was enjoying the same sensations, and maybe Tony too, but he was so little. All at once I wanted to punch Mike in the nose, the evil-minded little fool.

"Why don't you beat it?" I said.

"So you can have the whole window to yourself? Nothing doing! We're staying—aren't we, Tony? Aren't we, Hugo?"

Hugo barked, and Tony warned: "I'll cry again."

"Okay," I said, pinching his arm viciously and butting Hugo out of the way. "Stay, and see if I care." Hugo got hold of my pants leg and started tugging, growling and shaking his head. I patted him and he quieted.

Papa was talking. Not only that, but Papa had his hand on Coletta's knee now, patting it and roaring with laughter. "So the minute Pat got under the bed, Mike came in." He laughed some more, bending over and letting it sputter out of him, patting and squeezing her knee. It was contagious laughter. Coletta laughed with him, and so did Dino, and then the three of us at the window were laughing and laughing, Hugo barking and barking, and none of us knew why. On and on we laughed, until Tony fell off the box and rolled on the grass, his arms squeezing his waist, Hugo straddling him and growling happily, and Mike and I watched him, and still more laughter came from the room, wild brutal laughter, impossible to understand.

It ended as quickly as it began, and I thought Mamma and Clara had come into the room, but they hadn't. Once more Tony climbed up on the box. Now there seemed no more laughter in the world, and a grimness set the faces of Papa and Coletta, who polished her nails against her thigh and pretended to be very busy with this task. Papa had removed his hand from her knee. He sat like Dino, his arms crossed stoically, rolling the cigar between his teeth, and Dino's face was as smiling as ever, showing simple gratitude for being one of them.

Silence held the room. Dino looked toward the kitchen. "But what of Maria?" he asked. "Ah — we should have helped her."

They listened until there was the sound of pans rattling in water. Dino got up and bowed.

"If you will excuse me, please."

They watched him walk out of the room. A moment later we could hear him in the kitchen talking to Mamma and Clara, and we knew he was helping them with the dishes. Papa and Coletta were alone now. Papa winked at Coletta through the smoke of his cigar. He bent close and spoke softly. We couldn't hear it from the window. His left eye squinted as he talked, and it was evident he was talking about Dino. Papa had a certain way of squinting his eyes for every subject he talked about. We could look at his face and know unmistakably if he was talking about politics. Or about war. Or women. Or money. Now we knew Papa was talking about money. Not his money — we knew he didn't have any — but Dino's money. He kept nodding his head and his squint sharpened. Coletta played with the bracelets on her wrists and smiled wistfully. We looked at one another, our way of disapproving what was being plotted in that room, even though we couldn't hear a word of it.

As soon as he heard footsteps, Papa got to his feet. In a loud voice that was almost a yell he said: "And so I said to him, I said, 'George, what this town needs is an honest mayor, because if we don't have honesty at the top you can't expect it at the bottom.' "

Coming into the room, Mamma shook back her hair and smoothed it with reddish hands. Her cold eyes were for Coletta and Papa, telling them she had nothing to say to either of them. Coletta arose.

"I must go now," she said. "It was a wonderful dinner, Mrs. Toscana. I enjoyed it so much."

Papa grinned. You could see he felt highly complimented. He put his arm around Mamma's waist and patted her seat. "You ain't tasted nothing yet, Coletta. This old girl can really cook." Then he laughed. "What do you think I married her for? Maybe she don't look like you, but, oh, boy, how she can cook!" Mamma backed away, her face white and tight. Dino took both Mamma's hands in his and opened the palms. He bent and kissed each of them lightly, in the middle.

"Thank you, my Maria," he said in his usual Italian. "These weary little hands are much too patient with all of us." The sharpness left Mamma's face, and for the first time she smiled. "Thank you, Dino," she said.

Papa left the room and returned with Coletta's fur. Hugo growled and we shut him up. Papa's eyes were bright as he held the fur, and you could see his fingers were startled by the rich softness. He was awed as he held it out to Coletta, holding it out in his two hands as though it were an animal that mystified him. Like a black leopard she walked across the room to the edge of the divan, where she had left her handkerchief. All of us, those in the house and we at the window, stared in amazement and marveled at the miracle of her wonderful movements.

Then Papa spoke. "As long as you're going toward town, Coletta, why don't you give Dino a lift?"

"Of course!" she said.

Dino protested: it was too much trouble, he felt like walking, he loved the night air, he needed exercise, his rooms were only a few blocks away. We turned from the window to look at the car, which stood directly in front of our house, the sleek lines melting into the night. It seemed as it should be, that car. Coletta belonged in no other car but that one; it was as much a part of her as the dark hair, the black fur, the leopard-like movements.

Dino's protests got him nothing. Both Coletta and Papa pooh-poohed his desire for exercise, and when Papa handed him his hat Dino shrugged in defeat.

"Go on, you two," Papa said. "Hop out there."

He took Dino's left hand and slipped it under Coletta's right arm. Dino looked at Mamma for help, and Mamma understood, but she couldn't do anything. Coletta dropped her eyes shyly, looking down at Dino, because she was taller and in every way larger than he.

She said: "There doesn't seem to be anything we can do about it, does there, Dino?" And Dino smiled to hide his embarrassment. Papa got behind them, put his arms around both of them, and almost knocked them down when he crushed them together and shoved them toward the door.

"Go on, you two!" he said. "Get out there under the moon and under them there stars and really get to know one another!"

Tony looked at the sky.

"What's he talking about? There ain't any stars."

"No moon, neither," Mike said.

"Shut up," I said.

We heard them on the front porch. We ran around the side of the house and threw ourselves on our bellies in the strawberry patch. Coletta and Dino stepped off the porch, their arms locked, and walked up the path toward the car. Gently Dino tried to remove his hand. It brought a yell from Papa on the porch.

"No you don't, Dino! What's the matter? Can't you act like a gentleman for five minutes?" and Papa laughed.

We were so disgusted with Papa that we buried our faces in the strawberry patch, and I was so disgusted I tore out grass with my teeth. When they reached the street Dino did take his hand from her arm as he stepped toward the big car and briskly opened the door. But Coletta scarcely saw him as she walked past the shiny monster and stopped before a tattered jalopy parked behind it. The wreck was an old Ford, top gutted, fenders smashed, paint peeling. It was such a wreck that we hadn't even noticed it.

"No, Dino," Coletta said. "Poor little me. *This* is my car."

Shocked, disillusioned, incredulous, the three of us sat up. We didn't care if we were seen or not. Coletta got behind the wheel and Dino got in beside her. The engine started with a series of plups and flups and the choke rod squealed hideously as Coletta pumped it. The car rattled down the street, Hugo chasing it and barking bitterly while we stood sneering at the wake of dirty exhaust smoke almost concealing an Illinois license plate.

"Pah," Mike said. "She's a phony."

"I hate her," Tony said.

"A frill," I said.

Hugo came back to where the car had been parked. Very busily he smelled around here and there and, when he looked up the street where they had gone, his hair stood up on his neck and he growled menacingly.

For a week after Coletta's visit our house was a pretty hard place to live in. Mamma got careless with her hair, and she stopped using face powder, and she kept wearing the same blue gingham dress with the white dots. That was the way with things at our house. Mamma and Papa would have a quarrel, and Mamma would let herself crumble and waste away.

It was just the opposite with Papa. Oh, he got spruced up more than ever. He took to shining his shoes and whistling all the time, as though something exciting were going to happen that night, like a dance or a banquet at the Little Italy Club.

While Mamma cooked dinner he would be very gentle with us, giving Clara a nickel for brushing his suit or going after ten-cent cigars, because at those times of strife with Mamma, Papa always smoked Chancellors, perfuming the house with their rich Papa-like smell. Then we would have dinner, Papa all frisked up in a white shirt without a tie, and he would laugh and talk to us, wonderfully heroic with tales of what he did years ago, when men were men and bricklayers were really artists, when he had built a whole church with his own hands.

89

We worshipped him then: he was exciting, and he answered all our questions with rich stories that ended in ways undreamed of. We sometimes got mad at Mamma, because she would push back her chair and leave the table in the middle of one of his stories. A shadow would cross his face as he watched her go, and we would plead loudly with him to tell us some more, and he would shake himself as if it were all a dream, saying: "Oh, yes, where was I?" We would tell him and he would sigh and finish the story.

But his stories were always better if Mamma listened. We couldn't understand why Mamma stayed mad at him; we sometimes blamed Mamma, yet in a way we were glad they were quarreling, because Papa never told those wild tales of his past unless he and Mamma were not on speaking terms. I used to think about it a great deal in those days, and I used to say how foolish Mamma was, and I used to think if I were she I could never be mad at a man as exciting as Papa.

Four nights after Coletta's visit, Papa came home drunk. It must have been about five in the morning, because when we woke up it was almost daylight through the bedroom window. We heard him stumbling around in the living room, singing "*La Donna è mobile.*" All at once there was a crash of furniture, and then quiet. The lights flashed on, we jumped out of bed, and Mamma and all of us hurried to the living room to find Papa sprawled on the carpet, lying on his back with a pleasant smile on his face. Hugo walked up and licked Papa's nose, and Papa said woo-woo-woo and tried to kiss Hugo. In the corner, still rocking back and forth, was Mike's football, swished there after Papa had stepped upon it. We knew he wasn't hurt or he wouldn't be smiling so happily. Hugo had smelled Papa's breath and sauntered away in disgust.

"Papa's drunk," Tony said, and we looked at one another and smiled. Old Papa, just plastered to the gills and very happy, and we grinned knowingly, feeling sophisticated and mature. Papa often got drunk. He was so generous when he got drunk. We liked him very much when he got drunk. But Mamma felt different. She detested him like that. She looked down at him, her teeth clenched.

"Look at him," she said. "Just look at that shameless man, father of four innocent children!"

We didn't like to be called innocent, so we defended Papa, and Mike surprised Mamma when he said: "A man's got a right to get drunk once in a while."

"Let's wake him up," Tony said. "Maybe he'll give us some money."

"Look!" Clara pointed. "Blood! There's blood all over his shirt."

We fell on our knees around him. Tony and Mike began to cry, and that started Hugo whimpering. "Papa's hurt," Mike said. "Our papa's injured. He's dead, he's dead." I told them to shut up, and while Mamma unbuttoned Papa's coat they became so interested they stopped crying.

"Funny blood," Clara said. "Looks kinda pink."

Below Papa's collar was the imprint of pressed lipstick, forming a woman's mouth. They didn't know it, Mike and Tony and Clara, but Mamma did, and so did I. We looked at each other, and I had to turn away from the gray fury of Mamma's eyes. Without a word she got up and walked into the bedroom. She threw herself upon the bed and lay rigid and silent.

"Somebody bit him," Tony said.

Papa came awake long enough to grin, look around, and ask the time. We told him, and Tony said: "Papa, are you dead or not?" He shook his head serenely and closed his eyes once more. " 'La donna è mobile,' " he tried to sing, but his tongue was so heavy he laughed at himself and was content to hum it feebly as he drifted back to sleep, his thick work-scarred fists holding Tony's small hand with the same tenderness he might have shown a chick.

"Papa," Mike said, "kin I have a dime?"

"Sure. You can have anything you want. You just come to Papa when you want something, and you'll be sure to get it. 'Cause your papa loves you lots more than your mamma loves you."

"Gimme," Mike said.

Papa fumbled at his pants, searching for the pockets. Tony was glad to assist him, taking Papa's limp hand and pushing it into the pocket. There it remained, for Papa fell asleep at once, a slumber from which he could not be roused though we shook him violently; and Mike cupped his hands at Papa's ear and shouted: "Hey, Papa! What about the dime?"

91

It was in vain. He slumbered with a wide grin across his face, and after a moment he snored loudly. The hand could not be moved. We thought of throwing water in his face, but we were afraid that would make him so sober he would get his razor strop. We were pushing him this way and that across the floor, Hugo gnawing his shoes, when Mamma came back to the room. She had been crying. Carefully she removed his hand from the pocket and drew out a few coins. She gave each of us a dime, and went back to bed.

In a while she called me. I got up and it was bright morning, cold. She had undressed him, pushed blankets under him, a pillow under his head, and covered him there on the floor. His clothes were folded on the rocking chair, all but his shirt, which lay in a heap where she had rolled it up and thrown it into the corner.

"You saw what it was?" she asked.

"I know," I said. "But I won't tell."

"Good boy." Though she spoke calmly, the tears seeped from her eyes. "It's that woman," she said. "I know it's that woman."

"It ain't nothing serious."

"Maybe not," she said. "A kiss. No—that's nothing. But this is serious, this, what he does to me here," and she pressed her heart. Papa awakened, groaned, and rolled himself, blankets and all, across the floor.

"What's going on around here?" he said. "What's all these women doing in my bed?"

It made me laugh. I felt sorry for Mamma, but I went back to bed laughing at what Papa had said.

At seven o'clock we got up to go to school. Papa wasn't on the floor. We looked in the bedroom, but he wasn't there either. We had breakfast in the kitchen. There was Mamma, polishing the stove. She worked in a fury, the sweat clinging like mist across the lines of her forehead. The stove was very hot, in some places it was red-hot, and the kitchen had the pungent smell of stove-black and burning rags. We sat down and crammed ourselves with eggs and toast.

"Where's Papa?" Clara said.

"He's gone," Mamma panted. "He went to work."

Mike held his nose.

92

"Pheeeeeew! Something stinks!"

We looked at the rag in Mamma's hand. Mike and Tony and Clara didn't notice it, but I could tell by what remained of the buttons that it was Papa's shirt of the night before. I glanced at Mamma's face. It shone with vengeance. It made the toast clog my throat like sand. It frightened me, and I looked away.

At school we had choir practice, and I didn't get home until six o'clock. On the front porch was Papa, sound asleep in the rocking chair, his eyelids raw and sickly, his mouth wide open, his lunch pail beside him on the floor. The smears of mortar on his hands and arms showed how hard he had worked that day. From under his hat a curl of hair was pasted against his forehead, sweat-dried and pathetic.

He hurt me, Papa did, he hurt me, the way he looked there, his bones aching, his knotty hands deformed yet so brave, outraged by years of toil. Oh, he hurt me deeply in my chest, a cry there, a wail I wanted to send floating into the warm twilight. And all of a sudden I hated Mamma.

I ran into the kitchen and threw my books down. I smelled fish, which meant Friday, baked fish. Mamma stood over the stove, her face as sullen as it was that morning.

"Why do you do it?" I said. "Why do you leave him out there by himself? He's lonesome. Why don't you talk to him?"

She didn't answer.

"You're wicked. You're mean to him. He didn't do anything serious. Look how hard he works every day."

She lifted a pot of boiling potatoes from the stove and carried it to the colander in the sink, steam from the pot hiding her face. "Please stay out of my way," she said. While she mashed the potatoes I sat at the table, watching the set face, the changeless line of her lips. I couldn't understand it: day after day the same even flow of anger, the constant blaze in her eyes. It was all right to get mad once in a while and stay that way for a while, but why stay mad all the time? After all, what did *we* have to do with it, Mike and Tony and I? We had to live there too.

She drew the baked fish from the oven and tested it with a fork. It was ready. She went to the back porch and called Mike and Tony and Clara, who were pitching horseshoes in the back yard. They marched in and and sat at the dining-room table without washing their hands and faces, and their hands were the color of dust. Mamma didn't care. Mike and Tony began to pick at the fish with their hands, tossing chunks to Hugo under the table. She didn't say a word. I kicked Hugo out and tried to make them wash their hands and faces, but they thumbed their noses at me and said I wasn't anybody important. It made me so mad I didn't wash, either. We sat in a circle, every place taken but Papa's.

"What about him?" I said.

"Call him," Mamma said. "That is, if you really want him."

I went out to the porch and shook Papa awake. He staggered inside, his muscles aching. At the kitchen sink he bent over and washed his face, gasping from the cold water. Then he combed his hair before the little wall mirror and came into the dining room and sat down. The sight of him made Mamma pale. She pushed back her plate and went into the bedroom, locking the door behind her. We ate in silence. The fish was burned, the mashed potatoes were watery; there weren't any napkins, and every few minutes one of us got up to get something that should have been there.

As soon as dinner was finished, Papa walked into the bedroom. Immediately Mamma walked out of the bedroom and went into the kitchen. We could hear Papa dressing in the bedroom. He felt better now, he was whistling, and we could hear him moving around with more quickness.

He was whistling *"La Donna è mobile"* when he left, wearing his new suit and whistling for all the world like a man without troubles. It made Mamma so furious that she took the large fish platter and sent it crashing over the floor. Hugo howled in fright and came dashing out of the kitchen, to hide himself under the bed. Mamma kicked the pieces aside and rushed back to the bedroom. Hugo crawled from under the bed and went back and ate the fish on the floor. After a while Mamma returned to the kitchen, swept up the broken pieces, and finished the supper dishes.

We sat around the dining-room table, playing casino. Mamma

went back to the bedroom and locked the door. After an hour she called me. I went in and stood at the bedside in the darkness. I could smell her grief and tears in the room, filling the room.

"Go down to Dino's," she said. "Tell Dino to come here right away."

"What for?"

"Do what I tell you."

I pulled on my sweater and started out. Dino's barber shop was next to the alley on Osage Street, a block from the Platte River Bridge. You could hear and smell the river from Dino's. It was a one-chair shop, not much bigger than our dining room. Next to the shop was the North Pole Recreation Club, where Papa played a card game called *pangini* and sometimes got drunk. Dino's shop was closed, a dim blue light burning over the opened cash register. Dino lived in a bedroom and kitchen behind the shop. Many years ago this place had been a blacksmith shop, and when you were inside you could still smell horsehide and burned horses' hoofs.

I went around the alley to the back door. Lights shone from the two kitchen windows. I climbed the fence. From inside came laughter, the rich deep laughter of Coletta and the sharp brash laughter of my father. I crept to the window and looked inside. They sat at a small table in the middle of Dino's white, immaculate kitchen, a bottle of wine between them: Coletta, Dino, and Papa. Dino sat as though by himself, a little apart from Coletta and Papa, who were close together, their chairs touching. That other time she had worn black. Tonight she was in white, but color made no difference—she still looked beautifully naked. I swallowed slowly. Holy cow! What a honey!

Papa was swinging his arms as he talked, sometimes hugging her, talking all the time.

"Look at him there!" Papa said. "He ain't no man, Coletta. He's half a man, that's what."

Dino smiled indifferently.

"Don't laugh," Papa warned. "We know you, you impostor, you *ingannatore.*You just ain't got the guts to go out and get a woman. That's his trouble, ain't it, Coletta?"

Coletta dropped her eyes and wouldn't answer.

"Look, Dino. Let me show you."

Papa's arm went around Coletta's shoulder, pulling her against him. "You see? You don't have to kiss a woman, Dino. All you have to do is show them who's the boss. And not a cockroach."

Dino raised his wine glass, sipped, and blinked his eyes in amusement. Plainly Papa's advice was having no effect. This enraged him. He jumped out of his chair, rushed over to Dino, and, with arms outstretched and fingers trembling under Dino's nose, he pleaded in Italian.

"Dino Rossi, in the name of San Rocco, get some sense. I am your beloved friend, Dino. This is Guido Toscana talking to you, one who loves you more than life itself. I would give you my tongue, tear it out by the roots, if you asked. I am trying to help you, Dino. Awake, Dino! *Avanti!* Do not snout about the highways and byways looking for a mate. I have found her for you, Dino. She is here before you, a flower from the hills of Sorrento. Act, Dino. This is your friend talking to you, Guido Toscana who knew your stupid mother, your worthless father, and your idiotic brothers."

This was too much for Coletta. She arose and demanded that Papa shut up. With lean cat-like strides she crossed the room and stood with her hands on her hips. her lips in an indignant pout. Papa was on his knees before Dino, and as she spoke he sat back on his heels to listen.

"I think I've got something to say about this," she said. "I happen to be a decent woman, and not the kind to throw herself at the feet of any man who comes along."

"You see what you've done, Dino?" Papa said. "Insulted her. Made a fool out of her."

Dino reddened.

"But I—"

"But—nothing!" Papa said, "Friend or no friend, I ought to punch you in the nose."

"Don't you dare!" Coletta said.

It made Papa speechless, confused.

"Please, dear lady," Dino said, his hands out, "I ask you to forgive me. I am so worthless, so rude. I meant no offense. It is only that I do not wish to—"

"There he goes!" Papa said. "He's off again. He wants you to forgive him. That's all he knows: forgive me, forgive me, forgive me." Papa chanted it sarcastically. It hurt Dino. He stared at the floor and chewed his lips.

"Forgive me! He's been saying that ever since he was born. Fifteen years ago he tried to marry my wife." Papa laughed in scorn. "Him! Trying to take a woman away from me! He was saying the same thing: forgive me, forgive, forgive. I forgived him, all right! I took Maria right out from under his nose — *that's* how I forgived him!"

It was like a stiletto between Dino's ribs. He twisted in his chair, the cords in his neck standing out like ropes. Then I saw his eyes, and he was crying. Papa looked at Coletta in astonishment. She too was surprised. Dino sobbed and dropped his head to his chest, trembling out his misery.

"Poor Dino," Coletta said. "You've hurt him."

From behind she twined her long arms around him. "Poor Dino, poor, poor Dino." She put her cheek against his, her throat at his neck. "Poor Dino, poor gentle Dino." Papa studied them suspiciously. Coletta's finger went in and out of Dino's hair. Her voice crooned in his ear, and a long sigh came from Dino. He closed his eyes and relaxed in her arms.

"That's the boy, Dino!" Papa said. "That's the way to do it."

At once Dino broke again, sobbing into his hands. Coletta tried to comfort him, but he wept without shame. Coletta shook her head, and Papa was full of impatience.

"What the hell's he crying for?"

It brought spasms and chokes from Dino. Through drowning eyes he looked at Papa bitterly. Coletta's handkerchief fluttered as she dabbed away his tears. He smiled and raised his face to her.

Coletta said: "You'd better go, Guido."

Papa had already picked up his hat. Dino protested that Papa should stay, and while they got into a fierce argument about it I jumped the fence to the alley and ran down the street. I was home in five minutes. It was a warm night; there was a moon. I found Mamma sitting in the rocker on the front porch. She stood up when I turned into the yard.

"Where's Dino?" she said.

97

"I couldn't find him."

Half a block down the street we heard heels clicking and the whistling of *"La Donna è mobile."* Along came Papa, swaggering home. I hurried inside and watched from the front door. Papa and Mamma looked at each other, but they didn't say anything. Then Papa sat down on the porch steps and Mamma went back to the rocker. For an hour they were outside in the moonlight. Crickets chirped, and now and then a car swooshed by, but Mamma and Papa never said a word about anything. They came inside together and went to bed together, and still they didn't say a word.

It was three days later that they spoke to each other again. It happened so casually that we scarcely noticed it. We were all at dinner, everyone eating and nobody talking, when Mamma's eyes searched the table for something. The bread plate was at Papa's elbow. He saw her looking around, but he didn't seem to care. Then it happened.

"Guido," Mamma said, "please pass the bread."

Papa looked around, pretending to be very confused."The bread? You said bread?" He glanced over his shoulder and all around the room, as though the bread had legs and was about to stumble through the door. "Oh, the bread! Sure, the bread. Here it is, right here." He passed it to her, and from that instant the whole house seemed to lift itself back to life like a dying person who had at last opened his eyes and would survive after all.

"This is good cabbage," Papa said. "You put bay leaf in it?"

"A little bit," Mamma said. "Personally, I don't believe in too much bay leaf. I prefer rosemary. But you have to be awfully careful with rosemary. Sometimes you put too much in and it ruins everything. I've seen it happen time and time again."

"You're right," Papa said. "Absolutely. You know what I like? I'll tell you." He pinched his fingers to denote a very small amount. "I like oregano. Just a pinch of it. I think you ought to try oregano some time. It's a fine spice."

"Why, Guido! I didn't know you liked oregano! Why, you should have *told* me! Well, now isn't that funny! Why, I have lots and lots of oregano, Guido. Just lots of it."

"Wonderful spice. Back in the old country we used it all the time."

"Is that so, Guido? Why I've got a whole box of it in the pantry." Papa was amazed, dumfounded.

"A whole box! Pheeeew! I sure wish you'd use it some time."

"Why, of course, Guido. Wait. I'll show you."

She hurried into the pantry and we could hear her fussing frantically through boxes and papers. She came back with a small green box, her face sparkling with excitement. Papa took the box and studied it in wonder. Aloud he read the writing on the box: " 'Oregano. Five ounces. A Schilling product. Price, ten cents. Packed in California, U.S.A. Schilling Spice Products Company, Los Angeles, California, U.S.A.' " Papa nodded. "This is the stuff, all right. This is her, sure enough."

He looked at us kids, and that old glitter had come back to his eyes. He was no longer the teller of heroic tales, the dispenser of coins and kindness. He was himself once more. For a week he had exhausted himself in gentleness toward us. That was all over. Now the pendulum had swung. Now he was going to be tough again.

"You," he said, pointing at me. "Why didn't you get the coal and kindling this morning?"

"But I did," I whined, lying.

"You did not. I saw your poor mother carrying a bucket of coal this morning. Come here."

I got up and stood before him. In the corner Hugo stood up, the fur rigid on the back of his neck.

"Around," Papa said.

I turned around and bent slightly. Hugo whined. The flat of Papa's hand resounded against my rump. I yelled, not in pain but in order to exaggerate the effect. Hugo yelped piteously. Mike and Tony cackled joyously. I didn't care. Their turn was coming too. I got three more wallops, but none stung like the first. Pretending to be in great torment, I staggered back to my chair and began eating again. Hugo came up and nuzzled me with his nose, comforting me. Mike and Tony were very quiet now. Papa was looking at them.

"You," he said to Mike.

"I never done nothing." Mike said.

Hugo began to whine again.

"How do I know that?" Papa said. "Do you help your mother with the work around here? No. You run around all day, and you let her slave her life away. How you going to prove you never done nothing?"

"Ask Mamma," Mike said. "Mamma, did I do anything wrong? Haven't I been a good boy?"

But Mamma was too pleased with Papa to intervene.

"This is between you and your father, Mike. You'll have to settle it yourselves."

Mike began to cry, "You crook, you. You dirty crook!"

"Ho!" Papa said. "So that's how it is! So your mother's a dirty crook, is she? I'll teach you to show some respect around here. Come here!"

"I never did a single thing," Mike said, getting to his feet, "not a single thing."

"Oh, no," Papa sneered. "You insult the person who brought you into this world, but you never did a thing. I'll show you. Around!"

He and Hugo were bawling as he took his position, blinking tears from his eyes and staring at Mamma accusingly. Papa slapped him lightly, the blows resounding; they must have stung somewhat, but hardly enough to merit his screams. I knew he cried not from pain but from the belief that Mamma had betrayed him. Two minutes later, eating jello for dessert, he had stopped crying, and while Hugo licked his hand he looked up to see Mamma smiling at him, and a shadow of revenge crossed his face.

Tony was next. He was such a little boy, and he made so much noise and trouble, that he was crying even before Papa accused him. There he sat, crying in his jello, and Papa hadn't said a word. But Tony was Papa's favorite and rarely, no more than seven or eight times a year, did he get a licking. Nor were they bona fide lickings. It was the noise that scared Tony, for Papa would clap both hands loudly against Tony's seat, and Tony would scream in agony.

"And now you," Papa said.

"You better not," Tony said. "I'll leave home. I'll take Hugo, and we'll run away and never come back."

"Listen to who's talking," Papa said.

"I will too," Tony said. "I'll run away and join the circus. Me and Hugo. Won't we, Hugo?"

Hugo looked very unhappy.

Anything about circuses frightened Mamma, who loathed snakes and shivered even at their pictures in the newspapers. "Don't you dare!" Mamma said. "Don't you try it."

"Then you better tell him not to lick me."

But he got his licking, anyway, the same loud, painless licking he always got, and he was angry and humiliated before Mike and me.

"We're leaving for the circus," he wept, staggering into the bedroom. "Come on, Hugo, let's run away from this awful house." Hugo followed him into the bedroom and the door closed. "I'm packing my suitcase now," he informed us, and we heard him dragging something across the floor. Hugo was growling and tearing at something. "I'm putting my things in now," Tony wailed. "Here goes my shoes, and here goes my sweater, and here goes my socks, and I'm not going to take any underwear either, and maybe I'll catch cold and die." We laughed, and so did Papa, but Mamma's forehead was choppy with zigzag lines of concern. She started to get up. Papa shook his head.

"Here we come," Tony announced. "We're all packed and now we're coming out. Here we go to join the circus. Come on, Hugo."

We watched the door open. He emerged with his back to us, dragging a suitcase as big as himself, so heavy he couldn't lift it, Hugo tugging at a strap from the other end, his paws slipping on the linoleum. "Good-by, everybody," he wept. "Here we go to join the circus. Good-by, Mamma, good-by, Papa, good-by, Mike, good-by, Clara, good-by, Jimmy. They treat you good at the circus. They don't give you lickings, and you get to feed the animals. Good-by, everybody."

We laughed as he tried to tug the heavy suitcase toward the front door, Hugo's powerful neck tensing as he slowly pulled Tony back toward the bedroom. Our laughter made Tony so angry he cried the more, wasting his strength in savage tugs and

101

jerks that Hugo easily parried. Then Mamma couldn't bear it any longer. She got up and threw her arms around him.

"I'll give you a nickel if you don't go away," she said.

He sniffed, wiped his arm across his nose, and considered her offer. "Make it a dime," he said.

Mamma lifted him off the floor and kissed him, and Hugo barked joyfully. Papa whispered Clara's name. She sobbed, ran to him, and he lifted her to his lap and kissed her.

Again there was peace at our house. Papa growled and complained, but that was a good sign: it meant that he was on good terms with the universe. Mamma lived in the clouds, her lips smiling, her thoughts far away from us. Every night at dinner she wore her expensive Sunday dress, the one Auntie Louise had given her. She was good to us; she let us take Hugo into the bathtub with us, warning us not to tell Papa about it.

When we nailed barrel hoops on the front-room walls and had a basketball game, she never said a word. We broke a window and smashed a vase, but she stood at the kitchen stove, stirring polenta, her face like an angel's, her thoughts far away, and she didn't even hear the noise. Nor did she say anything when we shot away the chin of Benito Mussolini, whose picture hung over Papa's desk. Papa saw the mutilation from the supper table that night, but luck was with us, because Papa had just read something in the evening paper that made him mutter: "That damn bum of a Mussolini!" and when he lifted his eyes to find the Duce's chin shot away he blinked several times and seemed pleased with the result. He and Mamma had always discussed Dino Rossi, but now they never even mentioned his name. As for Coletta Drigo, all of us sensed that the very thought of her was explosive.

Sunday morning, the first Sunday after the peace, we got up to go to church. It was the one morning in the week when Papa slept late. We had to talk in whispers and walk around on tiptoe. That was bad enough. What made it worse was that we had to do it in our Sunday clothes, new shoes pinching, neckties strangling us. Mamma fixed breakfast. We didn't pay any attention to her. Then we put on our coats and started for church.

As I stepped out of the house I felt something was wrong.

Something was screwy, something was missing, and I didn't notice it until then. I went back to the living room and stood there. Then I felt it clearly, the house telling me of it: Papa's absence, instinct telling me Papa was not in the house. I opened the bedroom door. Mamma had gone back to bed. Beside her, Papa's place was empty, smooth: he had not slept in it the night before.

It sickened me. I felt like rushing across the room and punching the empty place. Mamma turned and opened her eyes. Before she could speak I closed the door and walked out. I wasn't going to church that morning. I was going to find my father and tell him this had gone far enough.

I dog-trotted all the way to Dino Rossi's barber shop. Reaching the back fence in the alley, I became scared and confused. After all, what could I ever say to Papa? Who was I to order his life? He wouldn't tolerate it; he'd give me a licking for sure. Just the same, I could tell him to come home. I could say it politely, in a way not to arouse him.

Dino answered my knock. He wore a white nightgown and a funnel-shaped nightcap. He rubbed his sleepy face and told me to come inside.

"Where's my father?" I said.

"You mean he did not come home last night?"

"He didn't."

He smacked his lips. "Bad. Very bad."

"Where could he be?"

He opened his hands. "Who can say?"

"I bet he's with her — that Coletta dame."

He pressed my lips with his two fingers. "You must not say such things about your father. No, no. Never about your father."

"Just the same, I bet he is."

"No," he said vaguely. "It is impossible."

"He hadn't ought to do things like that, Dino." I felt mature and full of ancient wisdom. "A man's place at night is with his wife and children." Then I remembered something else Papa was fond of saying. "That's just the trouble with the world nowadays, Dino. No more family life."

He patted my shoulders.

"Go home," he said. "I'll find your papa."

103

But he didn't find Papa. That night at ten he came to our house, his face weary, his feet aching. Mike and Tony and Clara had gone to bed, but they were making a lot of noise. I went into the bedroom. It was full of floating feathers. In the corner was Hugo, mangling what was left of a pillow.

"Watch!" Tony said.

He picked up the pillow and threw it across the room. "Go get Coletta, Hugo! Go get her!" The dog jumped across the bed and lunged into the pillow, ripping it savagely. I made them shut up. I turned off the light and kicked Hugo out of the room.

In the kitchen Dino had removed his shoes. He had searched all over North Denver, every poolhall and every cardroom, every bowling alley and saloon, but there was no trace of Papa. Mamma fixed a tub of warm suds and Epsom salts; Dino sank his feet into the tub, moaning with pleasure.

"There is no need to worry," he said. "Guido can take good care of himself."

"He certainly can," Mamma said. "The father of four children, chasing after a she-wolf!"

Dino shook his head violently.

"No, no, Maria! You must not say such things. You have no proof. Guido is a reckless man, but he is a good man, Maria. A family man."

"Sure," Mamma said. "Everybody's family."

But Mamma wasn't crying. She looked as though she had spent a lot of time thinking things over, and had finally made up her mind. Her face was unsmiling, but it was soft and calm. There wasn't much to say. Dino worked his toes in the water, staring absently at the ripples. He seemed anxious to speak his heart, but to Mamma alone, and I could feel that my presence worried him, and that he felt I was too young to become involved. Mamma understood his glances at me.

"Jimmy is my oldest," she said. "I want him to understand these things."

"Ye gods, Dino," I said, "I wasn't born yesterday!"

Dino was still skeptical.

"It's okay," I said. "You can say anything you want in front of me, Dino. I'm fourteen, going on fifteen."

104

This did not fetch him, either, and the three of us lapsed into hopeless silence.

I said: "Look, Mamma. We're not getting anywhere, just sitting here. Let's have some action. What do you intend to do? A man like that, I think you ought to sue him for divorce."

Mamma turned green at the word. She looked at me in horror. Right away I knew I shouldn't have said that, because we were Catholics, and in our Church there is no such thing as a divorce. I felt Dino's kindly gaze, the trace of a smile on his lips. You see, he seemed to say, you don't understand such things after all.

"Okay, wise guy Dino," I said. "You're so damn smart, what would *you* do?"

"A divorce!" Mamma gasped. "Did you hear what he said, Dino? Just a child, and talking like that!"

"Somebody's got to do *something!*" I said.

"Shame on you!" Mamma said. "Your own father and mother. Shame on you!"

"I thought you was sore at him," I said.

"Shame on you," Mamma said. "Shame, shame, shame!"

"Shhhh," Dino said. "Listen."

In the distance we could hear it, faintly, but growing louder, someone — no one but Papa — whistling *"La Donna è mobile"*; then the boom-boom of heels on the front porch, the turn of the lock, and we craned our necks to watch him enter the living room. Before closing the door, he hesitated. We saw his face, reddish, gay, stimulated, his eyes as bright as a squirrel's. He wasn't exactly drunk, but the tilt of his hat and the swagger of his shoulders told us he had not spared the Burgundy.

"Hello!" he waved. "Hello, hello, hello! And how's my happy family tonight? My sweet-tempered wife, my angelic children?"

"Woooo," Mamma groaned. "The beast that he is!"

"So Dino's here too!" Papa said. "Good old Dino, close friend of the family. He's here too."

He leaned in the doorway, a hand on his hip, his hat tilted back. He winked at me, but Mamma watched me closely and I was afraid to wink back.

"Please don't tell me where you slept last night," Mamma said. "Please don't. I'm just your wife. I have no right to question you."

"Oh!" Papa said. "So you want to be sarcastic!"

Mike and Tony came to the bedroom door. "Hey, Papa," Tony said. "Kin we have a dime?"

Papa turned. "Kin you have a dime! You can have *ten* dimes. Here!"

He handed Tony a dollar bill, and Tony accepted it fearfully, backing away, excited and in doubt, the dollar bill like something incredible in his hands. We saw him run, and then we heard him squeal with joy as he leaped into bed, Mike and Hugo following. We listened to them, Hugo barking, Mike shouting: "I get half, I get half!"

"Who loves you the most?" Papa shouted. "Your father or your mother?"

"Our father!"

Grinning, Papa faced Mamma.

"There," he said, opening his hands. "You see?"

Mamma's rage nearly tore her apart. She stood trembling at the sink, biting her lips. "You—you—you vagabond! You—you—you dog, animal!"

She turned in a circle, seeking something, her hands groping for anything in reach. They came upon the soap dish over the sink, and in a flash she grabbed the big White King bar and heaved it. Papa grunted when the bar hit him squarely in the chest, then it bounded to the floor. He was so startled it sobered him. Still Mamma turned round and round, her hands searching again.

"So that's how it is!" Papa said. "So that's the thanks I get for sweating my life away!"

He was backing away as he said it, for Mamma had found the salt and pepper shakers on the stove. Dino jumped up to stop her, but thought it advisable to duck aside as her arm swung. The shakers shot through space, far over Papa's head, and Papa kept backing toward the front door, his head covered defensively, like a boxer's, shouting in Italian to Dino: "You saw this, Dino! You bear witness to the fact that she attacked me in my own home!"

Mamma darted into the pantry and emerged with her hands full of cups and saucers. Papa bolted and ran for the front door.

"You saw it, Dino! You saw it all!"

As he disappeared, Mamma collapsed like a ruin, her body shuddering. She buried her face, and her sobs made the table tremble. Dino bent to comfort her, but she shook her head and asked to be left alone. Her grief filled the room.

"Little Maria," Dino whispered. "My own little Maria. Do not cry, little one. All will be well."

Mamma sat up, blinked the tears away, and blew her nose delicately into the hem of her apron. Dino too began to cry. One look at his wet eyes and Mamma moaned and let herself go again. They both wept, Mamma gasping and choking, Dino in silence, swallowing his misery. Pretty soon I was crying with them, not for Mamma but for Dino: because he was such a good little man, because he was so fond of Mamma and had always seen her suffer, without being able to do anything about it. He took one of her hands in his white fists and gently stroked the calluses that had come with years of housework.

"Weep not, little Maria. We will solve this together. God will help us."

"What can God do? It's him, Dino. And that woman. That terrible *puttana!*"

Dino blew his nose and picked up his hat.

"There is a way," he said. "Somehow we will find one."

On the way out he patted my shoulder: my crying had pleased him. "Good boy, Jimmy." Quietly he walked through the house to the front door. In a moment he returned, and I was laughing and crying, because he walked away barefoot, and I had to clench my teeth to keep from laughing while he put on his socks and shoes. Then he walked away again, and I heard his feet in the street.

I tried to make Mamma go to bed, but she hid her face and pushed me away with one hand. I undressed and crawled into bed. Hugo was in my place, chewing the tattered pillow case. I kicked him out, and he crawled under the bed, dragging his victim with him. After a while the kitchen light went out, and I knew Mamma sat in the darkness. Faintly I heard her crying. I felt I should be crying too, and I tried to make the grief come, but there was none, until I thought of what would happen

107

to us if Papa really went away, how we would be poor and other kids would laugh at our old clothes, and as I fell asleep I felt so sorry for myself I made the pillow sticky with tears.

Shouts awoke me, feet stamping, the slamming of doors, laughter, someone singing. Lights burst on in the middle of the house. We kids sat up. It was three o'clock in the morning, and the singer was Papa, the song was "Here Comes the Bride," and the laughter was Coletta's.

We slipped out of bed and went to the door just as Mamma appeared from the kitchen, her eyes like bacon.

"Welcome to my house!" Papa shouted. "The future Mrs. Dino Rossi!"

They marched in, Papa's arm locked inside Coletta's. Coletta's chin was high, her eyes defiant. Behind them was Dino, and he seemed scared to death.

"Get your coat," Papa said to Mamma. "They're getting married right now. Me and you are witnesses."

"It can't be," Mamma said, hiding her words with the back of her hand. "It's impossible."

"That's what you think," Papa said. "Come on, get your coat. We're going to Golden and get them married."

Dino took Mamma's hands in his.

"Maria, we ask your blessing, Coletta and I."

"Ah, Dino," Mamma said. "You mustn't do this. You mustn't!"

Coletta stepped up. Her face was furious.

"You keep out of this!"

Mamma ignored her. "No, Dino, You mustn't."

Suddenly Coletta rushed between Dino and Mamma, and her hand clamped Mamma's mouth. Mamma backed away, but Coletta came after her. Mamma tried to breathe and speak, and her cheeks puffed out and her face was pink. Hugo growled. We stood frightened. Papa and Dino tried to tear Coletta's hands away from Mamma's face.

"Go get her, Hugo!" Tony said. "Go get Coletta!"

His teeth showing, Hugo dove between Papa and Dino. His jaws sank into Coletta's rump, nipping her. She screamed, and both her hands went to her seat. Furiously she attacked Hugo,

108

kicking at him. He retreated under the table, barking at her. Coletta turned and faced all of us.

"Nice people!" she said. "My God, what people!"

"Please," Dino said. "Let us not quarrel."

"Oh, shut up," Coletta said. "You runt. You little fool."

"Now look," Papa said.

"You too!" Coletta said. "You ape!"

"Who's an ape?" Papa said.

"*You're* an ape!"

"You get out of here!" Papa said. "Nobody can call Guido Toscana an ape. Beat it!"

Coletta looked at all of us, slowly, carefully, shaking her head. "Such people! Such terrible people."

She turned and walked out of the house proudly, her chin in the air. Dino went after her, pleading with her to come back. At the door she swung around and faced him. Then she laughed, shrilling it as she looked Dino up and down. We heard her laughing all the way to her car. Then the engine banged and blasted and she drove away.

Papa laid his hand on Dino's shoulder.

"Forget her, Dino. She's no good."

"Ah, but—"

"Stay single, Dino. You're better off."

"*Si, Si.* But—"

"Forget her. Dino. Nothing but trouble when you get married. Kids. Trouble. Debts. Stay single, Dino. Take my advice."

Dino looked at Mamma, and Mamma was smiling. Dino smiled too. Then Hugo came out from under the table, his ears down, his tail between his legs. Dino bent and patted his head.

"Gooda dog," he said in English. "Nicea pooch."

"You kids," Papa said, "get back to bed."

Dino dug into his pockets. He gave each of us a quarter. But Tony got two quarters.

"Some hamburg for the dog," Dino said.

Dino went home, and after the lights were out we could hear Mamma and Papa talking in the bedroom.

"Where were you last night?" Mamma said.

"Uptown."

"And who was with you?"

"Nobody!" He shouted it with such savagery that Mamma didn't dare answer.

The Road to Hell

WHEN YOU GO to Confession you must tell everything. Anyone who hides a sin gets into trouble right away, for though you fool the priest it is not easy to fool God. In fact, it can't be done. Every Friday at St. Catherine's we have instructions on the confessional. Our teacher is Sister Mary Joseph, and she is the one who told us about God's omniscience, which means knowing all things. She proved it with the story of the Kid who actually tried to hide a sin in the confessional.

Sister Mary Joseph told us this fellow was a pretty good Kid. He studied hard and got good grades. He obeyed his father and mother, and said his morning and evening prayers. He didn't cuss, and all his thoughts were pure. Every Saturday he went to Confession, and every Sunday morning he received Holy Communion. As you can see, there was nothing wrong with a Kid like that.

But it was like everything else. As soon as a fellow is coasting along smooth, here comes the Devil, meaning Temptation. Even a good Kid like this one had plenty of it. Sister Mary Joseph said one day this Kid was walking along downtown, minding his own business, when he came to a window full of baseballs and catcher's gloves. He was a poor Kid. He already owned a catcher's mitt, but it wasn't much good. Well, he'd always wanted a new one. In the window he saw a honey, and right away he wanted it bad. If you want a thing bad, specially something you can't get, it's called Temptation. He wanted that mitt, but he knew he couldn't buy it, and so he should have forgotten about it. But no. He stood in front of that window, and, sure enough, along came the Devil. I know how that Kid felt, because I have listened to the Devil plenty, and it seems he is always in front of store-windows waiting for a fellow to come along, specially a fellow who wants a new glove, or a gun, or anything that costs lots of money.

The Devil said to the Kid: "My boy, don't be a sap. You want that glove and it costs five dollars. Now tell me where *you'll* get five dollars! It's a cinch your father hasn't got it. So use your head. Go into that store and swipe the glove. It's a sin, but so what! You've been a good boy right along now, but what have you got from it? Nothing! Get smart!"

The Kid stared at the glove and saw himself making sensational one-hand catches with it. He saw all the other Kids in town crowding around, feeling the soft leather, asking him a lot of questions, begging him to play on their teams.

Then the Kid's Guardian Angel stepped up. Sister Mary Joseph said the Guardian Angel was very soothing and patient with that Kid. The Guardian Angel said: "My sweet child, remember that you are a good boy, and God is well pleased. All the baseball gloves on earth, and all the baseball bats, are not equal to one second of the bliss in Paradise. If you steal that glove, God will be very angry. He will punish you, for nothing can be hidden from our Blessed Lord."

Suddenly Sister Mary Joseph stopped. Our whole class was listening with mouths wide open. The girls were on one side of the room, the boys on the other. We could hardly wait for the story to go on. Sister Mary Joseph folded her hands and smiled.

"And now," she said, "who can tell me what that boy did? Were the words of Satan more powerful than the words of his Guardian Angel? Did the boy steal that glove, or did he remain in the state of sanctifying grace by resisting temptation? Who will venture an answer?"

Every hand in the classroom went up and waved like a flag. We were all given a chance to say something. Then a strange thing happened. All the girls said the Kid *didn't* steal that glove, and all the boys said he *did*. We argued back and forth. It was going hot and heavy, with the boys winning all the way because we figured the Kid in the story was like us, and nearly all of us had stolen things.

Clyde Myers said: "Sure he stole it! He's a funny guy if he didn't."

"Why, Clyde Myers!" Sister Mary Joseph said.

Then my turn came. My folks were poor people, so I knew what to say, because I'd swiped a lot of things in my life, things that cost money. What I mean is this: I never did have enough candy because it was so expensive, so I always swiped it from the Ten-Cent Store. But there were a lot of things I never even thought of stealing, because we had plenty at our house. Like spaghetti. Well, my folks were poor but there was always plenty of spaghetti, so I never even thought of swiping spaghetti. But if spaghetti was as good as candy and as hard to get, I would have swiped it plenty.

"He went in and stole the glove," I said. "He was poor, and that's what he did."

Clyde Myers and I were pals. His folks were not poor, but they wouldn't buy him a ball glove because they were afraid he would break his neck or something playing baseball. So what happened was, Clyde had swiped a glove, not a new one out of a store but an old one out of the gym.

Clyde said: "No. The reason he swiped it was because his folks wouldn't let him have one."

So what happened was, the boys put themselves in the Kid's shoes, and everyone had a different reason why the Kid swiped the glove. But they were all very good reasons. The girls didn't have a chance. They didn't want the Kid in the story to be a thief, so they just said he wasn't. But it didn't cut much ice. The girls didn't like it at all, because they knew they were losing the argument. It got to be a kind of a fight. Then the girls got sulky and mean. After a while they wouldn't raise their hands. They pretended they weren't even listening.

And Sister Mary Joseph went on with the story. "Unfortunately," she said, "the boys are correct in this case. The hero of our little story did succumb to temptation. Heedless of the warnings of his Guardian Angel, he entered the store and, when the proprietor's eyes were not upon him, he gave himself to his temptations, thereby committing a flagrant violation of God's precept in the Eighth Commandment. Despite the anguish and

113

protestations of his beloved Guardian Angel, despite the torture of his own conscience, he fell before his own weakness, and spurred on by the coaxing of Lucifer, he fell into grievous sin . . ."

By all of that Sister Mary Joseph meant that the Kid walked into the store, saw that the coast was clear, shoved the glove under his sweater next to his belly, and then ran for it. Next day he showed up on the school grounds with a swell, brand-new catcher's glove. Just as he figured, all the boys were nuts about it. The trouble began when they asked him where he got such a swell glove. He told them his father had got it. That was Lie Number One. Somebody asked him how much it was worth. The Kid said he didn't know. That was Lie Number Two, for the glove had been priced at five dollars. Lie Number Three followed immediately; the Kid now saw his chance to make the boys green with envy, and he told his friends the glove was really a present to his father from Babe Ruth. This led the boys to ask the Kid how come his father knew a great ball player like Babe Ruth. The kid gave them Lies Number Four and Five by saying his father and Babe had gone to school together in San Francisco, where they played on the same team. Lie Number Six was even worse. The Kid told his pals that Babe Ruth considered his father good enough for the big leagues. Lie Number Seven was terrible. The Kid said that, as a matter of fact, his father had once been a big-league ball player with the Boston Red Sox.

By the end of the week the Kid had told so many lies that only God, who knows all things, had any record of their exact number. The Kid had learned that the fateful way to fame and the things of the flesh was in stealing and then lying about it. He was like a snowball rushing downhill, gaining speed at every turn. There was no stopping him. He was on the Road to Hell.

II

When Saturday arrived, the Kid had a chance to go to Confession, tell his sins, and return once more to the Road to Paradise and sanctifying grace. Sister Mary Joseph paused again. Everyone in that class was worried about the Kid now. We felt better when

Sister said he did go to Confession that Saturday. Ah, but something terrible happened. He had been too long a companion of Lucifer. When he entered the confessional, a great fear came over the Kid. He simply couldn't tell the priest he had swiped a ball glove. He was under the Devil's spell. He coughed and stammered, finally giving up. The priest didn't know the Kid was holding back, so he pronounced Absolution and made the sign of the cross. The Kid left the church bathed in sweat, and Satan laughed like a fiend, for Satan knew he had pulled a fast one on the priest.

But not on God, because that can't be done. All night long the Kid thought of what he had done. His conscience gnawed like a fat rat, and he couldn't sleep a wink. Before him yawned the jaws of Hell, and far behind him flickered the bright lanterns on the path to Eternal Bliss. Was this Kid doomed, or wasn't he? Sister Mary Joseph took off her glasses and wiped them, and her face was set and kind of sad. From that we knew something awful was coming. She put on her glasses and spoke. It was tough on the Kid.

Concealing a sin in the confessional is bad enough and a mortal sin, but actually to go to Holy Communion afterward is the worst sin possible — a sacrilege. Sunday morning the Kid got up and walked bleary-eyed to Mass with his parents. They were pious, humble folks who always received Holy Communion on Sunday morning. Now the great test arrived. Would the Kid brave the shocking disappointment of his parents and not go to Holy Communion, or would he sink deeper into the grasp of Lucifer? The Kid was in a tough spot. If the Kid didn't go to Communion, then his folks would know something was wrong, and after services they would make him come clean. That would mean the loss of his new ball glove, plus a shellacking from his father, who was a pious man with a horror of evil. But if he kept his mouth shut and went to Communion, he would fool his folks and still have the glove. Oh, yes, but could he fool God? *That* was the question.

And it was here that the Kid made his big mistake. So far he had deceived his friends, the priest, and his parents. Drunk with power, and deep in the spell of Satan, he now challenged

115

the Supreme Being. And there, kneeling beside his humble parents, he made the decision which was to prove a fatal mistake. Sin or no sin, God or the Devil, he loved that ball glove. He decided that no matter what happened, he would go to Communion.

After the Consecration he walked down the aisle and knelt at the Communion rail. Side by side with his humble parents, he awaited the Blessed Sacrament. Would the priest know the black horror of that Kid's soul? Would a miracle happen? Would God in His wrath strike down this sinner who had sold out to Lucifer? Nobody in the class could guess. It was Sister Mary Joseph's story, and we couldn't guess the end. But it certainly looked bad for the Kid.

The priest came down from the altar and gave Holy Communion to members of the congregation. The Kid's mother and father received, bowing their heads in humility and piety. Then it was the Kid's turn. He lifted his face, and the priest placed the Communion on his tongue. Nothing happened except that Lucifer snickered, and the Kid bowed his head. That is, nothing happened right away.

But after he got back to his pew, a slow change came over the Kid. He felt a stiffness in his bones, starting at his feet. It moved upward. It reached his knees. Then his waist. Gradually it crept to his shoulders. Now it was in his neck and heading for his eyes and ears. On and on it moved. Finally it covered him all the way. God had answered the challenge of Lucifer. The Devil didn't sneer any more; he fled. For the Kid had turned to stone!

When we heard that, we were like stone too. The whole class was dead quiet. Than we realized Sister Mary Joseph's story was over. She sat up there and smiled.

"And the moral of that story is this," she said. "Always tell the truth, whether it be in the confessional or out of it. Avoid Temptation. Never harbor thoughts of stealing. Never tell little lies, or big lies, or any kind of lies. Be truthful to the very end."

The class sighed. Some of us said pheeeew! We were sure glad that story was over.

III

After school, Clyde Myers and I walked downtown. We fooled around, staring into shop-windows. The hardware-store window was chock-full of baseball supplies: balls, bats, and gloves.

"Let's go in," Clyde said. "We'll say we're just looking around."

Clyde walked down one aisle and I walked down the other. The clerks didn't pay any attention to us. There was a whole basketful of baseballs. I could have got plenty but I didn't feel like it. At the back of the store we passed each other, and Clyde walked up my aisle and I walked up his. Then we met at the front door and walked out.

"Did you get anything?" Clyde said.

"No," I said.

"Me neither."

For quite a while we stood out front and stared at the baseball supplies in the window.

"Do you think that Kid was really turned to stone?" Clyde said.

"Nah," I said. "It's a lot of baloney."

"Yeah," he said. "It's a lot of bunk."

"Well," I said, "so long."

"So long," he said. "See you tomorrow."

One of Us

My mother had just carried the last of the supper plates into the kitchen when the doorbell rang. All of us rose like a congregation and rushed to answer the call. Mike reached the door first. He threw it open and we pushed our noses against the screen. There stood a uniformed boy with his cap in his hand and a telegram at the bottom of it.

"Telegram for Maria Toscana," he said.

"Telegram, Papa!" Mike shouted. "Somebody's dead! Somebody's dead!"

A telegram came to our house only when one of our family passed away. It had happened three times in the lives of us kids. Those three times were the death of my grandfather, of my grandmother, and then the death of my uncle. Once, though, a telegram came to our hose by mistake. We found it under the door when we came home late one night. We were all greatly surprised, for it contained birthday greetings to a lady named Elsie, whom none of us knew. But the most astonishing thing about that telegram was that it was not a death notice. Until then it did not occur to us that a telegram might have other uses.

When my father heard Mike shouting, he dropped his napkin and pushed back his chair. We at the door pranced up and down in excitement. In a paralysis of anxiety, Mother stood in the kitchen. My father walked with an important air to the door, and, like a man who had spent his whole life signing for telegrams, he signed for this one. We watched him tear open the yellow envelope so that the paper would separate enough for his heavy fingers to reach the message inside. He frowned at us and walked to the center of the living room, under the chandelier. He held

119

the message high, almost over his head. Even jumping, we kids could not put our eyes upon it, and my little brother Tony, who was a shrimp and too little to read anyhow, climbed up the side of my father as if the man were a tree, and my father shook himself and Tony fell to the floor.

"Who died?" we asked. "Who died?"

"Down, down," my father said, like one speaking to leaping puppies. "Quiet, there. Down, down."

Squinting his eyes, he folded the ominous yellow paper and returned to his place at the table. We trailed after him. He told us to go away, but we swarmed around his shoulders, and Tony climbed the chair rungs and burrowed his fingers into his shirt at the collar. My mother stood in the kitchen door biting her lips. Worry crushed her face. Her hands turned round and round like kittens under her checkered apron.

Breathlessly we waited. Breathlessly we tried to guess whom the sad news might concern. We hoped it wasn't our aunt Louise, because she always sent us such wonderful Christmas presents. We didn't mind if it was our aunt Teresa, though, because what good was she around Christmas time? No good whatever. All we ever got from her was a greeting card, and we knew it cost only a penny because that was the very kind our mother bought. If she was dead she deserved it for being so stingy.

Father shook himself from us. Emphatically he told us to go back to our places. My mother quietly took her seat. She held her small worried face between spread fingers like a woman gathering strength for an ordeal. She had many brothers and sisters whom she had not seen since girlhood, for she had married when yet very young. We could see that my father's mind was reaching here and there to find the quickest and best way of releasing the sad shock when at length my mother was ready to receive it. She raised her face and looked at him with eyes opened all the way.

"Who, Guido?" she asked. "Who is it?"

"Clito," he said. "Your sister Carlotta's boy."

"Dead?"

"Killed. He was run over. He's dead."

For many silent moments my mother sat like a statue in

gingham. Then she lifted her face to that place she believed contained life eternal. Her lips were distended as in a kiss of farewell. Her eyes were too grieving to stay open.

"I know his little soul is beautiful in the sight of God," she whispered.

He was our cousin, the only child of Uncle Frank and Aunt Carlotta, my mother's oldest sister. They lived in Denver, thirty miles south of our small town. Clito was but a day older than our Mike, second in age among us kids. Clito and Mike were born in the same Denver hospital ten years before. They were brought to life by the same physician, and — wonderful thing! — the two boys were remarkably similar in face and form. Among the many members of our scattered clan they were always referred to as the Twins, for they were inseparable when our family lived among the Italians of North Denver three years before, and, though they often quarreled, there seemed a deeper kinship between them than between Mike and me, or between Mike and Tony. But, three years before our family had moved from Denver to the small town in the mountains, and Mike had not seen his cousin since then.

These were the reasons why, in the silence after my father had spoken, my mother stared so passionately, so possessively at Mike, her eyes slowly beginning to float. Mike felt her gaze. He was yet too young to realize the tragic significance of Clito's death, but he felt my mother's eyes upon him, as if to draw him into them, and he fidgeted nervously, glancing at my father for clarity and sustenance. My mother pushed back her chair and went into the bedroom. We heard her lie down, and then we heard her sobbing.

"I bet Clito's in Heaven," Mike said. "I bet he didn't have to stop off in Purgatory."

"Sure," my father said. "He was a good boy. He went right straight to Heaven."

My mother called from the bedroom.

"Mike," she called, "come here to Mamma."

He didn't want to leave the table. But he looked at my father, who nodded, and then he got up and went hesitantly away. We heard my mother draw him beside her upon the bed, and we heard the wet, violent kissing of his face and neck. We heard the wild sound of smacking lips and my mother's possessive moans.

"But it ain't me!" Mike was saying. "See! I'm not dead."

"Thank God! Thank Almighty God!"

After my father left the table, the telegram lay open at his place, one corner of it in the salad bowl, the yellow paper drawing salad oil into itself like a blotter. We kids dove for it. I got it first and held it above me, out of reach of my tiptoed sister Clara's clawing fingers. I climbed up on my father's chair and held the paper almost to the ceiling. My sister climbed right up on the chair beside me. Over my head I read the message while she hung on and my little brother Tony tugged at my pants in an effort to dethrone me.

"Let me read it!" he shouted.

"You little fool!" Clara said. "You can't read yet! You're not even in school."

"Yes, I can too! You don't know everything, so there!"

The message read: "Clito struck by truck while riding bicycle. Died this afternoon four o'clock. Funeral Sunday three o'clock."

I let it go from my fingers and it floated zigzagging toward the floor. Clara and Tony fell upon it and instantly it was in shreds, all over the floor. The commotion on the linoleum brought my mother and Mike in a hurry from the bedroom. My mother saw the shredded telegram lying about, and, drying her eyes with the hem of her apron, she said: "I didn't get to see it. How did he die?"

"He was run over by a bicycle," I said.

My father was in the front room, reading the paper.

"No," he corrected. "The boy was run over by a truck."

"No, he wasn't," I said. "He ran into the truck."

"The truck ran into him."

So, with constant interruptions, we lost all conception of what had actually taken place. Before long I was insisting that our dead Clito had been riding in the truck bed, the bicycle at his side, and that he had fallen out when the machine struck a bump in the road. My father was quite as inaccurate. He said that little Clito had been knocked down and killed by a man riding a bicycle. Now we were guessing recklessly. Even Tony had an

122

interpretation to offer. He insisted that he too had read the telegram, but he said that Clito had been killed by a German aviator who dropped bombs from an airplane. In the confusion nobody had anything more to offer.

Then Clara said: "Maybe you're all wrong. Maybe he was run over by a motorcycle."

In despair my mother asked if there was any mention of a funeral.

"Tuesday."

"Monday."

"Friday."

"Wasn't it Sunday?" Clara said.

While we quibbled hopelessly, my mother and Mike gathered up the bits of yellow paper and pieced them together on the table.

II

After supper my mother wouldn't let Mike go out. The rest of us did, but Mike had to stay in the kitchen with her. He could hear us shouting in the front yard, and he cried and kicked the stove, but my mother was never so firm. Even my father was surprised. When he walked into the kitchen and told her she was crazy and unreasonable, she turned on him, her eyes still crying, and told him to go back to his newspaper and mind his own business. Sucking a toothpick, he stared at the floor, shrugged his shoulders, and then went back to his reading.

"But, Mamma," Mike said over and over, "I'm not the one that's dead! See?"

"Thank God. Thank Almighty God."

That evening Uncle Giuseppe and Aunt Christina came to our house. Aunt Christina was the youngest sister of my mother and Aunt Carlotta. She too had received a telegram. My mother dried her wet, dish-watery hands when she saw Christina enter the front door, and the two women locked bosoms in the dining room and stood there crying. My mother put her nose into Aunt Christina's shoulder and sobbed, and Aunt Christina sobbed and stroked Mother's hair.

"Poor Carlotta!" they said. "Poor Carlotta!"

Nobody was watching Mike in the kitchen. He saw his chance and sneaked out the back door. He ran around the house and joined us in the front yard. Our cousins, Aunt Christina's two kids, had come with her, so the whole bunch of us got up a game of kick-the-can.

My mother forgot about Mike. She and my father and Aunt Christina and Uncle Giuseppe sat in the front room, talking about Clito's death. The two women sat side by side in rocking chairs. My mother still held her dish towel, and she let her tears splash into it. Aunt Christina cried into a tiny green handkerchief that smelled of carnations. Over and over they said the same thing.

"Poor Carlotta! Poor Carlotta!"

My father and Uncle Giuseppe smoked cigars in silence. Death was the supreme mystery to these people, and the women feverishly resigned themselves to the workings of the Almighty. But the men clung to those ancient platitudes, ancient as the mind of man. Since he was not a son of theirs, the passing of the little boy did not move them noticeably. They were sorry he was dead, but they were sorry only because it was the proper thing to be, so their sorrow was etiquette and not out of their hearts.

"Ah, well," my father said, "you never know. Everybody has to go some time."

Uncle Giuseppe's dark head and screwed-up lips agreed slowly.

"Too bad," he said. "It's too bad."

"But he was so young!" Mother said.

Wistfully my father answered: "Maybe he's better off."

"Ah, Guido! How can you say that? How do you suppose his poor mother feels? And poor Frank?"

"A man never thinks what's in a woman's heart," Aunt Christina said. "No, they don't know. They never will know. Men are so selfish."

My father and uncle stared at their cigars in dismal confusion.

"Well," my father said, "all I know is we all have to go some time."

Uncle Giuseppe was trying hard to feel grief. He closed his eyes and said, "No. We never know. Tomorrow, the next day, tonight — next year, next month, we never know."

"Poor Carlotta," my mother said.

"Poor woman," Aunt Christina said.

"Too bad for Frank," my father said. "He'll miss the boy."

Uncle Giuseppe sat in a helpless way, uncomfortable in a straight-back chair. Many times he looked at the ceiling and walls as though he had never seen them before. Then he would examine his cigar, as though that were a curious object too. My father sat more at ease, since this was his house. He sat with his cigar between his teeth, his feet spread stiffly in front of him, his thumbs in his sweat-stained suspenders, his eyes squinting to evade the curl of cigar smoke. He would have liked to say something different on this subject of death, but there was nothing new he could think about.

"The best of us have to die," he ventured.

"How true that is," my uncle said.

My Aunt Christina blew her nose many times and then wrung the tip of it until it was as red as a radish. She was a stout woman who tried but never could cross her fat little legs.

"How does Mike feel?" she asked. "He and Clito were such good friends. They loved one another so."

My mother's eyes opened in fright, and she turned in her chair and looked behind her in a kind of terror.

"Mike!" she called. "Where are you, Mike?"

No response. She twisted her body and peered tensely into the kitchen. She saw no one. Rising, she slipped her fingers into her deep hair and screamed.

"Mike!" she screamed. "Where are you, Mike? Come back to me, Mike!"

My father jumped to his feet as though he had seen a ghost. He took her into his arms.

"*Dio!*" he panted. "Calm yourself, woman!"

"Find Mike! In God's name, find Mike!"

Uncle Giuseppe went to the front door, and in the twilight he saw us playing our game beneath the black trees of the front yard. Mike was a little apart from the rest of us, leaning against the biggest tree, partly hidden in its shadows.

"Your mother is calling you," Uncle Giuseppe said. "Can't you hear her?"

All he said was: "Aw, what does she want?"

"Go on, Mike," we said. "Go see what she wants." For my mother's screams had stopped our game like an unexpected crash of lightning. Then the screen door was flung open violently, and it banged against the wall that supported it, and my mother dashed wildly from the house. She stooped and lifted Mike like an infant high above her, and, laughing and crying, she kissed him and kissed him and cooed into his throat.

"Mamma's own little boy," she moaned. "Never leave me. Never, never, never, never leave me."

"I'm not Clito," he said. "I'm not the one that's dead."

She carried him back to the front room, and they all sat down again, and, though Mike hated it, he had to sit in her lap and be kissed about a million times.

We slept together in the same bed, Mike and I, and very, very late that night — some time after midnight — my mother came to our room and softly slipped between us, but it was still Mike she worried about. And, lying with her back to me, she awakened him by petting him so much. When she went back to her own bed, I had to turn my pillow over because it was so wet from her tears.

III

Who would go to the funeral? Sunday morning in the kitchen there was a fierce argument between my father and mother on this question. My mother wanted to take Mike with her, but my father wanted her to take me.

"No," my mother said. "I want Mike to come."

"What's the idea?" my father said. "There's no use making it harder for those people. You know how Carlotta and Frank will feel when they see Mike."

"Oh," my mother scoffed, "what on earth are you talking about?"

"I know what I'm talking about," my father said. "What the devil's the matter with you women?"

"I said Mike was coming with me," my mother said. "And he is. If Jimmy wants to come, he can."

126

"What about me?" Clara said.

"Nothing doing," my father said.

"Me and Jimmy and Mike," Tony said.

My father looked at him contemptuously.

"Pooh!" he said. "And who are you?"

"Aw," Tony said. He was so little he never could answer that question.

The telegram said the funeral was to be at three o'clock. It was only an hour's ride on the electric to Denver, but when any of our family went anywhere we had to turn the house upside down. Mother couldn't find her hairpins and Mike couldn't find his new necktie. When he did find it in the pantry the mice had eaten a hole in it so he had to wear an old one of my father's.

Tucking the endless cravat into his waist, he howled: "I don't like it! Look how big it is! It's an old man's tie."

"Who said it was an old man's tie?" my father said. "Wear it and keep still."

But my mother wanted him to look nice. She didn't pay any attention to how I looked, but she wouldn't let Mike wear that necktie. She made Tony go over to Oliver Holmes's and borrow a light blue one for Mike, and while I was gone to borrow hairpins from Mrs. Daley she sat on the bed in her petticoat, her hair streaming down and tangling her fingers as she sewed a button on Tony's coat.

When at last we were ready to go, she couldn't find her hat. Weary and fretting, she stood in a pile of boxes in the clothes closet, calling everyone to search for her black hat. My father found it clear on the other side of the house, under my sister Clara's bed, but Clara said she didn't know how it got there, and that was quite a lie, because Clara is always secretly wearing my mother's things. When my father pushed the hat over my mother's lumps of hair, he sighed and said: "Good God, wipe that powder off your neck. You look like you been baking a cake."

She wet the end of her handkerchief with spittle and dabbed the powder away. Then she grabbed Mike by the wrist and hurried out the door. I ran after them, her purse in my hand, for she had forgotten it.

My father and Clara and Tony stood on the front porch and

127

watched us walk down the street. When we were half a block away, my father whistled to us. We three turned around.

"Hurry up!" he yelled, loud enough for even that deaf old Miss Yates to hear and throw open her window and look out. "Hurry up! You only got five minutes to make the train."

My mother squeezed Mike's hand and walked as fast as the worn heel of her right shoe would permit her, and I could see from the way Mike winced as he scratched his belly that he hated the whole thing and was ready to break into tears.

IV

We reached the electric on time, and an hour later we arrived at the Denver Union Station. From there we took a yellow street car to Aunt Carlotta and Uncle Frank's house. As soon as she sat down in the street car, my mother started to cry, so that her eyes were red-rimmed when we got off at Aunt Carlotta's street. We stopped on the corner a minute while Mother fastened her garter and Mike and I went behind the hedge to wee-wee, and then we started up the street.

There were so many people and automobiles at my aunt's house that it was the biggest funeral in the history of our family, and there was such an abundance of flowers that some of the bouquets had to be spread on the front porch, and you could smell the funeral as soon as you got off the street car.

We went up the front stairs to the little cloakroom, where dozens of Italians in Sunday suits stood with sad faces peering over the shoulders of one another to the parlor where the bier was placed in the center of the scent-suffocated room, the lid off, the waxen and shining face of Clito's corpse sleeping in infinite serenity amid the moans and gasps and supplications of black-draped, dark-skinned, choking women who sometimes knelt and sometimes arose first on one knee and then on the other to kiss the rosary-chained, icy hand of the small thin corpse in the gray box with silver-plated handles.

Mike and I saw it all between the legs of the men in the

cloakroom as my mother dragged us through the crowd and up the stairs to Aunt Carlotta's bedroom.

My aunt arose from the bed, and the two sisters fell upon each other and wept helplessly. Aunt Carlotta had wept so much that her face was as raw as a wound. Her arms were around my mother's neck, the hands hanging loosely, the fingernails gnawed until there were tiny blood tints at the quick. I closed the door, and Mike and I stood watching.

Then we saw Uncle Frank. He was at the window. He did not move when we entered, but stood with his hairy hands in his back pockets. He had seldom spoken to us, but he was gentle and generous, and each year he sent us pajamas for Christmas. We didn't know much about him, except that he was an electrician. He was a tall man with a thin neck; his spinal column rounded out like a rope beneath his brown skin, so that he always seemed to have a trim haircut. His body was not quivering from sobs, and when we saw the dry-eyed reflection of his thin face in the windowpane it amazed us that he was not shedding tears. We could not understand it.

"Why doesn't he cry?" Mike whispered. "He's the papa, isn't he?"

I think Uncle Frank heard him, for he turned around slowly and skeptically, as one turns to heed the note of a new bird. He saw my mother and me, and then he spied Mike. Instantly his knees seemed to buckle, and he backed against the window and clapped his hand over his mouth. The look of him made my brother shriek, and he grabbed my mother around the waist and hid his face in the small of her back.

Uncle Frank moistened his lips.

"Oh," he said, pressing his eyes. "Oh, it's you, Mike."

He sat on the bed and panted as he ran his two hands in and out of his hair. Aunt Carlotta saw Mike then, and she spread herself across the bed, her face vibrating in the depths of the pink coverlet. Uncle Frank stroked her shoulder.

"Now, now," he murmured. "We must be brave, *mia moglia*."

But he was not crying, and the more I thought of it the stranger it seemed.

My mother bent down to straighten Mike's crooked tie.

"Be a good boy," she said, "and give your Uncle Frank and Aunt

Carlotta a big kiss. You too, Jimmy."

I kissed them, but Mike wouldn't go near Uncle Frank. "No, no, no!" he screamed. "No, no!"

He followed me when I walked to the window that overlooked the back yard. We looked out upon the hot Sunday afternoon and saw what Uncle Frank had been staring at when we came in. It was the twisted bicycle. It leaned against the ashpit, a bundle of bent and knotted steel. Mike kept looking over his shoulder at Uncle Frank, as if expecting a blow, and when Uncle Frank arose from the bed and came to the window and stood beside us, Mike crept into my arms and began to whimper in fear. Uncle Frank smiled tragically.

"Don't be afraid. I won't hurt you, Mike."

He patted my hair, and even through it I felt the dryness of his hand and how sad it was.

"See?" he said. "Jimmy's not afraid of his Uncle Frank, are you, Jimmy?"

"No, Uncle Frank. I'm not afraid."

But Mike cringed from the man's melancholy hands. Uncle Frank tried very hard to smile, and then of a sudden he drew two half-dollars from his pocket. I took one, but Mike hesitated, looking at my mother on the bed. She nodded. A soft smile broke on the boy's face, and, sniffing, he accepted the coin and went into Uncle Frank's arms.

"Little boy Mike," Uncle Frank said. "Little boy Mike, so like my little boy Clito." But he was not crying.

He sat Mike upon his lap, and by the time the procession to the graveyard was ready to begin, my brother was deeply devoted to him. They went down the stairs to the parked cars, Mike holding his hand and looking up at his face in curiosity and admiration.

Uncle Frank was the only one who did not cry during the burial. He stood a little back from the head of the grave, my sobbing Aunt Carlotta clinging to him, his eyes closed, his jaw hard. Around the grave the throng hovered, the men with their hats in their hands, the handkerchiefs of the women fluttering in the lifeless afternoon heat, sobs bursting like unseen bubbles, the priest sprinkling holy water, the undertaker standing in professional dignity in the background, the bier sinking slowly, the while my brother and I stood side by side and stared at the black ground appearing as the box descended, our eyes flowing and flowing, our chests hurting, our hearts breaking in terror and first grief as the life of Clito rushed from our memories for the last time, vividly, distressingly; our mother whimpering as she chewed her handkerchief, the straps around the box crackling, the silver pulleys squeaking, the sun brilliant against them, the priest murmuring on and on, men coughing in shame, women wailing, Aunt Carlotta weak and near fainting, clinging to Uncle Frank, and he there with a hard jaw and closed, arid eyes, thinking the thoughts of a father, thinking—God knows what he thought.

Then it was over.

We went back to Aunt Carlotta's, and we sat in the living room, Aunt Carlotta still weeping and my mother consoling her. Dazed and white, Uncle Frank stood at the window, Mike watching his face.

Mike said: "Don't you ever cry, Uncle Frank?"

The man only looked down and smiled feebly.

"Well, don't you?"

"Mike!" my mother said.

"Well, why doesn't he? Why don't you, Uncle Frank?"

"Mike!"

"Keep still, Mike," I said.

"Well, why doesn't he cry?"

Uncle Frank pressed his temples.

"I am crying, Mike," he said.

"No, you're not."

"Mike!"

"Well, he's not."

"Shut up, Mike," I said.

"But you didn't cry at the graveyard, and everybody else did."

"Mike!"

"He was the only one who didn't cry, because I was watching."

"Mike! You go outside."

He went out indignantly, and sat in the rocker before the window, his back to Uncle Frank. He began to rock furiously, stiffening his legs with the motion backward. Uncle Frank turned

131

from the window and went outside and bent over Mike's chair, smiling down at him. Then he spoke. I was watching from the window, but I couldn't hear what he said. Mike grinned, and the two of them went down the porch steps and on down the street.

"Where are they going?" my mother asked.

"I don't know," I said.

A half-hour passed without their return, and my mother and aunt sent me in search of them. I went down the street to the drug-store on the corner, and that was where I found them. They were in an ice-cream booth, Mike drinking a malted milk, sucking it down greedily. Uncle Frank sat across from him, his face cupped in his hands, great tears rolling off his cheeks and falling on the table as he watched Mike sucking down the malted milk.

The Odyssey of a Wop

I PICK UP little bits of information about my grandfather. My grandmother tells me of him. She tells me that when he lived he was a good fellow whose goodness evoked not admiration but pity. He was known as a good little Wop. Of an evening he liked to sit at a table in a saloon sipping a tumbler of anisette, all by himself. He sat there like a little girl nipping an ice-cream cone. The old boy loved that green stuff, that anisette. It was his passion, and when folks saw him sitting alone it tickled them, for he was a good little Wop.

One night, my grandmother tells me, my grandfather was sitting in the saloon, he and his anisette. A drunken teamster stumbled through the swinging doors, braced himself at the bar, and bellowed:

"All right, everybody! Come an' get 'em! They're on me!"

And there sat my grandfather, not moving, his old tongue coquetting with the anisette. Everyone but he stood at the bar and drank the teamster's liquor. The teamster swung round. He saw my grandfather. He was insulted.

"You too, Wop!" said he. "Come up and drink!"

Silence. My grandfather arose. He staggered across the floor, passed the teamster, and then what did he do but go through the swinging doors and down the snowy street! He heard laughter coming after him from the saloon and his chest burned. He went home to my father.

"*Mamma mia!*" he blubbered. "Tummy Murray, he calla me Wopa."

"*Sangue della Madonna!*"

Bareheaded, my father rushed down the street to the saloon.

133

Tommy Murray was not there. He was in another saloon half a block away, and there my father found him. He drew the teamster aside and spoke under his breath. A fight! Immediately blood and hair began to fly. Chairs were drawn back. The customers applauded. The two men fought for an hour. They rolled over the floor, kicking, cursing, biting. They were in a knot in the middle of the floor, their bodies wrapped around each other. My father's head, chest, and arms buried the teamster's face. The teamster screamed. My father growled. His neck was rigid and trembling. The teamster screamed again, and lay still. My father got to his feet and wiped blood from his open mouth with the back of his hand. On the floor the teamster lay with a loose ear hanging from his head. . . . This is the story my grandmother tells me.

I think about the two men, my father and the teamster, and I picture them struggling on the floor. Boy! *Can* my father fight!

I get an idea. My two brothers are playing in another room. I leave my grandmother and go to them. They are sprawled on the rug, bent over crayons and drawing-paper. They look up and see my face flaming with my idea.

"What's wrong?" one asks.

"I dare you to do something!"

"Do what?"

"I dare you to call me a Wop!"

My youngest brother, barely six, jumps to his feet, and dancing up and down, screams: "Wop! Wop! Wop! Wop!"

I look at him. Pooh! He's too small. It's that other brother, that bigger brother, I want. He's got ears too, he has.

"I bet *you're* afraid to call me Wop."

But he senses the devil in the woodpile.

"Nah," says he. "I don't wanna."

"Wop! Wop! Wop! Wop!" screams the little brother.

"Shut your mouth, you!"

"I won't neither. You're a Wop! Wop! Woppedy Wop!"

My older brother's box of crayons lies on the floor in front of his nose. I put my heel upon the box and grind it into the carpet. He yells, seizing my leg. I back away, and he begins to cry.

"Aw, that was sure dirty," he says.

134

"I dare you to call me a Wop!"

"Wop!"

I charge, seeking his ear. But my grandmother comes into the room flourishing a razor strop.

II

From the beginning, I hear my mother use the words Wop and Dago with such vigor as to denote violent distaste. She spits them out. They leap from her lips. To her, they contain the essence of poverty, squalor, filth. If I don't wash my teeth, or hang up my cap, my mother says: "Don't be like that. Don't be a Wop." Thus, as I begin to acquire her values, Wop and Dago to me become synonymous with things evil. But she's consistent.

My father isn't. He's loose with his tongue. His moods create his judgments. I at once notice that to him Wop and Dago are without any distinct meaning, though if one not an Italian slaps them onto him, he's instantly insulted. Christopher Columbus was the greatest Wop who ever lived, says my father. So is Caruso. So is this fellow and that. But his very good friend Peter Ladonna is not only a drunken pig, but a Wop on top of it; and of course all his brothers-in-law are good-for-nothing Wops.

He pretends to hate the Irish. He really doesn't, but he likes to think so, and he warns us children against them. Our grocer's name is O'Neil. Frequently and inadvertently he makes errors when my mother is at his store. She tells my father about short weights in meats, and now and then of a stale egg.

Straightway my father grows tense, his lower lip curling. "This is the last time that Irish bum robs me!" And he goes out, goes to the grocery-store, his heels booming.

Soon he returns. He's smiling. His fists bulge with cigars. "From now on," says he, "everything's gonna be all right."

I don't like the grocer. My mother sends me to his store every day, and instantly he chokes up my breathing with the greeting: "Hello, you little Dago! What'll you have?" So I detest him, and never enter his store if other customers are to be seen, for to be

135

called a Dago before others is a ghastly, almost a physical, humiliation. My stomach expands and contracts, and I feel naked.

I steal recklessly when the grocer's back is turned. I enjoy stealing from him — candy bars, cookies, fruit. When he goes into his refrigerator I lean on his meat scales, hoping to snap a spring; I press my toe into egg baskets. Sometimes I pilfer too much. Then, what a pleasure it is to stand on the curb, my appetite gorged, and heave *his* candy bars, *his* cookies, *his* apples into the high yellow weeds across the street! . . . "Damn you, O'Neil, you can't call me a Dago and get away with it!"

His daughter is of my age. She's cross-eyed. Twice a week she passes our house on her way to her music lesson. Above the street, and high in the branches of an elm tree, I watch her coming down the sidewalk, swinging her violin case. When she is under me, I jeer in sing-song:

> *Martha's crooooooss-eyed!*
> *Martha's crooooooss-eyed!*
> *Martha's crooooooss-eyed!*

III

As I grow older, I find out that Italians use Wop and Dago much more than Americans. My grandmother, whose vocabulary of English is confined to the commonest of nouns, always employs them in discussing contemporary Italians. The words never come forth quietly, unobtrusively. No; they bolt forth. There is a blatant intonation, and then the sense of someone being scathed, stunned.

I enter the parochial school with an awful fear that I will be called Wop. As soon as I find out why people have such things as surnames, I match my own against such typically Italian cognomens as Bianchi, Borello, Pacelli — the names of other students. I am pleasantly relieved by the comparison. After all, I think, people will say I am French. Doesn't my name sound French? Sure! So thereafter, when people ask me my nationality, I tell them I am French. A few boys begin calling me Frenchy. I like that. It feels fine.

Thus I begin to loathe my heritage. I avoid Italian boys and girls who try to be friendly. I thank God for my light skin and hair, and I choose my companions by the Anglo-Saxon ring of their names. If a boy's name is Whitney, Brown, or Smythe, then he's my pal; but I'm always a little breathless when I am with him; he may find me out. At the lunch hour I huddle over my lunch pail, for my mother doesn't wrap my sandwiches in wax paper, and she makes them too large, and the lettuce leaves protrude. Worse, the bread is homemade; not bakery bread, not "American" bread. I make a great fuss because I can't have mayonnaise and other "American" things.

The parish priest is a good friend of my father's. He comes strolling through the school grounds, watching the children at play. He calls to me and asks about my father, and then he tells me I should be proud to be studying about my great countrymen, Columbus, Vespucci, John Cabot. He speaks in a loud, humorous voice. Students gather around us, listening, and I bite my lips and wish to Jesus he'd shut up and move on.

Occasionally now I hear about a fellow named Dante. But when I find out that he was an Italian I hate him as if he were alive and walking through the classrooms, pointing a finger at me. One day I find his picture in a dictionary. I look at it and tell myself that never have I seen an uglier bastard.

We students are at the blackboard one day, and a soft-eyed Italian girl whom I hate but who insists that I am her beau stands beside me. She twitches and shuffles about uneasily, half on tip-toe, smiling queerly at me. I sneer and turn my back, moving as far away from her as I can. The nun sees the wide space separating us and tells me to move nearer the girl. I do so, and the girl draws away, nearer the student on her other side.

Then I look down at my feet, and there I stand in a wet, spreading spot. I look quickly at the girl, and she hangs her head and looks at me in a way that begs me to take the blame for her. We attract the attention of others, and the classroom becomes alive with titters. Here comes the nun. I think I am in for it again, but she embraces me and murmurs that I should have raised two fingers and of course I would have been allowed to leave the room. But, says she, there's no need for that now; the thing for

137

me to do is go out and get the mop. I do so, and amid the hysteria I nurse my conviction that only a Wop girl, right out of a Wop home, would ever do such a thing as this.

Oh, you Wop! Oh, you Dago! You bother me even when I sleep. I dream of defending myself against tormentors. One day I learn from my mother that my father went to the Argentine in his youth, and lived in Buenos Aires for two years. My mother tells me of his experiences there, and all day I think about them, even to the time I go to sleep. That night I come awake with a jerk. In the darkness I grope my way to my mother's room. My father sleeps at her side, and I awaken her gently, so that he won't be aroused.

I whisper: "Are you sure Papa wasn't *born* in Argentina?"

"No. Your father was born in Italy."

I go back to bed, disconsolate and disgusted.

IV

During a ball game on the school grounds, a boy who plays on the opposing team begins to ridicule my playing. It is the ninth inning, and I ignore his taunts. We are losing the game, but if I can knock out a hit our chances of winning are pretty strong. I am determined to come through, and I face the pitcher confidently. The tormentor sees me at the plate.

"Ho! Ho!" he shouts. "Look who's up! The Wop's up. Let's get rid of the Wop!"

This is the first time anyone at school has ever flung the word at me, and I am so angry that I strike out foolishly. We fight after the game, this boy and I, and I make him take it back.

Now school days become fighting days. Nearly every afternoon at 3:15 a crowd gathers to watch me make some guy take it back. This is fun; I am getting somewhere now, so come on, you guys, I dare you to call me a Wop! When at length there are no more boys who challenge me, insults come to me by hearsay, and I seek out the culprits. I strut down the corridors. The smaller boys admire me. "Here he comes!" they say, and they gaze and gaze. my two younger brothers attend the same school, and the smallest, a little squirt seven years old, brings his friends to me and asks me to roll up my sleeve and show them my muscles. Here you are, boys. Look me over.

My brother brings home furious accounts of my battles. My father listens avidly, and I stand by, to clear up any doubtful details. Sadly happy days! My father gives me pointers: how to hold my fist, how to guard my head. My mother, too shocked to hear more, presses her temples and squeezes her eyes and leaves the room.

I am nervous when I bring friends to my house; the place looks so Italian. Here hangs a picture of Victor Emmanuel, and over there is one of the cathedral of Milan, and next to it one of St. Peter's, and on the buffet stands a wine pitcher of medieval design; it's forever brimming, forever red and brilliant with wine. These things are heirlooms belonging to my father, and no matter who may come to our house, he likes to stand under them and brag.

So I begin to shout to him. I tell him to cut out being a Wop and be an American once in a while. Immediately he gets his razor strop and whales hell out of me, clouting me from room to room and finally out the back door. I go into the woodshed and pull down my pants and stretch my neck to examine the blue slices across my rump. A Wop, that's what my father is! Nowhere is there an American father who beats his son this way. Well, he's not going to get away with it; some day I'll get even with him.

I begin to think that my grandmother is hopelessly a Wop. She's a small, stocky peasant who walks with her wrists criss-crossed over her belly, a simple old lady fond of boys. She comes into the room and tries to talk to my friends. She speaks English with a bad accent, her vowels rolling out like hoops. When, in her simple way, she confronts a friend of mine and says, her old eyes smiling: "You lika go the Seester scola?" my heart roars. *Mannaggia!* I'm disgraced; now they all know that I'm an Italian.

My grandmother has taught me to speak her native tongue. By seven, I know it pretty well, and I always address her in it. But when friends are with me, when I am twelve and thirteen, I pretend ignorance of what she says, and smirk stiffly; my friends daren't know that I can speak any language but English. Sometimes this infuriates her. She bristles, the loose skin at her throat knits hard, and she blasphemes with a mighty blasphemy.

139

V

When I finish in the parochial school my people decide to send me to a Jesuit academy in another city. My father comes with me on the first day. Chiseled into the stone coping that skirts the roof of the main building of the academy is the Latin inscription: *Religioni et Bonis Artibus*. My father and I stand at a distance, and he reads it aloud and tells me what it means.

I look up at him in amazement. Is this man my father? Why, look at him! Listen to him! He reads with an Italian inflection! He's wearing an Italian mustache. I have never realized it until this moment, but he looks exactly like a Wop. His suit hangs carelessly in wrinkles upon him. Why the deuce doesn't he buy a new one? And look at his tie! It's crooked. And his shoes: they need a shine. And, for the Lord's sake, will you look at his pants! They're not even buttoned in front. And oh, damn, damn, damn, you can see those dirty old suspenders that he won't throw away. Say, Mister, are you really my father? You there, why, you're such a little guy, such a runt, such an old-looking fellow! You look exactly like one of those immigrants carrying a blanket. You can't be *my* father! Why, I thought . . . I've always thought . . .

I'm crying now, the first time I've ever cried for any reason excepting a licking, and I'm glad he's not crying too. I'm glad he's as tough as he is, and we say good-by quickly, and I go down the path quickly, and I do not turn to look back, for I know he's standing there and looking at me.

I enter the administration building and stand in line with strange boys who also wait to register for the autumn term. Some Italian boys stand among them. I am away from home, and I sense the Italians. We look at one another and our eyes meet in an irresistible amalgamation, a suffusive consanguinity; I look away.

A burly Jesuit rises from his chair behind the desk and introduces himself to me. Such a voice for a man! There are a dozen thunderstorms in his chest. He asks my name, and writes it down on a little card.

"Nationality?" he roars,

"American."

"Your father's name?"

I whisper it: "Guido."

"How's that? Spell it out. Talk louder."

I cough. I touch my lips with the back of my hand and spell out the name.

"Ha!" shouts the registrar. "And still they come! Another Wop! Well, young man, you'll be at home here! Yes, sir! Lots of Wops here! We've even got Kikes! And, you know, this place reeks with shanty Irish!"

Dio! How I hate that priest!

He continues: "Where was your father born?"

"Buenos Aires, Argentina."

"Your mother?"

At last I can shout with the gusto of truth.

"Denver!" Aye, just like a conductor.

Casually, by way of conversation, he asks: "You speak Italian?"

"Nah! Not a word."

"Too bad," he says.

"You're nuts," I think.

VI

That semester I wait on table to defray my tuition fee. Trouble ahead; the chef and his assistants in the kitchen are all Italians. They know at once that I am of the breed. I ignore the chef's friendly overtures, loathing him from the first. He understands why, and we become enemies. Every word he uses has a knife in it. His remarks cut me to pieces. After two months I can stand it no longer in the kitchen, and so I write a long letter to my mother; I am losing weight, I write; if you don't let me quit this job, I'll get sick and flunk my tests. She telegraphs me some money and tells me to quit at once; oh, I feel so sorry for you, my boy; I didn't dream it would be so hard on you.

I decide to work just one more evening, to wait on table for just one more meal. That evening, after the meal, when the kitchen is deserted save for the cook and his assistants, I remove my apron and take my stand across the kitchen from him, staring at him. This is my moment. Two months I have waited for this moment. There is a knife stuck into the chopping block. I pick it up, still staring. I want to hurt the cook, square things up.

He sees me, and he says: "Get out of here, Wop!"

An assistant shouts: "Look out, he's got a knife!"

"You won't throw it, Wop," the cook says. I am not thinking of throwing it, but since he says I won't, I do. It goes over his head and strikes the wall and drops with a clatter to the floor. He picks it up and chases me out of the kitchen. I run, thanking God I didn't hit him.

That year the football team is made up of Irish and Italian boys. The linemen are Irish, and we in the backfield are four Italians. We have a good team and win a lot of games, and my teammates are excellent players who are unselfish and work together as one man. But I hate my three fellow-players in the backfield; because of our nationality we seem ridiculous. The team makes a captain of me, and I call signals and see to it my fellow-Italians in the backfield do as little scoring as possible. I hog the play.

The school journal and the town's sport pages begin to refer to us as the Wop Wonders. I think it an insult. Late one afternoon, at the close of an important game, a number of students leave the main grandstand and group themselves at one end of the field, to improvise some yells. They give three big ones for the Wop Wonders. It sickens me. I can feel my stomach move; and after that game I turn in my suit and quit the team.

I am a bad Latinist. Disliking the language, I do not study, and therefore I flunk my examinations regularly. Now a student comes to me and tells me that it is possible to drop Latin from my curriculum if I follow his suggestion, which is that I fail deliberately in the next few examinations, fail hopelessly. If I do this, the student says, the Jesuits will bow to my stupidity and allow me to abandon the language.

This is an agreeable suggestion. I follow it out. But it backtracks, for the Jesuits are wise fellows. They see what I'm doing, and they laugh and tell me that I am not clever enough to fool them, and that I must keep on studying Latin, even if it takes me twenty years to pass. Worse, they double my assignments and I spend my recreation time with Latin syntax.

142

Before examinations in my junior year the Jesuit who instructs me calls me to his room and says:

"It is a mystery to me that a thoroughbred Italian like yourself should have any trouble with Latin. The language is in your blood and, believe me, you're a darned poor Wop."

Abbastanza! I go upstairs and lock my door and sit down with my book in front of me, my Latin book, and I study like a wild man, tearing crazily into the stuff until, lo, what is this? What am I studying here? Sure enough, it's a lot like the Italian my grandmother taught me so long ago — this Latin, it isn't so hard, after all. I pass the examination, I pass it with such an incredibly fine grade that my instructor thinks there is knavery somewhere.

Two weeks before graduation I get sick and go to the infirmary and am quarantined there. I lie in bed and feed my grudges. I bite my thumbs and ponder old grievances. I am running a high fever, and I can't sleep. I think about the principal. He was my close friend during my first two years at the school, but in my third year, last year, he was transferred to another school. I lie in bed thinking of the day we met again in this, the last year. We met again on his return that September, in the principal's room. He said hello to the boys, this fellow and that, and then he turned to me, and said:

"And you, the Wop! So you're still with us."

Coming from the mouth of the priest, the word had a lumpish sound that shook me all over. I felt the eyes of everyone, and I heard a giggle. So that's how it is! I lie in bed thinking of the priest and now of the fellow who giggled.

All of a sudden I jump out of bed, tear the fly-leaf from a book, find a pencil, and write a note to the priest. I write: "Dear Father: I haven't forgotten your insult. You called me a Wop last September. If you don't apologize right away there's going to be trouble." I call the brother in charge of the infirmary and tell him to deliver the note to the priest.

After a while I hear the priest's footsteps rising on the stairs. He comes to the door of my room, opens it, looks at me for a long time, not speaking, but only looking querulously. I wait for him to come in and apologize, for this is a grand moment for me. But he closes the door quietly and walks away. I am astonished. A double insult!

I am well again on the night of graduation. On the platform the principal makes a speech and then begins to distribute the diplomas. We're supposed to say: "Thank you," when he gives them to us. So thank you, and thank you, and thank you, everyone says in his turn. But when he gives me mine, I look squarely at him, just stand there and look, and I don't say anything, and from that day we never speak to each other again.

The following September I enroll at the university.

"Where was your father born?" asks the registrar.

"Buenos Aires, Argentina."

Sure, that's it. The same theme, with variations.

VII

Time passes, and so do school days. I am sitting on a wall along the plaza in Los Angeles, watching a Mexican *fiesta* across the street. A man comes along and lifts himself to the wall beside me, and asks if I have a cigarette. I have, and, lighting the cigarette, he makes conversation with me, and we talk of casual things until the *fiesta* is over. Then we get down from the wall and, still talking, go walking through the Los Angeles Tenderloin. This man needs a shave and his clothes do not fit him; it's plain that he's a bum. He tells one lie upon another, and not one is well told. But I am lonesome in this town, and a willing listener.

We step into a restaurant for coffee. Now he becomes intimate. He has bummed his way from Chicago to Los Angeles, and has come in search of his sister; he has her address, but she is not at it, and for two weeks he has been looking for her in vain. He talks on and on about this sister, seeming to gyrate like a buzzard over her, hinting to me that I should ask some questions about her. He wants me to touch off the fuse that will release his feelings.

So I ask: "Is she married?"

And then he rips into her, hammer and tongs. Even if he does find her, he will not live with her. What kind of a sister is she to let him walk these streets without a dime in his pocket, and

144

she married to a man who has plenty of money and can give him a job? He thinks she has deliberately given him a false address so that he will not find her, and when he gets his hands on her he's going to wring her neck. In the end, after he has completely demolished her; he does exactly what I think he is going to do.

He asks: "Have *you* got a sister?"

I tell him yes, and he waits for my opinion of her; but he doesn't get it.

We meet again a week later.

He has found his sister. Now he begins to praise her. She has induced her husband to give him a job, and tomorrow he goes to work as a waiter in his brother-in-law's restaurant. He tells me the address, but I do not think more of it beyond the fact that it must be somewhere in the Italian quarter.

And so it is, and by a strange coincidence I know his brother-in-law, Rocco Saccone, an old friend of my people and a *paesano* of my father's. I am in Rocco's place one night a fortnight later. Rocco and I are speaking in Italian when the man I have met on the plaza steps out of the kitchen, an apron over his legs. Rocco calls him and he comes over, and Rocco introduces him as his brother-in-law from Chicago. We shake hands.

"We've met before," I say, but the plaza man doesn't seem to want this known, for he lets go my hand quickly and goes behind the counter, pretending to be busy with something back there. Oh, he's bluffing; you can see that.

In a loud voice, Rocco says to me: "That man is a skunk. He's ashamed of his own flesh and blood." He turns to the plaza man. "Ain't you?"

"Oh, yeah?" the plaza man sneers.

"How do you mean—he's ashamed? How do you mean?"

"Ashamed of being an Italian," Rocco says.

. "Oh, yeah?" from the plaza man.

"That's all he knows," Rocco says. "Oh, yeah? That's all he knows. Oh, yeah? Oh, yeah? Oh, yeah? That's all he knows."

"Oh, yeah?" the plaza man says again.

"Yah," Rocco says, his face blue. "*Animale codardo!*"

The plaza man looks at me with peaked eyebrows, and he doesn't know it, he standing there with his black, liquid eyes, he doesn't know that he's as good as a god in his waiter's apron; for he is indeed a god, a miracle worker; no, he doesn't know; no one knows; just the same, he is that — he, of all people. Standing there and looking at him, I feel like my grandfather and my father and the Jesuit cook and Rocco; I seem to have come home, and I am surprised that this return, which I have somehow always expected, should come so quietly, without trumpets and thunder.

"If I were you, I'd get rid of him," I say to Rocco.

"Oh, yeah?" the plaza man says again.

I'd like to paste him. But that won't do any good. There's no sense in hammering your own corpse.

Home, Sweet Home

I AM SINGING NOW, for soon I shall be home. There will be a great welcome for me. There will be spaghetti and wine and salami. My mother will spread a great table piled high with the delicacies of my boyhood. It will all be for me. The love of my mother will come over the table, and my brothers and my sister will be happy to see me among them again, for I am to them the big brother who never errs, and they will be a little envious of the welcome that is poured upon me, and how they will laugh at the things I say, and how they will smile when they see me swallow those squirming forkfuls of spaghetti, and shout for more cheese, and roar my pleasure. For they are my people, and I will have returned to them and to the love of my mother.

I shall pass my glass to my father, and I will say: "More of that wine, Pa," and he will smile and pour the red stuff with a sweet taste into my glass, and I will say: "Atta boy!" and I will swallow it slowly and deeply, feeling it warm my belly, tingling my heart, singing a song to my ears. And my mother will say: "Not too fast, my son," and I will look upon my mother, and I will see the same eyes that I have caused to weep so many, many times, and my bones will get that blunt feeling of remorse, but it will endure only a second, and I will say to my mother: "Ah, Ma, don't you worry about this guy, he'll be all right," and my mother will smile with the happiness that only my mother knows, and my father will smile a little too, for he will be looking at his own flesh and blood, and I will get a throb in my chest, and I will avoid my father's eyes, for they will not be able to conceal their happiness.

That will make me feel very tenderly jubilant, but I will not show it in my face, but my eyes, looking down at the yellow

147

spaghetti, will not be able to hide it, and my father will catch the twinkle there, but he will look away in a flash, for it will make him as bashful as a boy, and I bet he will do some retrospecting, and think about me in the years of my boyhood, and he will see every minute and second of my twenty-one years in the fleeting glance of my eyes, and I will think exactly the same thoughts, for we are of the same flesh and bone, and the stuff of my brain and spine is the stuff of his, and so we will think the same things together, and each will know that the other is thinking the same things.

Our thought will be of a day in Colorado and another welcome spread, when both my father and I got very drunk, and yet remained brutally sober, and I began to curse him for neglecting my mother, and he cursed me for the misery I had flung upon her, and we grew angrier and angrier, and my mother tried to make peace, and presently my father lost himself in an insane passion to make me suffer for the things I had said, and at that same second I too saw scarlet before my eyes, and the two of us leaped upon each other, and we were like two animals, and I knocked my father to the floor, and he fell with a thud, and, lying on the floor, began to cry like a little child.

I was but eighteen then. I looked at my fist that had knocked my father to the floor, and I looked up to the ceiling, my heart pounding, and I lifted my fist to the ceiling, and I saw a blue mark on the knuckles, and I screamed: "Jesus Christ, what have I done? Oh, Jesus Christ, cut my arm off! Quick! Quick! Oh, Jesus Christ, cut it off!" And there on the floor my father lay, and he was crying, and it was not the weeping of the sentimental drunk, but it was the weeping of a man who had seen his little god of wax melt in the blistering sun. And there stood my mother with her hands pressed to her temples, and the gray hair that my father gave her, and the wrinkles and sad eyes that were gifts from me, and my mother knew not what to do, for there were her son and her man fighting over old scars.

The scars could not be healed, but they could be soothed, and now the flesh of her flesh and the man of her life were at each other's guilty throat in the way of fanatics, and in the anger of each there was no defense of her glorious wifehood and

148

motherhood, but only the beastly whining and snarling of two who shouted at each other and bruised each other. "It is you who are the cause!" "No! It is you." My mother saw me there, eighteen years out of her womb, and my father was on the floor, and I was his little wax god who had melted in the blistering sun.

So that is why I will not look into the eyes of my father after I gulp my electrifying wine, and that is what each of us will think, and we will not have forgotten, but our spirits will be at peace, and in a whirl of bitter silence that scene of three years past will go through us, and I will make a boisterous pretense at nonsense, and my father will be ready to leap into the unimportance of it, and in the hearts of my brothers and sister will come a merriment that will not last long, and in the mind of my mother. . . . Ah, God, forgive my father and me!

II

But the wine from fresh grapes, purple-red and bitter-sweet, will bring delight to that hour of welcome, and we shall all have a fill of it. Even my youngest brother, who does not like it, will be allowed to drink perhaps two glasses. He will watch me closely. He will hold his glass as I hold mine, and he will say "Ahhh" when he feels the last drop of it in his mouth, just as I will say it. And he will rub his belly, concealing the unpleasantness, and say: "Boy! That's swell stuff. Gimme some more." And my mother will say softly: "No more, my son." And my father will yell: "Hey! Who the hell do you think you are?"

My sister, who has spoken only a little, will primp for me. She will be seated next to my mother, and I will steal glances at her, and I will see that she is becoming more beautiful with every breath. I will be amazed again at the loveliness of her immense brown eyes, which are like those of some giant squirrel, and she will know that I am peeping surreptitiously at her, and she will be inwardly singing with happiness, and I will see that her beauty is that which drew my father to my mother when he came to America thirty years before, a conceited young Italian, conceited even as I am. My mother will be at my sister's side at the table, and I will study the faces of the two, and I will vow that my sister shall not have the agony which has been my mother's, and I will see my sister lift her chin disdainfully at the remarks of my little brother, and he will shout: "Aw, you're not so smart. You needn't show off just because Jimmy is home." My sister's face will turn pink-scarlet, and she will look suddenly at me, and I will be delighted by her squirrel eyes, and she will glare at my brother and say: "And what about you? What about you, playing like you like wine, just because he's home?" And my little brother will say: "Aw, keep still." And my father will say: "Hey! How many times do I have to tell you to cut out that talk?" And my brother will say: "Well, she started it." And my mother will say softly: "Let's all be nice today. Let's not have one fight."

My plate will be empty now, the tomato sauce and shreds of cheese having been skillfully mopped up with a lump of bread. My mother will see its glistening emptiness, and she will look at my cheeks and say: "You look awful thin, Jimmy. You better eat a lot." And I will battle with another dish of the stringy, cheesy spaghetti, for my mother will be injured within if I do not eat until I am left gasping for breath. There will be, too, a dish of salted anchovies to pick at, and there will be salami, the casing already peeled away, and there will be more and more wine, and there will be tomatoes prepared especially for me, drowned in yellow olive oil, touched with the zestful tang of garlic juice, and at my father's plate will be a saucer filled with garlic, toasted to a crisp.

He will eat it with great noise, and as always my sister will say, and we will all laugh: "There goes the garlic!" My father will grin and say the same old thing: "You people don't know what's good. . . . Try it!" And my sister will turn her lips and draw away from the table and close her big, squirrel eyes and go "Grrrrrrr!" And of course we will all then listen to my father's story of his boyhood when he had nothing to eat but garlic for a week, and long before he has finished we will have gone ahead of him in his story and said aloud the words which he will laboriously, eventually come to, and he will threaten to kill us, and my mother will try to be composed and impartial, but she will not be able to resist the feathers which tickle all but my father, and soon

150

the table will shake with our laughter, and my father will roar like a wild beast.

My brother Tony will then say: "Cutton, cutton, cutton, where's the cutton?" And that will bring even lustier laughs, for he is mimicking the crippled English of my father, who says "cutton," but means "cotton." And then my sister will say: "I love warmelon." Laughter, laughter, laughter. For that is my father's way of saying "watermelon." My father will grind his garlic in his teeth and be silent. And my brother will say: "Bose of you are dutty, hoggly hanimals."

Oh, man! That will be the end of our joy, for my father will now rise from his place and seize my brother by the ear, and kick him in the seat with each step as he leads him to the back porch. My brother will rub his seat and laugh and cry, and my father will return to his place at the table. My brother will shout through the door: "Papa's han hanimal! Papa's han hanimal!" And my father will scrape the chair legs on the floor, and my brother will hear them, and off he will go to his friends, laughing and shouting as he runs: "Papa's han hanimal!"

We will eat in silence for a while, no sound save the tinkling forks and knives, We are settled to the business of eating now, and no one speaks.

My father will say: "Where's the napkins?"

My mother will say, innocently: "Oh, didn't you get one?"

"What kind of a house is this, without napkins?"

My sister will go for the napkins.

"Bring me one," I will say.

"All right."

"Me too," my brother Mike will say.

"What's wrong?" my sister will ask him. "Are you crippled?"

And so I will be among my people, sitting at the welcome supper my mother has prepared, and my father, my sister, and my younger brother will be gathered around the table. My youngest brother, who is thirteen, will have gone away laughing at the stumbling language of my father, who is fifty-two. At his side will be seated my sister, who is seventeen, and next to her my brother Mike, who is nineteen, eating in silence, and my mother, whose eyes are far too large, who is forty-nine, who has a broken body, who has gray hair at her temples, who is daily losing her hearing. And I am twenty-one, and I understand my people better than they understand one another.

III

I will look at my father over the rim of my wine glass. I will see myself. I will know again the streak of cruelty and treachery within me by looking at my father. I will look at the hands of my father, and a turning and a grinding will go on within me, for my father still has the seeds of greatness in him, but they have been choked by the treachery and cruelty that I know — always too late — crouch in me. My father will catch the feeling in me, and in his eyes it will come out for me to look upon, and he will see the same lurking in my eyes, and we will not have strong enough chins to glare at each other, and let those two pairs of eyes collide, and kill that lurking which lies in both our eyes.

Another feeling will come across the table, and we will not know what to do with it, for we loathe it, and that will be shame. We will sense it, and we will be hurt by it, but we have not hands to slug it or to caress it. And so we will look away, and we will sneak glances at each other. And I know it shall always be so, and my father knows. My father will keep on filling my wine glass, and together we will drink, and we shall always feel that kindredness which is a gorge neither of us can leap.

I will look at my father's hands.

I will say: "Are you working?"

He will answer: "No, I'm not working."

"No work here, eh?"

"No, no work here."

"Any work in Sacramento?"

"No, no work in Sacramento."

I will be silent then, for I will know I have touched a painful spot, and he will not have sympathy. He will fight it away.

I will speak about myself. I will make my father envious. He knows that I, too, have the seeds of greatness in me, but my father believes they will be choked up by the treachery which is the

152

heritage of both father and son. I am younger than my father: my hopes scream to the skies. His have dwindled to despair. I know my father sees me at fifty-two, and I at fifty-two am my father. What I will say will please him and yet sadden him.

I will say: "Well, in a few days there'll be a check in the mail for me." I will say this to my father about the manuscript I am now writing.

"You say that a lot."

I will grow angry at this from my father.

"Yes, yes. Moreover, you'll hear it plenty more."

My father will drink more wine, and as he lowers his glass I will see a smile turning his lips faintly. He will be amused by my pugnacity.

My mother will say: "Please. Let's all be happy. Let's all hope for the best, and not quarrel."

I will say: "I'm not quarreling, Ma."

My sister will say: "I read your story in the magazine. I knew you'd write against the Church."

I will say: "Don't be dumb. That wasn't against the Church."

This will not interest my father, for he does not care what I write, nor does he read it. I will drink wine now, for I must prepare myself for the question which my mother will now ask.

She will say: "Do you go to Mass every Sunday, my Jimmy?"

I will answer: "Sometimes, Ma. Sometimes." I will be lying.

She will ask: "Do you still read books against God?"

I will say, lying again: "Not any more, Ma."

And I will look at the face of my mother, and I will remember a night when we lived in the South, and I came home, and I saw my mother in tears, and sick unto death, and the doctor was called, and he saved my mother, and he came out of the room wherein my mother lay, and he held a book in his hand, and he handed it to me, and he said: "This is the cause. If you must read such stuff as this, do it where your mother can't see you." When I looked at the book, I saw that it was the *The Anti-Christ*. Now I will be home soon, and my mother will ask if I read books against God, and I will answer that I do not.

My sister will say: "Why do you write about your family all the time?"

I will shrug. "Why not?"

"You haven't any pride."

"Sez you."

I will be conscious of the splendid beauty of my flowering sister, and will be proud that she has accused me of unpride.

My taciturn brother Mike will assert himself now. He will tell of his feats on the diamond.

He will say: "Pitched a three-hit game last Sunday."

My father, who roots for my brother and gets great praise for the ability of my brother, will say, "He's some boy, that Mike. The best pitcher in this town."

I will say then: "Well, if Mike can do it, I guess I'm able to hold them to *two* hits."

My father will not answer, for he knows that I am a better pitcher than my brother, and my brother knows it too, but I have put baseball behind me now, and they know it, and they respect me, and they will not comment.

Now my mother will ask if all are finished, the plates will be passed to her, and she will scrape them and carry them into the kitchen. My sister, her squirrel eyes flashing over the tablecloth for spots, will rise and help my mother. My father will refill the wine glasses. We will drink in silence, conscious that my sister and mother have gone.

IV

Then will come the triumph of the meal — a sweetmeat made by my mother. It will be a cake of eggs, cheese, lemon peel, and cinnamon. We will shout when my mother carries it in, her face happy in this, her little moment.

She will say: "For Jimmy." I will leap to my feet and kiss my mother where her shoulder curves to meet her neck, where a kiss tickles, and she will laugh in ecstasy, and I will turn her face to look upon it, and there will be tears, and she will say: "Thank God for my Jimmy!"

My father and my brother will not look at us, for neither of them has ever gone away to return to sentimental embraces.

154

Those are things which they see only in picture shows.

I will say to my mother. "Thank whatever gods there be for you."

"Listen to the atheist," my sister will say.

I will answer: "Atheist? When I use the plural? You mean polytheist."

"I told you a million times I don't know what that means."

"Look it up, squirrel eyes." And that will bring smiles.

And my father will surely say: "You better leave them books alone."

My brother Mike will say: "Do you think the Yanks have a chance?"

My sister will now say what she has been bubbling to tell all this time.

"I have a new boy friend. Gee, he's keen!"

And then the whole family will attack her.

My mother: "You're too young for boy friends."

My father: "I'll kill that bum if he hangs around here."

My brother: "Aw, he's no good."

How my sister will defend her new boy friend! Her face will change to pink, her arms will grow hard, and her white teeth will bite the words. She will threaten to run away and never return. She will seize her napkin, twisting it in her fingers. She will fire denunciations at each reviler, and I will understand that she is right, and that my people are unfair and wrong.

I will say: "Why don't you bring him here to meet your father and mother? Maybe that would help."

And she will stare at the four bare walls, at the stiff furniture, the curtainless windows, the carpetless floors gone gray with age and with the cracks between boards pressed smooth with dirt.

I will say nothing. No one will speak, but around the table will be four people who feel the great pain of poverty, and my father, whose hopes are despairs, will be hurt most painfully.

Maybe, as he sometimes does, he will say: "Ah, well, better days are coming." But that, I will remember from Nietzsche, is hope — the first sign of defeat. My father will tremblingly, avidly drain his glass, fill it, and drain it again. His hand will go out to my sister, and he will chuck her under the chin.

155

"Your father's no good," he will say.

And my sister: "Don't be silly."

My mother will cut away a huge piece of cake and carry it into the kitchen. That will be for my little brother Tony, who has run laughing at the bungling speech of my father. Tonight he will come home and find his cake in the pantry. Maybe before he returns I will go into the pantry and steal it for myself. Everyone but my mother will be likely to do that.

The dinner will be ended now. The wine pitcher, a huge thing with a capacity of half a gallon, will be drained. Outside, darkness will be coming. A car or two will pass, with lights glassy and glaring.

My brother will say: "I wish we had a radio."

My father will put on his hat, and in shirt-sleeves he will go away to the poolhall.

My mother will come out of the kitchen to the front door and say to my father as he descends the porch steps: "Aren't you going to stay home this one night when Jimmy is home?"

"What for?" he will answer. "There ain't nothing for me here."

And I will hear him, and I will know that he is right. He will go down the street, and I will know what is in his mind. Maybe he will meet my little brother, and my brother will run, and my father will shake his fist at him and shout: "Dutty hanimal!"

In the kitchen, my mother and sister will wash the dishes, my sister singing as she dries them, my mother before the sink, her apron with a round wet spot where she presses against the sink. My brother Mike will go to the back yard to oil his ball glove.

I will go to the front yard, light a cigarette, lie on my back on the lawn, and grow restless. The stars will begin to twinkle, and I will think of a favorite line in *The Mysterious Universe*: "And the total number of stars in the universe is probably something like the total number of grains of sand on all the seashores of the world." I will linger with the words, and wish that I could have written such a line. I will think about my girl Claudia, who is far away, and I will see her in a red dress, and I will think about kissing her. She will come between me and the stars, and the whole sky will be filled with her.

156

I will get up on my feet and flip my cigarette, and wish I were with her, and not in this goddamned, godforsaken, one-horse town.

The Wrath of God

CLAUDIA'S APARTMENT was the last on the second floor. Fifteen minutes before the first quake I sat reading in the living room, but I wasn't interested in the book because Claudia was so near. She was a woman who impulsively loved to cook, and now she was in the kitchen making marmalade. It was turning out with such success that every few minutes she exclaimed so, and I sat there pleased with her happiness.

She always came without a sound, and coming from the kitchenette she stood in the door. I thought how beautiful she was, and yet I knew she was fading. In her thirty-sixth year, her beauty was dying like the setting sun coming across the Pacific and pouring so richly through the chintz curtains behind her. She wore the green dress I always requested because it did such wonderful things to her figure.

"Come and see!" she said. "Hurry!"

I tossed the book on the chesterfield and got up. Instantly her hands went to her hips.

"Jimmy! Put that book back in the case! How many times must I tell you that?"

"I'm not through with it," I said.

"It doesn't matter."

I put the book in the case, but it got me. I couldn't stand it when she harped on small details. Her requests were always expressed as demands, and they implied that big difference in our ages. The clock on the bookcase said ten minutes to six, and I was hungry. We usually ate at five but today she had closed her millinery shop an hour later. I followed her into the kitchenette that blended so well with her green dress. She stirred the

159

marmalade with a bright spoon. Leaning upon her from behind,
I dovetailed my hands across her waist and pressed her carefully.
She lifted her Slavic face and rubbed her forehead into my throat.
I knew she could never possess me, this small woman who I liked
to believe had lured me from my Faith. Ever since I was a kid
who served at Mass I had wanted a sinful woman, someone to
lure me like a siren. Now I was tiring of it. The feeling of sin-
fulness was all right for a while, but in the end it was tiresome.
I felt a need for Confession again, for Holy Communion, symbols
which Claudia thought stupid and superstitious and barbaric.

"Look!" she said. "Isn't it wonderful?"

I put my finger into the golden marmalade and tasted it. She
waited breathlessly for my verdict. I thought the mixture was
acrid, the apricots unripe and bitter.

"Not bad," I said.

Which was too prosaic. She had expected bombast and flattery, which was my style, but I had lost all feeling for it. She
looked at me and I saw the bluish-white spots where her temples
met her eyes, and again I told myself the Church would be amused
and shocked in the delight I took in those marks of maturity upon
a woman fourteen years my senior. Leaning against the sink, I
watched her sleek hips as she furiously stirred the marmalade.
I hadn't been to Confessions and Communion since I met her,
two years before. I hadn't been to Mass, either. I would have
a lot to tell Father Driscoll about her and me. I knew what he
would say, that cynical, intelligent priest. He would tell me that
two years with Claudia was not adultery but absurdity. He would
tell me it was not sinful but silly. He would raise hell about my
missing Mass for two years, though. He would say, take it easy,
Jimmy; and he would warn me about youthful excesses. As for
Claudia, he would think her ridiculous, a silly woman with
a crush on a kid. He was so wise; non-Catholic women were
so absurd to him, they were outside the Church and they
hadn't the intelligence to come in; they weren't like the women
inside the Church, who knew the answers, knew the ground upon
which they walked. He would say, if you've got to go helling
around, Jimmy, get yourself a Catholic girl—it's more fun,
you'll have more in common; and he would tell me Catholic

women had more on the ball; they were as women should be, sad and mystical.

At that moment the first tremendous shock came. Just before it hit there seemed a paralysis of death in the air. It seemed the atmosphere was palsied and even suffocating a tenth of a second before the shock came. Then it hit us.

Claudia looked around, eyes shrieking. The floor rolled. I spread my legs and clung to the sink. The floor rolled. The swaying was deep and beautiful, a colossal gracefulness. I felt like laughing, it was so beautiful. I heard creaking and cracking like the twisting of bones. Plaster fell. The floor was like a mad sea. Somewhere there was screaming. Claudia fell upon me, clawing my neck. The boiling marmalade fell to the floor, and I dragged her away from the toppling stove. The walls wept and wailed. There was a boom when the piano hit the floor. The carpets crept. Windows broke. Cupboards fell. Dodging dishes, we were knocked down.

"God save me!" Claudia screamed. "Earthquake!"

I got up and pulled her after me. In the corridor people were running. Clouds of dust and smoke wafted after them like ghosts through open doors. The swaying continued and the women screamed. We ran down the back stairs. The face of the earth was veiled in dust in the twilight. From everywhere came the gleeful laughter of breaking glass. When we reached the bottom I stared at the quivering earth and tried to subdue a revolution of thought and sensation. And the women screamed. Claudia lay on her back and panted. The dust hovering over the ground was like fog blooming from an agonized soil.

"God have mercy!" Claudia moaned.

We were in an empty parking lot surrounded by tall palm and eucalyptus trees. Beyond the line of trees to the south I noticed the gaping horizon, and at once I knew the tall Protestant church had been knocked down and out of sight. I wondered about Father Driscoll's parish and St. Vincent's. I turned quickly and looked beyond the trees to the north. It was still there—that golden cross. My blood howled with joy, but my thought raced up and I said, it's a coincidence; Aquinas would call it that, and so would Augustine, and St. Ignatius, and Father Driscoll, and

161

so must you; remember what Aquinas wrote about superstition; be rational. And I laughed because I was so scared, and because I was praying with instant familiarity a prayer I hadn't remembered for fifteen years:

In miseria, in angustia,
Ora, Virgo, pro nobis,
Pro nobis ora, in mortis hora,
Ora, ora pro nobis!

I had my Faith, it was still there, strong as ever, right there in my blood, fighting off my fear of the quake, beating it down with a forgotten Latin and making me laugh for joy that it should guard me so selfishly, protecting me in a film of blood-prayer.

The temblors were ceaseless. The earth quivered like a horse-rump flicking flies. It was a jabbing, sickening vibration, as though someone pulled wires fastened to your ankles. It stirred up that nausea that comes before retching. And the women screamed. With every shake they screamed. I saw a lot of grotesque stuff: the old lady embracing the palm tree with arms and legs, as though to shinny it; the woman slugging herself furiously with both fists; the dog crawling flat on his belly, his snout lifted beseechingly to the inscrutable sky.

Claudia lay with eyes wide to the twilight, her fingers tearing tufts of grass from the earth. She had got her breath at last.

"Afraid?" she asked.

"Scared to death," I said.

Kneeling, I lifted her head into my lap.

"I love you so much," she said.

How often she had said that, yet never had I the talent to believe her! It was simply not in me. She was an instrument of sin; my only talent with her was a capacity for willing to believe she had lured me awhile into a wasteland of evil, not too far from the outposts of my spiritual beginnings.

Suddenly in front of us in a circle a group of men and women gathered in prayer. There was a stout woman in a housedress in the center of the circle. Her arms stretched to the sky, she wept as she led their propitiations. Then they sang hymns. Claudia

162

joined in the singing. I had to smile: they seemed like savages crawling back to their pristine altars: they were denying intelligence and reason. I said, not for me this voodooism, not for me this slobbering at the feet of catastrophe; my Church fostered this civilization and if God wills that an earthquake destroy it I will at least refrain from singing hymns and acting like a Holy Roller. The praying folk were indeed like Holy Rollers. They kissed the earth with their faces, got dirt in their mouths, and let out weird noises to the first stars of that incredible night. I felt ashamed and turned my back on the scene.

It infuriated Claudia, and I could feel her shame before me, her anger that I should witness her sudden return to God, for a thousand times she had ridiculed all religion and proclaimed herself a fearless atheist. She lifted her head from my lap and sat up, her elbows on her knees. The temblors rocked her, and she spread her legs to keep from being bowled over, and when she did so one of the men in the circle looked at her hungrily, his eyes softening and he forgetting to pray as he stared at Claudia's spread legs. I pulled off my leather coat and threw it over her knees.

"Was that necessary?" she asked.

"You're corrupting his earthquake morals," I said.

"You prude!" she sneered. "You Catholic!"

While I laughed she glanced around the tree-confined lot. I knew she wanted someone different from me to sustain her, that she wanted to go nearer the group and give herself heart and soul to the prayers and hymns. I said something about the worst being over now, but she shrugged contemptuously and began polishing her nails against her thigh. Suddenly she jumped to her feet.

"My jewels!" she said. "Heavens! All my jewels are up there on the dressing table!"

The apartment building still stood, but all the windows were smashed and the walls were split asunder in a dozen places. The incinerator chimney lay in debris, much of the back wall torn away with it. The building had withstood the quake, but at the moment it was unsafe to enter it. Slight temblors kept knocking away brick and stucco, and a severe jolt could easily sink the upper floors. I thought it stupid to enter the building after her jewels; anyhow, they were not particularly valuable.

"You're a filthy coward!" she said.

"No one will touch the jewels," I said.

"But the fire!" she said. "They had a fire after the San Francisco quake, didn't they?"

"No danger," I said. "By now all gas mains and power lines are obviously disconnected."

She thought a moment. "Of course you left the door wide open."

"I don't remember."

"Of course you did! Someone will steal the jewels!"

"No thief will enter that building tonight," I said.

"Thieves aren't cowards."

I wanted to tear her to pieces.

"All right," I said. "I'll get them."

II

I started for the darkened apartment house. The late evening was bathed in the white light of the moon, and for the first time I saw the real havoc of earthquake. Across the street on the hotel lawn the dead were laid out in rows and covered with blood-soaked sheets. The wounded were on the other side of the lawn. The writhing of bodies bespoke great pain, but I heard only the drone of airplanes, the roar of automobiles, the wailing of sirens. For the wounded there was no escape, the earth still quivering in spasms everywhere within a radius of a hundred miles.

Then I saw the three newsreel cameramen. They were shooting a woman crushed to death beneath a fallen wall. Lying on her side, she was half buried in tons of masonry. The cameras were poised six feet above her, the boys standing with feet braced, red-tipped cigarettes in their mouths as they ground out the shot. It was like a bullet between the eyes to watch them. I buckled and ran inside the dark apartment. Lighting matches, I found my way to the stairs in the foyer. The floor was solid but buried in six inches of fallen plaster. Intermittent temblors sprinkled me with plaster. I was scared stiff, but I had to smile at the gush of forgotten Latin that came from memory. It was not prayer, for prayer means propitiation. It was memory set to the music of fine Latin stanzas. It was a beautiful way to be frightened and I was grateful. I wondered what Father Driscoll would say if he were to see me there, risking my neck for Claudia's jewels, and I knew he would laugh and call me a sucker.

Claudia's apartment was an impassable heap of overturned furniture, broken pictures, and fallen plaster. I found a candle under the table in the breakfast nook, and as I stepped back to the living room I felt the soles of my feet covered with sticky marmalade; it clung like dead fingers, as if to imprison me. I scraped it off on a chair rung.

Claudia's jewels were buried under a heap of perfume bottles. As I gathered them a shock came. I lost my balance and the candle wavered, and it seemed my heart sprang and struck me like a snake. But I got the jewels. At the door I stooped for one last look around. Before the fireplace I was surprised to find the chesterfield unmoved, the only piece of furniture undisturbed by the quake. A long time ago Claudia and I had christened it "The Field of Honor." We used to lie there by the hour, talking and sipping gin fizzes on hot summer afternoons. I went up to it and turned it over and shoved it across the room, thinking all the time of the laughter of Father Driscoll.

By the time I got downstairs and into the open again the Marines had taken charge and the town was under martial law. They ordered me away from the wrecked walls and I moved to the middle of the lot. I couldn't find Claudia. Someone had built a big bonfire, where the refugees of that district now huddled. I walked around the fire, looking into frightened, flame-shadowed faces. She wasn't there, so I began a systematic search of the lot, starting at one corner and walking down the crowded sidewalk. Then I heard my name called. I turned toward the street and saw Claudia seated with someone in a car. I walked over. A man was at the wheel beside her, but I didn't know him; I'd never seen him before. With eyes lowered, she open her palms and I emptied my pockets of the jewels.

"Who's the guy?" I asked.

She didn't answer.

"What're you doing here?" I said.

"All set?" the man asked.

"Claudia!" I said.

"I can't stay here," she said.

The engine started.

"Claudia!"

"I can't stay here! I can't!"

The car moved from the curb. I stepped back as it nosed into the sweep of traffic. Once more I called, but she didn't look back, and the last I ever saw of her was a white hand protecting the hair that flowed from her bent head. Then the traffic swallowed her. I leaned against a lamp post and lit a cigarette. I was glad she was gone.

A heavy hand grabbed my shoulder and shook me. I looked around quickly, and before me loomed the big figure of Father Driscoll. His black suit was grimy, his reversed collar awry. He wasn't wearing the usual soft black hat, and I noticed a trickle of blood near the line of his gray, curly head.

I said: "Hi, Father! Swell earthquake." Then I said: "Your head's bleeding."

He was a huge man, six feet five, and looking down at me he dusted the front of his coat and smacked at the dusty spots around his knees.

"Never mind me," he said. "How come I don't see you at Mass any more?"

"Busy," I said.

"I ought to knock hell out of you," he said.

"Save it," I said. "Your head's bleeding."

"You better get smart," he said, "you fifth-rate Huysmans!"

"Maybe I will."

He took out a handkerchief and dabbed the blood.

"Can't talk now," he said. "I'm needed at the hospital. You come to Mass Sunday, get me? I want to talk to you."

"Maybe I will," I said.

"No maybe about it," he said. "You come, get me?"

"Okay."

He smiled.

"So long, sucker. Look out for the girls."

166

He slapped me on the shoulder and hurried away, dabbing at his bloody head. I watched him break into a run as he crossed the street. Then I went the other way, walking slowly, mingling with the hysterical crowd, walking along and thinking I was alone, that soon my slate would be clean again, grateful that my Church was above all a good sport.

Hail Mary

HAIL MARY, full of grace, the Lord is with thee; blessed art thou among women, and blessed is the fruit of thy womb, Jesus. O Holy Mother Mary, I am now in Hollywood, California, on the corner of Franklin and Argyle, in a house where I rent a room at six a week. Remember, O Blessed Virgin, remember the night twenty years ago in Colorado when my father went to the hospital for his operation, and I got all my brothers and sisters down on the floor in our bedroom, and I said: "Now by gosh—pray! Papa's sick, so you kids pray." Ah, boy, we prayed, you Virgin Mary, you Honey, we prayed and my blood sang, and I felt big feelings in my chest, the ripple of electricity, the power of cold faith, and we all got up and walked to different parts of the house. I sat in the kitchen and smirked. They had said at the hospital that Papa was going to die, and nobody knew it but me and Mamma and you, you Honey, but we had prayed and I sat smirking, pooh-poohing at death because we had prayed and I knew we had done our share for Papa, and that he would live.

The rest of them wouldn't go to bed that night, they were afraid Papa would die, and they all waited, and already Grandma planned the funeral, but I smirked and went to bed and slept very happy, with your beads in my fingers, kissing the cross a few times and then dozing off because Papa could not die after *my* prayers, because you were my girl, my queen, and there was no doubt in my heart.

And in the morning there was wild joy to wake me, because Papa had lived and would live some more, a lot of years to come, and there was Mamma back from the hospital, beaming and sticky when she kissed us for joy, and I heard her say to Grandma:

169

"He lived because he has an iron constitution. He is a strong man. You can't kill that man." And when I heard that, I snickered. They didn't know, these people, they didn't know about you and me, you Honey, and I thought of your pale face, your dark hair, your feet on the serpent at the side-altar, and I said, she's wonderful, she's sure wonderful.

Oh, those were the days! Oh, I loved you then! You were the celestial blue, and I looked up at you when I walked to school with books under my arms, and my ecstasy was simple and smashing, crushing and mad and whirling, all these things across my chest, sensations, and you in the blue sky, in my blue shirt, in the covers of my blue-covered book. You were the color blue and I saw you everywhere and then I saw the statue in the church, at the side-altar, with your feet on the serpent, and I said and said a thousand times, I said, oh, you Honey, and I wasn't afraid of anything. . . .

Hail Mary, full of grace, the Lord is with thee; blessed art thou among women, and blessed is the fruit of thy womb, Jesus. O Holy Mother Mary, I want to ask a favor of you, but first I want to remind you of something I once did for you.

You will say that I am bragging again, and that you have heard this story before, but I am proud of it, and my heart is beating wildly and there is the rustle of a bird in my throat, and I could cry, and I am crying because I loved you, oh, I loved you so. That hot flash on my cheek is the course of my tears, and I flick it off with the point of my finger, and the finger comes away warm and wet, and I sit here and I am of the living, I am saying this is a dream.

His name was Willie Cox, and he went to Grover Cleveland. He was always razzing me because I was a Catholic. O you Mary! I have told you this before, I admit the braggadocio, but tonaight, one day removed from Christmas Eve, I am in Holywood, California, on the corner of Franklin and Argyle, and the rent is sex a week, and I want to ask you a favor, and I cannot ask until I tell you once more about this Willie Cox.

He chewed tobacco, this Willie Cox. He went to Grover Cleveland, and he chewed tobacco, and I went to St. Catherine's and we used to pass one another on the corner, and he used to

170

squirt tobacco juice on my shoes and legs and say: "*That* for the Catholics. They stink."

Willie Cox, where are you tonight? I am on the corner of Franklin and Argyle, and this is Hollywood, so it is quite possible that you are two blocks away, but wherever you are, Mr. Willie Cox, I call upon you to bear witness to the truth of my narrative. Willie Cox, I took a hell of a lot of your guff that spring. When you said the priests ate the nuns' babies, and then spat on my shoes, I took it. When you said we had human sacrifices at Mass, and the priest drank the blood of young girls, and you spat across my knees, I took that. The truth is, Willie, and tonight I admit, you scared me. You were very tough, and I decided to do as the martyrs did—to do nothing. To take it.

Hail Mary, full of grace! I was a boy then, and there was no love like my love. And there was no tougher boy than Willie Cox, and I feared him. Ah, but my days were celestial blues and my eyes had only to lift and there was my love, and I was not afraid. And yet, in spite of it all, I was afraid of Willie Cox.

How is your nose today, Willie Cox? Did your front teeth grow out again? He was on his way to Grover Cleveland and I was on my way to St. Catherine's and it was eight o'clock in the morning. He shifted the wad in his jaw, and I held my breath.

"Hi, Red Neck."

"Hello, Willie."

"What's your hurry, Catholic?"

"Gotta, Willie. I'm late."

"What'sa matter? Scared of the nunnies?"

"Don't, Willie. You're choking me."

"Scared of the nunnies?"

"*Don't*, Willie! I can't hardly breathe!"

"I heard somethin', Red Neck. My old man, he tells me you Catlickers think Jesus was borned without his mother having kids like other people have kids. Is that right?"

"It's the Immaculate Conception. Ouch!"

"Immaculate, crap! I bet she was a whore like all Catlickers."

"Willie Cox, you dirty dog!"

Mr. Thomas Holyoke, you are dead now, you died two years later, but even in death you may speak out tonight and tell what

171

you saw from your window, there on the lawn, fourteen years ago one morning in the spring. You may say what you said to the policeman who ran from the courthouse steps, you may say again:

"I saw the dark lad here struggling to get free. The Cox boy was choking him. I thought he'd hurt the boy, and I was about to intervene. All at once the dark lad here swung his fist, and the Cox boy went sprawling across my new spring lawn. I thought they were playing, until I saw the Cox boy didn't move. When I ran out his nose was bleeding and his front teeth were missing."

Hail Mary, full of grace! Here in Hollywood, on the corner of Franklin and Argyle, I look through my window and gaze and gaze at an unending pattern of celestial blue. I wait and I remember. O you Honey, where are you now? Oh, endless blue, you have not changed!

In her room next to mine, my landlady sits before the radio. Willie Cox, I know now that you are in Hollywood. Willie Cox, you are the woman in the next room playing the radio. You have given up the vulgar habit of chewing tobacco, but, oh, Willie, you had charm in those days, and you were not nearly so monstrous as you are now, slipping little pieces of paper under my door, telling me over and over that I owe you eighteen dollars.

Hail Mary, full of grace! Today when I talked to my agent he said there was a slump in Hollywood, that the condition was serious. I went down the stairs of his office and into the big, late afternoon. Such a blue sky! Such riotous blue in the Santa Monica mountains! I looked everywhere above, and I sighed, and I said, well, it won't rain tonight, anyway. That was this afternoon. Willie Cox, you are my landlady and you are a Slump in Hollywood.

Mary in the Sky, what has happened to me? O tall queen standing on the serpent at the side-altar, O sweet girl with waxen fingers, there is a Slump in Hollywood, my landlady slips little pieces of paper under my door, and when I gaze at the sky it is to form an opinion about the weather. This is funny. It is probably goddamn funny to the world and it is funny to me, but this gathering dust in my throat, this quiet in my chest where once there was whirling, this cigarette-clenching mouth that once

172

bore a smirk of faith and joy in destiny — there is no laughter in these things. Willie Cox has got me by the throat again.

Willie Cox, I am not afraid of you. I know that I cannot bloody the nose of a Slump in Hollywood or knock the teeth out of my landlady's mouth, but, Willie Cox, remember that I still look to the sky. Remember that there are nights like these when I pause to listen, to search, to feel, to grope.

Hail Mary, full of grace, the Lord is with thee, and blessed art thou among women. Holy Mary, Mother of God, I was going to ask a favor, I was going to ask boldly about that rent. I see it is not necessary now. I see that you have not deserted me. For in a little while I shall slip this into an envelope and send it off. There is a Slump in Hollywood, and my landlady slips little pieces of paper under my door, and once more I sit in the kitchen of my world, a smirk on my lips. . . .

Later Stories

A Nun No More

MY MOTHER WENT to a high school which was run by the nuns. After she got through she wanted to be a nun too. My Grandma Toscana told me. But Grandma and the whole family didn't want her to become a nun. They told her it was all right for girls in other families to become nuns, but not their daughter. My mother's name was Regina Toscana and she was so holy the holiness lit up her eyes. She had a statue of St. Teresa in her room, and when they kicked about her becoming a nun she stayed in her room day and night praying to St. Teresa.

"Oh beloved St. Teresa!" she prayed. "Grant me the light to see the path thou hast made for me, that I might do thy holy bidding. Visit me with sanctifying grace in the name of our Blessed Mother and the Lord Jesus, amen!"

Some prayer. But it didn't do any good because Grandma Toscana still said nothing doing. She told my mother to cut out acting like a sick calf and get some sense. They all talked to her like that, Uncle Jim, Uncle Tony, and Grandma and Grandpa Toscana. They were Italian people and they didn't like the way she was acting, because Italians hate it when their women don't want to get married. They hate it and they think something is screwy somewhere. It is best for the Italian women to get married. Then the husband pays and the whole family saves money. And that was the way they talked to my mother.

Then my Uncle Tony got an idea. One night he brought a man named Pasquale Martello to the house. Uncle Tony introduced him to my mother, and he had a hunch she would go for him and maybe marry him and forget about the nun business. My mother was a honey and I know it, because we have some pictures and I can prove it.

177

Pasquale Martello owned a grocery store and he was lousy with money, but otherwise he wasn't so hot for a girl like my mother. He sold fancy things in his store, like Parmesan cheese, salami, and a special kind of fancy garlic. He dressed real loud in green shirts with white stripes and red neckties. The only reason my mother went with him was on account of she was afraid of Uncle Tony, who raised hell if she didn't go out with him. Pretty soon Pasquale Martello got a crush on my mother and he tried to get her to marry him.

But he had so many bad habits that my mother got awfully tired of him pretty soon. For one thing, he ate too much fancy garlic and his breath was something fierce. He carried garlic around in a sack in his pockets and he used to toss it up in the air and catch it in his mouth the way you eat salted peanuts. He took my mother to different places, like Lakeside Park, and the dance, and to the movies. On account of that garlic you could smell him coming for miles. Every time they went to the movies people got up and found other seats. Any my mother wanted to become a nun! It was very embarrassing for her. After the show they used to sit in front of the big stove in Grandma Toscana's parlor and talk. He was so dumb that my mother yawned right in his face and he never did catch on that she was hinting and wanted to go to bed. She had to tell him to go home or he would still be in that parlor, talking.

Every morning Uncle Tony asked the same question.

"Well, well! And when's the marriage going to be?"

"Never," my mother said. "There isn't going to be any marriage."

"Are you crazy?" Uncle Tony said. "That guy's got money!"

"I'm sorry," she said. "My life is in another direction."

"Meaning?"

"My life is dedicated to the service of our Blessed Lady."

"My God!" Uncle Tony said. "Did you hear that one! I give up!"

"I'm sorry," my mother said. "I'm really sorry."

"*Sangue de la madonna!*" Uncle Tony said. "And after all I've done for her! There's gratitude for you."

My mother went up to her room and stayed there all day, until Pasquale came that night. He always brought my grandmother something from the store, cheese mostly and sometimes tomato

178

sauce in big cans, or Italian paste. Grandma Toscana liked him most on account of the Parmesan cheese, which was a dollar a pound in those days.

That night my mother told Pasquale it was too bad, but he would have to find another girl because she did not love him. He was crazy about her all right. He got down on his knees and kissed her hands, and he walked out of the house bawling. The next day he called Uncle Tony on the phone and told him my mother had given him the gate and wouldn't let him come around any more.

Uncle Tony got boiling mad. He ran home from work and raised hell with the whole family. When he came to my mother he shook his fist in her face and pushed her against the sideboard so hard it knocked the wind out of her.

"You crazy fool!" he hollered. "What good are you anyhow?"

"I'm sorry," she said.

"Good God!" he said. "Don't you know anything else but 'I'm sorry'?"

"I'm sorry," she said.

"Listen to her!" he yelled. "She's sorry!"

"But I am sorry," she said.

My Uncle Tony was in the grocery business too, but his store was a little one and he didn't sell Italian stuff, and he had it all figured out that when my mother and Pasquale got married he would merge his store with Pasquale's and they would all clean up. But Pasquale never came back to the house again. Before long he married a girl, and she wasn't an Italian either. She was an American and he didn't love her either. Grandma Toscana said it was a spite marriage. The Italians do that sometimes. A spite marriage is when you marry somebody else to get your real girl's goat and try to make her sorry she didn't marry you. But my mother wasn't sorry at all. The whole thing tickled her pink.

In North Denver is the Church of St. Cecilia's. This was where my mother spent all of her time. It is across the street from the high school, an old red church without a lawn in front of it or anything, just the street, and not even a tree around. Once I went there for Christmas Mass with my mother. It was a long time

179

after she got married. I mean, it had to be. The church is a big, sad church and the incense smells like my mother. It is a leery church. It scared me. I kept thinking I was not born and would never be born.

My mother knew all the nuns at St. Cecilia's. She used to bum around with them, and they put her in charge of the altars and she decorated them with flowers. She washed and ironed the altar linen and things like that. It was more fun than getting married. She was there all afternoon, so that Uncle Jim or Uncle Tony had to come for her at supper time. Uncle Jim didn't mind because it was only a block away, but Uncle Tony raised hell. He thought church was a lot of boloney.

He said, "Instead of fooling around here all the time, why don't you stay home and help your mother?"

But my mother was a good worker and she told him to be careful what he said. She did all the washing and ironing around the house, and Grandma didn't have any kick coming, and once in a while she cooked the meals, but not often because she was not a good cook. She always did her work before she went to St. Cecilia's. Her garden was in Grandma's back yard, and she grew peonies and roses for the altars. Uncle Tony told her to cut out the church stuff or he would wreck her garden.

"You go to the dickens!"

Oh oh, that got him mad. Italian girls are not supposed to sass their big brothers. Uncle Tony wouldn't allow anything like that.

"By God, I'll show you!" he said.

He ran out to the coal shed and got the spade. Then he took off his sweater and spaded every flower in the garden to pieces. It hurt my mother. She stood on the back porch and it hurt her. She was crazy about her garden, and when she saw him hacking it up she hung on the door and almost fainted. Then she ran out and screamed and screamed. She fell on the ground and kicked with her feet and hit with her hands. It scared Uncle Tony. He called Grandma. She kept screaming. He tried to lift her. She screamed and kicked him.

She was very sick. They carried her upstairs and put her to bed. The doctor came. He said she was a very sick woman. For a long time he came every day. They had to have a nurse. For a year she was sick and nervous. Everybody in the house had to be quiet and walk on tiptoe. It cost a lot of money for doctor bills. My mother cried and cried night and day. They couldn't stop her. Even the Sisters came, but they couldn't do anything. Finally Grandma Toscana called the priest. He gave her Holy Communion. Right away she felt better. Next day she was better than ever. Next day she was swell. Pretty soon she was able to get out of bed. Then she moved around more. All at once she was well again.

Grandma Toscana said it was a miracle. Uncle Tony felt like the devil. He told my mother how sorry he was, and he planted her a new garden. Everything was fine again. My mother liked the new garden better than ever, and Uncle Tony left her alone. Nobody bothered her any more.

She went on decorating the altars at St. Cecilia's. Also she taught school. She went on retreats. A retreat is when you pray and meditate for three days without talking to anybody. Once she went on a retreat for six weeks. Whatever the nuns did, she did. She was crazy about them. All they ever did was wash clothes, decorate altars, scrub floors, and teach kids.

Before long, sure enough Uncle Tony started kicking again, but not like before. He was afraid my mother would get sick again. He even brought more men to the house. He brought Jack Mondi, who was the biggest bootlegger in North Denver. He isn't any more because he got shot, but he was important when Uncle Tony brought him to meet my mother. He scared the whole family stiff. Before sitting down, he always put his gun on the table. Every few minutes he jumped up and peeked out the front window. He brought gangsters with him, and they waited for him on the front porch. Even Uncle Tony didn't know it was going to be that scary, so he tried to get rid of Jack Mondi, but he didn't try very hard. He was afraid he would get hurt.

Once Jack Mondi came to the house drunk and he bit my mother on the cheek. It was the first time anything like that ever happened to her, and she got mad and hauled off and slapped him. The whole family held their breaths and waited for Jack Mondi to shoot them down. Uncle Tony made a sign to my mother to go easy and not make Jack mad. But my mother didn't think he was so tough. She told him to get out of the house and never come back. He did it too. He stuck his gun in his pocket and walked right out without saying a word. For a long time they thought he would come back and shoot the whole family, but he never came back again. Uncle Tony was so scared he even went to church. But Jack Mondi never showed up again. After he got killed they read about it in the papers. My mother went to his funeral and prayed for the repose of his soul. She was the only woman in the church besides Jack Mondi's mother. Which proves my mother was a good sport.

Another guy with a crush on my mother was Alfredo di Posso. Uncle Tony brought him too. Whenever he found a guy he thought would make a good husband he brought him to dinner. There were others too, but I only know about Pasquale Martello, Jack Mondi, Alfredo di Posso, and a man named Murphy, but Murphy didn't cut much ice because he was Irish. Uncle Tony never did like the Irish.

Alfredo di Posso was a salesman for lima beans. Once in a while Alfredo comes to our town, so I know him. He doesn't sell beans in cans or anything like that. He sells them by the carload. When he comes to our town he stops to see my mother. He is a swell guy, always laughing. He gives me money, usually four bits. When my mother met him, he didn't have a religion. She made him join the Catholic Church, but he made fun of it; he made fun of everything. My mother got tired of it. She told him she could never marry him.

When my mother was twenty-one everybody in North Denver knew she was going to be a nun. Her favorite order was the Sisters of Charity. You have to take the train to their convent in Kentucky. For a long time you study stuff. Then you become a real nun. They cut off your hair and you wear black dresses, and you can't get married or have fun. Your husband is Jesus. Anyway, that's what Sister Delphine told me.

It was all set. My mother was ready to go. Uncle Tony hated it and so did the rest, but they couldn't do anything. Grandpa was disappointed. He had a shoe shop on Osage Street. He liked nuns. He thought they were swell people, he even did their shoe work for nothing, but he couldn't see why his own daughter had to get mixed up in it.

He promised to send my mother to Colorado U. if she would forget it. My mother wouldn't hear of it because she thought Colorado U. was an awful place. Right now my mother knows a Catholic who doesn't believe in God. He went to Colorado U. He was all right until then. Now the Catholics in our town are off him for life. They even kicked him out of the Knights of Columbus because he made smart cracks. So my mother wouldn't go to a school like Colorado U. It was Kentucky or nothing.

All day long Uncle Tony yelled at her, calling her a dumb cluck and a stupe. She almost had another nervous breakdown. He followed her around the house, yelling at her and trying to make her change her mind. Next door to Grandma Toscana's the Rocca people were building a new house. Uncle Tony had a big voice and he yelled so loud the bricklayers heard every word he hollered. They used to stop work on the scaffold and listen to him.

One morning two months before she was to leave for Kentucky my mother was eating breakfast, and Uncle Tony started right in on the same old argument. She didn't have any sense. Weren't they treating her all right at home? She wanted to bury herself in a hole and forget all the fine things her family did for her. Didn't she get enough to eat and plenty of clothes to wear? Then what more did she want? Why did she have to be so selfish? Think of her poor mother getting old without her around. Why couldn't she think those things out and realize the mistake she was making?

My mother put her head down and started to cry.

One of the bricklayers was watching from the scaffold. He climbed down the ladder and walked over to the kitchen window. He was an Italian too, but not the ordinary kind. He had a red mustache for one thing, and red hair. He knocked on the screen and my mother looked up. Uncle Tony wanted to know what he wanted. The man had a trowel in his hand. He shook it in Uncle Tony's face.

"If you say another word to that girl I'll knock your head off!"

The minute my mother saw him something happened. Uncle Tony got so mad he went into the front room without speaking. My mother kept looking at the man with the trowel and the little

183

red mustache. All at once they both started laughing. He went back to work, still laughing. At noon he sat on the scaffold looking down into the kitchen window. My mother could see him. He whistled. !She laughed and came to the window. What he wanted was some salt for his sandwich. That was how it got started. The man was my father. Every day he laughed and asked for something. If it wasn't salt it was pepper, and my mother laughed and got it for him. Another time he asked for some fresh fruit to go with his lunch. One day he came to the window and laughed and asked if she had any wine. Then he wanted to know if she could cook. My mother laughed and laughed. Finally she told him not to bring his lunch any more but to come over and eat with her. He laughed and said sure. Two months later, instead of going to Kentucky, my mother came to our town and got married.

My Father's God

UPON THE DEATH of old Father Ambrose, the Bishop of Denver assigned a new priest to St. Catherine's parish. He was Father Bruno Ramponi, a young Dominican from Boston. Father Ramponi's picture appeared on the front page of the Boulder *Herald*. Actually there were two pictures — one of a swarthy, short-necked prelate bulging inside a black suit and reversed collar, the other an action shot of Father Ramponi in football gear leaping with outstretched hands for a forward pass. Our new pastor was famous. He had been a football star, an All-American halfback from Boston College.

My father studied the pictures at the supper table.

"A Sicilian," he decided. "Look how black he is."

"How can he be a Sicilian?" my mother asked. "The paper says he was born in Boston."

"I don't care where he was born. I know a Sicilian when I see one." His brows quivered like caterpillars as he studied the face of Father Ramponi. "I don't want any trouble with this priest," he brooded.

It was an ominous reminder of the many futile years Father Ambrose had tried to bring my father back to the church. "The glorious return to divine grace," Father Ambrose had called it. "The prodigal son falling into the arms of his heavenly father." On the job or in the street, at band concerts and in the pool hall, the old pastor constantly swooped down on my father with these pious objurations which only served to drive him deeper among the heathens, so that the priest's death brought a gasp of relief.

But in Father Ramponi he sensed a renewal of the tedious struggle for his soul, for it was only a question of time before

185

the new priest discovered that my father never attended Mass. Not that my mother and we four kids didn't make up for his absences. He insisted that it had to be that way, and every Sunday, through rain, sleet and snow he watched us trek off to St. Catherine's ten blocks away, his conscience vicariously soothed, his own cop-out veiled in righteous paternalism.

The day after the announcement of Father Ramponi's appointment, St. Catherine's school droned like an agitated beehive with rumors about our new priest. Gathered in clusters along the halls, the nuns whispered breathlessly. On the playground the boys set aside the usual touchball game to crowd into the lavatory and relate wild reports. The older boys did all the talking, cigarettes dangling from their lips, while second graders like myself listened with bulging eyes.

It was said that Father Ramponi was so powerful that he could bring down a bull with one punch, that he was structured like a gorilla, and that his nose had been kicked in on an historic Saturday afternoon when he had torn apart the Notre Dame line. We younger kids stiffened in fear and awe. After the gentle Father Ambrose, the thought of being hauled before Father Ramponi for discipline was too ghastly to contemplate. When the first bell rang we rushed to our classrooms, dreading the sudden, unexpected appearance of Father Ramponi in the halls.

At 11:30, in the midst of arithmetic, the classroom door opened and our principal, Sister Mary Justinus, entered. Her cheeks shone like apples. Her eyes glittered with excitement.

"The class will please rise," she announced.

We got to our feet and caught sight of him in the hall. This was it. The awesome Father Ramponi was about to make his debut before the Second Grade class.

'Children,' Sister Justinus fluttered, "I want you to say 'Good morning,' to your new pastor, Father Bruno Ramponi." She raised her hands like a symphony conductor and brought them down briskly as we chanted, "Good morning, Father," and the priest stepped into the room.

He moved forward to stand before us with massive hands clasped at his waist, a grin kneading his broken face. All the rumors about him were true — a bull of a man with dark skin

186

and wide, crushed nostrils out of which black hairs flared. His jaw was as square as a brickbat, his short neck like a creosoted telephone pole. From out of his coat sleeves small bouquets of black hair burst over his wrists.

"Please be seated," he smiled.

The moment he uttered those three words the myth of his ferocity vanished. For his voice was small and sibilant, surprisingly sweet and uncertain, a mighty lion with the roar of a kitten. The whole class breathed a sigh of deliverance as we sat down.

For twenty seconds he stood there lost for words, his large face oozing perspiration. With the uncanny intuition of children we were on to him, knowing somehow that this colossus of the gridiron would never loose his terrible wrath upon us, that he was as docile as a cow and harmless as a butterfly.

Drawing a handkerchief from his pocket, he dabbed at his moist neck and we grew uneasy and embarrassed waiting for him to say more, but he was locked to the spot, his tongue bolted down.

Finally Sister Justinus came to his rescue, breaking the silence with a brisk slap of her hands. "Now children, I want each of you to rise and give Father your name so that he can greet you personally."

One at a time we stood and pronounced our names, and in each instance Father Ramponi nodded and said,"How do you do, Tom," or "How do you do, Mary," or "How do you do, Patrick."

At my turn I rose and spoke my name.

"Paisan," the priest grinned.

I managed a smile.

"Tell your folks I'll be around to meet them soon."

Even though he told most of the students the same thing, I sat there in a state of shock. There were some things I could tell my father and others I preferred to delete, but there was one thing I didn't dare tell him — that a priest was coming to visit him.

With my mother it didn't matter, and upon hearing that Father Ramponi was coming she lifted her eyes to heaven and moaned.

"Oh, my God," she said. "Whatever you do, don't tell your father. We might lose him for good."

It was our secret, my mother's and mine, and we paid the price, specially Mamma. All that was required of me was to keep the front yard clean, raking the October leaves and sweeping the front porch every day. She took on the rest of the house alone, and in the days that followed she washed the walls and ceilings, she washed the windows, she laundered and ironed the curtains, she waxed the linoleum, she dragged the frazzled rugs out to the back yard, flung them over the clothesline and beat them with a broom.

Every evening, home from work, my father strode through the house and paused, the smell of ammonia in his nostrils as he looked around and found some small new change. The gas heater in the living room polished and shining, its chrome gleaming like a band of dazzling silver, the furniture luminous as dark mirrors, the broken rocker repaired, the worn needlepoint replaced with a piece of blue wool from an old coat.

He crossed the linoleum that sparkled like a sheet of ice. "What's happening?" he asked. "What's going on around here?"

"House cleaning," my mother said, her face careworn, her hair coming loose from the bun in back, her bones aching. He frowned at her curiously.

"Take it easy. What's the good of a clean house if you end up in the hospital?"

Days passed and November showed up, bringing the first snow of winter. But Father Ramponi did not visit us. I saw him almost every day at school, and he always tossed a word or two my way, but he made no mention of the visit.

The snow fell steadily. The streets disappeared. The windows frosted. My mother strung clotheslines around the stove in the living room, in order to dry the washing. The cold weather confined the little ones indoors. Crayons were crushed underfoot, toys kicked beneath the furniture. My brother spilled a bottle of ink on the linoleum, my sister drew a pumpkin face with black crayon on the best wall in the front room. Then she melted the crayon against the side of the hot stove. Mama threw up her hands in defeat. If Father Ramponi ever visited us, he would have to take us for what we were—just plain, stupid peasants.

The snow was my father's deadly enemy, burying his job in desolate white mounds, engulfing brick, cement and scaffolding, robbing him of his livelihood and sending him home with an unopened lunch pail. He became a prisoner in his own house.

188

Nor was he the loving husband a woman could enjoy through long winter days. He insisted on taking command of a ship that was already on course through rough waters. Lounging in the kitchen he watched my mother's every move as she prepared meals, finding fault with everything. More salt, too much pepper, turn up the oven, turn down the oven, watch the potatoes, add some onion, where's the oregano, fry some garlic, and finally, "Let me do that!"

She flung down her apron and stalked out of the kitchen to join us in the living room, her arms folded, her eyes blazing. Oh God! If Father Ramponi didn't arrive soon she would be driven to the rectory to see him herself.

Our house on Sunday morning was chaos. I can still see my frantic mother dashing from bedroom to bedroom in her pink slip, her braided hair piled atop her head, as she got us dressed for ten o'clock Mass. She polished our shoes, fashioned knots in our neckties, sewed buttons, patched holes, prepared breakfast, ironed pleats in my sister's dress, raced from one of us to the other, picking up a shoe on the way, a toy. Armed with a washcloth, she inspected our ears and the backs of our necks, scraping away dirt, my sister screaming, "you're cruel, cruel!"

Lastly, in the final moments before we departed, she slapped talcum powder over her face and came out to the front room where my oblivious father sprawled reading the Denver *Post*. She turned her back for him to button up her dress.

"Fix me."

Chewing a cigar, he squinted as the curling smoke blurred his eyes and he worked the buttons through the holes with blunt fingers. It was the only contribution he made to those hectic mornings.

"Why don't you come to Mass with us?" she often asked.

"What for?"

"To worship God. To set an example for your children."

"God sees my family at church. That's enough. He knows I sent them."

"Wouldn't it be better if God saw you there too?"

"God's everywhere, so why do I have to see Him in a church? He's right here too, in this house, this room. He's in my hand.

189

Look." He opened and closed his fist. "He's right in there. In my eyes, my mouth, my ears, my blood. So what's the sense of walking eight blocks through the snow, when all I got to do is sit right here with God in my own house."

We children stood listening enthralled at this great and refreshing piece of theology, our collars pinching, our eyes moving to the window as the silent snow drifted down, shivering at the thought of plowing through the drifts to the cold church.

"Papa's right," I said. "God is everywhere. It says so in the catechism."

We looked imploringly at my mother as she put on her wool coat with the rabbit fur collar, and there was a sob in my sister's voice as she begged, "Can't we all just kneel down here and pray for a while? God won't mind."

"You see!" my mother glared at my father.

"Nobody prays here but me," he said. "The rest of you get going."

"It's not fair!" I yelled. "Who're *you?*"

"I'll tell you who I am," he said threateningly. "I'm the owner of this house. I come and go as I please. I can throw you out any time I feel like it. Now get going!" He rose in a towering fury and pointed at the door, and we filed out like humble serfs, heads bowed, trudging through snow a foot deep. God, it was cold! And so unfair. I clenched my fists and longed for the day I would become a man and knock my father's brains out.

In the seventh week of his pastorate Father Ramponi finally visited our house. He came in the darkness of evening, through a roaring storm, his arrival presaged by the heavy pounding of his overshoes on the front porch as he kicked off the clinging snow. It shook the house.

My father sat at the dining room table drinking wine and I sat across from him, doing my homework. We both stared as the wine in the carafe tossed like a small red sea. Mamma and Grandma came startled from the kitchen. We heard the rap of knuckles on the front door.

"Come in!" my father shouted.

Father Ramponi loomed in the doorway, hat in hand, so tall he barely made it through the door. Had the President of the

United States entered, we could not have been more surprised.

"Good evening," he smiled.

"Whaddya say there," Papa said, too astonished for amenities as Father Ramponi walked deeper into the house. All a twitter, my mother's face tingled with excitement as she hurried to take the priest's overcoat. He laid it across her arms like a massive black rug, so large that it dragged over the floor as she hauled it away to the bedroom.

By now the rest of us were on our feet, staring at the towering priest. Everything shrank proportionately, the room, the furniture, and the members of our family. Suddenly we were a tribe of pygmies confronted by a giant explorer from the outside world.

As they shook hands, Father Ramponi lowered a friendly paw on Papa's shoulder and spoke in his high, gentle voice.

"They tell me you're the finest stonemason in Colorado. Is it true?"

My father's face blossomed like a sunflower.

"That's the truth, Father."

"Fine, fine I like a man who's not ashamed of his worth."

Reeling with flattery, Papa turned and ordered the room cleared. "Everybody out!"

With grand pretensions of authority Mamma herded us into the living room, which didn't in the least add to the privacy since the two rooms were separated by French doors, only there weren't any doors. Just the hinges. The doors were out in the garage, for reasons nobody ever questioned.

We kids flung ourselves on the floor near the stove and Mamma settled into the rocking chair. Presently Grandma appeared, a black shawl around her shoulders, the rosary twined in her fingers, and she too found a chair. No more than four feet away, Papa and Father Ramponi had the entire dining room to themselves.

Those were the days of Prohibition and Papa's routine with guests never changed. Every caller was invited down into the earthen cellar where four fifty-gallon barrels of wine were stored—a hundred gallons matured, and a hundred in the fermentation process.

Through the trapdoor in the pantry he and Father Ramponi disappeared into the cellar. We listened to them down there under the house, their voices muffled, their laughter rumbling in the ground. Patiently we waited for them to reappear, like an audience expecting the return of the players to the stage.

As they came back Papa carried a fresh pitcher of wine, the beaded foam still bubbling. They sat at the table beneath light pouring down from a green metal shade. Papa filled two tumblers with wine and Father Ramponi lit a cigarette.

Raising his glass, the priest proposed a toast. "To Florence, city of your birth."

Pleased but dubious, my father shook his head. "I come from Abruzzi, Father. From Torcelli Peligna."

It surprised Father Ramponi. "Is that so? Now where did I get the idea you were a Florentine?"

"Never been there in my life."

"Maybe your relatives came from there."

"Maybe," Papa shrugged.

"You *look* like a Florentine."

"You think so?"

"A true Florentine, a craftsman in the tradition of that great city." He drained his tumbler.

We watched Papa expand with a sense of importance. It was as if Father Ramponi had sprinkled him with a holy water of magic powers. From that moment he was Father Ramponi's pigeon, eating corn from the good priest's hand. Then the subject matter changed quickly, and the real reason for the priest's visit became apparent.

"Nick," he said with a new familiarity, his voice softer than ever. "Why is it that I never find you at Mass on Sunday morning?"

Mamma and Grandma nodded at one another smugly. My father was a long time answering, kneading a kink in his neck, smiling as he sensed a trap.

"I been thinking about that," he said.

"Thinking about it? "

"About going."

"You should. As an example to your children."

There was an uncomfortable silence. My father put the tip of his fingernail in the wine glass and twirled it absently. "We'll talk about it some other time," he said.

"Come to the rectory tomorrow," Father Ramponi suggested.

"I'm gonna be pretty busy tomorrow."

"How about the day after tomorrow?"

"I'm pretty busy, Father."

"In this wretched weather?"

"Lots of figuring to do. Getting ready for Spring."

"Shall we make it next week?"

Papa frowned, rubbed his chin. "Too far ahead. You never know, one day to the next."

The priest sighed, lifted his hands. "Then I leave it entirely up to you. When would it be most convenient?"

My father found a cigar butt in the ashtray and went to a lot of trouble scraping and lighting it. "Let me think about it, Father." He produced clouds of smoke that hid his face. Then, to everyone's surprise, he said, "Let's make it tomorrow."

Mamma's gulp of delight sounded like a shout.

Father Ramponi rose and offered his hand. He was smiling in triumph and my father shook hands and squinted at him skeptically. Having committed himself, he seemed to regret it.

"Two o'clock tomorrow?" Father Ramponi asked.

"Not possible," Papa said.

"Three, then? Four?"

"Can't make it."

"Would you prefer to come in the morning?"

"How can I come in the morning? You don't understand, Father! I got things to do, people to see. I'm a busy man. All the time. Day and night!"

The priest did not press it. "I leave it up to you. Come when you can."

Papa nodded bleakly. "We'll see. I can't promise anything. I'll do the best I can."

The very next day my father began a series of talks at the rectory with Father Ramponi. The meetings left him in a somber mood, and a brooding calm settled over our house. We tiptoed around him, we talked in whispers. During meals he was completely silent, tearing bread and holding it uneaten in his hand. Even my little sister felt his melancholy.

"Are you sick, Papa?" she asked.

"Shhh!" Mamma said.

My father exhaled a sigh and stared, his forkful of macaroni dangling limply in mid air.

Every day he wore his Sunday clothes with a white shirt and a necktie. So intent was his concentration that he stopped talking altogether and merely gestured when he had some request. A wave of his hand could clear the room. A nod at his feet summoned his slippers. A flat stare and talking ceased among us. Moving furtively in the background, my mother and grandmother watched him with sympathetic, adoring eyes. The man of the house was in crisis, grappling with the devil, and the decision was in doubt. Every night at bedtime we left him alone in the dining room, seated under the light, sipping wine and writing on a jumbo school tablet with a stubby pencil.

A week of this, and suddenly the saturnine atmosphere of our home was shattered and my father was himself again. We awoke to hear him in the front yard, shoveling snow. Mamma called him to breakfast. He bounded into the house with scarlet cheeks and purple ears, his eyes snow-bright as he slapped his hands hungrily and sat down before his scrambled eggs. One mouthful and he scowled.

"Can't you even fry eggs?" he said.

We were happy again. Papa was complaining like his old self.

As I prepared for school, my mother followed me into the living room and brought my mackinaw from the closet. She buttoned me up while my father stood watching. He had a bulky envelope in his hand.

"Give this to Father Ramponi," he said, handing it to me. I said okay and folded it to the size of my pocket.

"Not like that," he said, taking it from me. He opened the mackinaw and stuffed the envelope under my T shirt. "Guard it with your life," he warned.

"What the heck is it?"

"Never mind. Just give it to Father Ramponi."

"Tell him," Mamma said. "So he'll know how important it is."

"You talk too much!" he snapped.

"It's your father's confession," Mamma said.

I suddenly felt it there against my flesh, and sucked in my stomach. It was incredible, impossible, sacrilegious.

"You can't *write* your confession!" I wailed. "You have to *tell* it. In the confessional!"

"Who says so?"

"It's the rule. Everybody knows that!"

"He won't get me in that confession box."

"It's the rule!" I cried, ready to burst into tears. "Mamma! Tell him, please! He doesn't understand!"

"That shows how much you know," Papa said. "He told me to write it: so what do you think of that!"

I searched my mother's face for the truth. She smiled. "Father Ramponi said it was all right this way."

I looked at my father accusingly.

"Why can't you be like everybody else?"

"No, sir. You can't get me in that box!"

Dazed and angry and disgusted, I walked out into the cold morning, my lunch pail rigid in one hand, my books in the other, my father's cold envelope freezing my stomach. Who the hell did he think he was? Why didn't he take his damned confession to the priest himself? Why should I be forced to walk the streets with it? They weren't *my* sins, they were his, so let him carry them to the priest.

The frozen air took my breath and whirled it into ostrich plumes and I walked afraid, like a glass vial, fearful of spilling my burden. I knew my father had not been to confession for thirty years, not since he was a boy of my age.

All of this wickedness, every human being he had injured, every sin against God's commandments were congealed in a block of ice burning against my stomach as I crossed town, under dripping maple trees, around grey mounds of mud-splattered snow, my toes picking their way with the delicacy of bird's feet, across the town, the awful responsibility of my burden hurting my flesh, too sacred, too heavy for my life.

195

As I reached St. Catherine's Father Ramponi drove up and parked in front of the stone steps leading to the main entrance. I waited for him to step out, pulling the envelope from under my shirt as the bell sounded and stragglers raced up the stairs.

"Oh, yes," he smiled, taking the envelope. "Thank you." He seemed in a great hurry and at a loss as to what to do with the envelope. Opening the car door, he tossed the envelope on the seat and dashed away, taking the stairs three at a time.

I watched in dismay as he disappeared. How could he do such a thing? That document was no trifling thing. It was my father's confession, a matter sacred to God, and there it lay on the car seat, cast aside like a rag.

What if someone came by and filched it — one of the older boys? The school was full of thieves who stole anything not nailed down. Suddenly I was in a panic as I imagined the confession being passed around, being read in the lavatory, touching off raucous laughter spilling into the halls, the streets, as the whole town laughed at my father's sins.

Guard it with your life, my father had warned, and guard it I did. For three hours I posted myself beside Father Ramponi's car, my feet numbed with cold, my ears burning like ice cubes as I stayed out of school and scorned the wrath of Sister Justinus.

At last the noon bell sounded and the students burst from the doors and down the stairs. I concealed myself as Father Ramponi appeared. He slid under the steering wheel and drove away, and the minuscule pinching pain in my stomach vanished at last.

That night Father Ramponi made his second visit to our house. It was very late and Papa was turning out the lights when the priest knocked. Papa welcomed him and they came into the dining room. Through the open bedroom door I saw them as I lay beside my sleeping brother. Father Ramponi stood huge as a black bear under the green lampshade. Then my father noticed the open bedroom door and he closed it, and I was in darkness save for a ribbon of light under the threshold. I slipped out of bed and peered through the keyhole.

Papa had seated himself before the wine, but Father Ramponi was still on his feet. He drew the envelope from his overcoat and tossed it on the table.

"You deceived me," he said quietly.

My father lifted the envelope and tested it in his fist. "It's all there, Father. I didn't forget a thing."

"It's long enough. God knows."

"Some things I wrote, they were very hard, but it's all there, over thirty years, the bad things in a man's life."

"But you wrote it in Italian . . ."

"What's wrong with that?"

Father Ramponi sank gloomily into a chair, his hands thrust deeply into his overcoat pockets. "I don't speak Italian," he sighed. "Or read it. Or write it. Or understand it."

My father stared.

"Bruno Ramponi, and you don't speak Italian? That's terrible."

The priest sank deeper in his chair and covered one eye. "It simply never entered my mind that you'd make your confession in Italian."

"The pope speaks Italian," my father said. "The cardinals, they speak Italian. The saints speak Italian. Even God speaks Italian. But you, Father Bruno Ramponi, don't speak Italian."

A moan from the priest. He pushed the envelope toward my father. "Burn it."

"Burn it?"

"Burn it. Now."

It was an order, angry and incontrovertible. My father rose and took the envelope into the kitchen. I heard the lid of the stove open, then close, and then he returned to the dining room where Father Ramponi now stood and draped a purple stole around his neck.

"Please kneel for penance and absolution," he said.

My father's joints cracked like sticks as he knelt on the linoleum. He clasped his hands together and lowered his eyes. Father Ramponi made the sign of the cross over him and murmured a Latin prayer. Then he touched my father's shoulder.

"As a penance, I want you to say The Lord's Prayer once a day until Christmas."

My father lifted his eyes.

"Until Christmas, Father? That's sixty days."

"You can say it in Italian."

It pleased my father and he lowered his eyes. Father Ramponi absolved and blessed him, and the little ceremony was concluded. My father got to his feet.

"Thank you, Father. How about a glass of wine?"

The priest declined. They moved toward the front door. Suddenly my father laughed. "I feel good," he said. "Real good, Father."

"Next time I'll expect you to come to the church for your confession."

"We'll see, Father."

"And I'll expect you at Mass Sunday."

"I'll try and make it, Father."

They said good night and the door closed. I heard Father Ramponi's car drive away. My father returned to the dining room. Through the keyhole I watched him pour a glass of wine. He raised it heavenward and drank. Then he turned out the light and all was darkness.

Scoundrel

Sister Mary Agnes had been my principal for eight years at St. Vincent's. She knew more about me than my mother. But Mamma was like that.

For instance, it was Sister Agnes who got me out of jail for breaking street lamps. The police sergeant called Mamma, but Mamma didn't believe him. Sergeant Corelli had caught Jack Jenson and me red-handed. I was standing right there when Sergeant Corelli telephoned Mamma. I could hear her voice in the receiver.

"There must be some mistake," she said, "my son Jimmy would never do a thing like that."

"I tell you this is your boy," Sergeant Corelli said, "he's right here. James Kennedy."

"Oh no," Mamma said, "I know you've made a mistake. There are lots of Kennedys in this world. My Jimmy isn't like that."

She hung up. Sergeant Corelli shook his head.

"You sure got her buffaloed," he said. Then he asked me where I went to school.

I told him I was in the eighth grade at St. Vincent's. He telephoned Sister Mary Agnes because she was principal and Sister Superior. She hopped into a cab and came right down to the city hall.

Jack Jenson's father got there about the same time. We didn't get along, Mr. Jenson and I. He shook his finger at me. "You're responsible for this."

"I broke two lamps," I said, "Jack broke the other two."

"That's a lie," Jack said, "I got that one on the corner of Ninth and Pine, and you know it. You only got one. I got three."

"Why Jack," I said, "that ain't so."

"Heck it ain't."

"I don't know who busted what," Sergeant Corelli said, "all I know is—four lamps is broke. City property."

Sister Agnes clucked like a hen. "It's scandalous," she said to me, "perfectly scandalous. To think that you, a Catholic boy, of Catholic parents, educated in a Catholic school, should go around destroying public property. James, if I've warned you once, I've warned you a thousand times—stay away from bad company."

Mr. Jenson's mouth and eyes popped open. "Now wait a minute, miss," he said, "you can't call my boy 'bad company.' You may be a holy lady, miss, but I'm not going to stand here and let you call my boy a criminal."

Just then Jack stuck out his tongue at Sister Agnes.

"I didn't *say* he was a criminal," Sister Agnes said.

"Let's quit arguing and get to the bottom of this," Sergeant Corelli said. "Now then: Why did you kids do it?"

Jack looked at me. "Go ahead and tell him."

"To settle a bet," I said.

Sister Agnes took a deep breath. "Why, James Kennedy. Gambling too. You know gambling is a sin."

"Not a very big sin," I said. "We were gambling for small stakes."

"Of all the brazenness!" she said.

"What was the bet?" Sergeant Corelli asked.

Jack told him: "I bet him a couple of cigars against a pack of cigarettes that I could bust more lamps than him."

"Cigars!" Mr. Jenson said. "So that's where my cigars been going."

"Cigarettes!" Sister Agnes said. "So you've been smoking again."

We didn't say anything. We were being honest, but nobody seemed to pay the least attention or to appreciate it at all.

"There you are," Sergeant Corelli said. "They admit everything. Now—what's to be done with these kids?"

Mr. Jenson opened his mouth and his teeth were like wolf fangs. "I know what *I'm* going to do," he said.

Jack swallowed and rolled his eyes around.

"And I think I can handle this young man," Sister Agnes said.

200

Jack left the city hall on tiptoe. Mr. Jenson had a strong grip on his left ear. I felt sorry for poor Jack. He was so sensitive, so easily hurt, and his father wasn't. Jack could play the piano and he sang in the choir at the Methodist Church. Mr. Jenson was foreman of a construction gang with the state highway.

"I'm taking you to see Father Cooney," Sister Agnes said to me. She asked Sergeant Corelli to call a taxi. The sergeant said he would be glad to have someone drive us back in the police car. This shocked Sister Agnes.

"I couldn't do that," she said, "but thank you so much, Sergeant. You've been very kind."

The sergeant picked up the phone and called for a taxi. Sister Agnes and I sat on a bench in front of the window and waited. I was slumped forward, trying to think of something pleasant to say. Sister Agnes kissed the crucifix at the end of the brown beads which hung from her belt and began to say the Rosary.

"Sit up straight," she whispered.

I sat up and folded my arms.

"Aren't you going to pray?" she asked. "You ought to be grateful to Almighty God that you're not behind bars. You should be on your knees, offering up thanks and begging Him to forgive you for this day."

"Right here?" I asked. "In the police station?"

"At least pray in your heart," she said closing her eyes.

I closed my eyes and thought out a prayer: Dear Lord, thanks a lot for getting me out of this mess. I think the whole thing is a bluff and they can't do much to me because I'm only fourteen. But things could have been a lot worse. So thanks again. And please, dear Savior, try to fix it up so Sister Agnes won't phone my old man. Please, Lord. If you ever did a fellow a favor, please, please, don't let her tell my old man.

Bill Callen owned the Boulder Taxi Company. He drove it up to the curb and we went outside and down the city hall steps. A long time before, Bill had been one of Sister Agnes' pupils. He opened the cab door and helped her inside.

"Anything wrong, Sister?" he said. "Anything I can do?"

"Nothing, Bill," sister smiled. "Nothing at all. Just take us back to the convent, if you please."

"Him too?"

She smiled again.

I got in beside Sister Agnes. Bill looked at me and said it all over again — "If there's anything I can do, Sister, just any little thing at all, just let me know."

"Thank you, Bill."

He kept looking at me and I knew he was remembering the time we put the goat in his cab on Halloween. "Don't forget now, Sister. Just any old time."

"You heard her," I said, "you drip. Get this jalopy up to the convent — if it'll go that far."

"Listen," he said, "I don't like you."

"Aw," I said, "now my feelings are hurt."

"I don't like any little rat who commits a crime and has to have a sister of our Lord keep him outa the penitentiary."

It made me mad but I didn't let him know it.

"You cad," I said, "you nasty man."

He slammed the door and got into the driver's seat. Sister Mary Agnes sat with her long white hands folded. We drove down Pearl Street and through the middle of town. It was almost summertime, the last week of school, just a few days before graduation.

"What are we going to do now, Sister?" I asked.

"First I'm going to take you to Father Cooney."

That wasn't bad. Father Cooney didn't deliver very good sermons but he was a sucker for penitence. All you had to do was hold your head down and make a sad face, and he'd give you the shirt off his back.

"Father Cooney'll be very disappointed in me," I said. "I'd rather do almost anything than face him."

"It's my duty to report this," she said.

"I know. I'm awfully ashamed. Poor Father Cooney."

"And then of course I must tell your father."

"My father? You mean, my father?"

"Your father."

Father Cooney was one thing, but my father was something else again. My father was the strong silent type. He was mostly strong and he liked to throw his weight around. He wasn't particularly silent, either. Something else: he lacked imagination. There was only one way he dealt with situations of this kind. It was very unpleasant to think about.

"I'll phone him tonight," she said.

I laughed. Not a loud laugh. Softly.

She glanced at me. "Why are you laughing?"

"It's kinda funny," I said shaking my head. "Just a little while ago I said a prayer to our Lord. I asked Him to please not let my father know about this. And now you're going to tell him."

"Of course I am."

"I know," I said. "You have to. It's your duty. It wouldn't be right if you didn't tell him. Still, at the same time, the Catechism says that all things come to him who prays. I know you have to tell my father. I know that. But still, it only goes to show that sometimes the things you learn in the Catechism don't work out in real life."

She watched me with her big blue eyes. I curled my mouth and slouched down in the seat and smiled like a man who is sad but not afraid, and ready for anything. All the way up the hill to St. Vincent's she sat there watching the trees and houses floating past, not saying a word. Now and then she bit her lip and looked at me. I didn't say anything either.

Father Cooney was eating supper. He told his housekeeper, Mrs. Hanley, she could be excused. Sister Mary Agnes and I watched her go away. Father Cooney had started his dessert, which was chocolate cake. He was a tall heavy man with a bald spot on the top of his head. He pointed to the other chairs around the table.

"Sit down," he said, "please do. You like chocolate cake, Jimmy?"

"Boy — do I!"

Sister Agnes did not sit down. Father Cooney took up the cake knife and cut off a big slab for me.

"After what this young man has done," Sister Agnes said, "I don't think he should be rewarded with a piece of chocolate cake."

"Indeed?" Father Cooney said looking at me. "What's this Jimmy? What've you done?"

"I got into trouble."

"Trouble? What kind of trouble?"

I hung my head and didn't say anything. Father Cooney put the piece of cake on a dish in front of me. Sister Agnes folded her arms. The look on her face said: Leave the cake alone. I sneaked down into the chair and sat with my hands in my lap. Father Cooney was watching us. I lifted my hand from under the table and picked up a fork. The cake was devil's food, with about a foot of chocolate icing. I took one quick look at Sister Agnes. She was daring me to try it. When I moved the fork toward the cake she stepped up to the table and put her hand on my arm.

"You haven't told Father Cooney why you're here," she said.

I didn't put down the fork but I hung my head in shame. "I was arrested, Father. Another kid and me got picked up for busting street lamps."

"Indeed," Father Cooney said.

I told him how it had happened.

"He wasn't a Catholic boy," I said. "I should of known better than associate with him."

"There's no reason why you shouldn't associate with non-Catholics," Father said, "provided they're good boys."

"He wasn't exactly a bad boy," I said. "Only thing is, he said he could break more lamps than any Catholic kid in town."

"Who won?" Father said.

"It was a tie. Two apiece."

"Humph."

He ate another mouthful of cake and sipped some coffee. He was thinking it over. I moved my fork toward the dish again. This time Sister Agnes didn't stop me. The cake melted in my mouth. I sat back and tasted the thick sweet chocolate on my teeth and tongue, tasted it all the way down into my stomach.

"Super," I said.

Father Cooney tried again to make Sister Agnes sit down.

"Do try this cake," he said. "It's marvelous."

204

"No thank you, Father. My own supper is waiting for me at the convent. I brought this young man here because I feel he should be reprimanded. Destroying public property is a very serious offense."

"It *is* a serious offense," Father Cooney said. "It most certainly is. And I intend to punish him severely."

Right away Sister Agnes felt better. But I wasn't worried. We had a man named Phipps in our parish who was arrested for beating up his wife. Father Cooney said he was going to punish him severely too. But all he did was get Phipps out of jail and pay for his rent and grocery bills.

"I shall phone Mr. Kennedy immediately," Sister Agnes said.

"A splendid idea," Father said.

All at once the cake had a flat taste. I couldn't swallow any more. Sister Agnes said good-by to Father Cooney. At the door she stopped to say she wanted to see me before I went home. I felt better after she was gone. Father Cooney got me a glass of milk, and he gave me another piece of cake. For a long time we ate without talking. Then I finished my cake and sat back. Father Cooney lit a cigar.

"Last night I was reading the life of St. Paul," he said. "A wonderful man — truly wonderful."

It was coming. It was going to be a sermon about St. Paul and everybody in the parish agreed that Father Cooney's sermons were the worst of any priest in the whole diocese.

"The Apostle Paul believed in the doctrine not of faith alone, but of faith by good works. Not mere lip service to our Blessed Savior, but piety as well, and good works; setting a fine example among the early Christians as well as the heathen."

"Yes, Father."

He tipped the ash off his cigar and leaned forward. "Let me put it this way, my boy: How would it have been if, in the early days of the struggling young Church, the blessed apostle, instead of setting an example by good works, had gone about the country-side breaking street lights? What chance would Christianity have had?"

"Not a chance," I said.

"Indeed not."

205

"Did they have street lights in those days, Father?"

"Perhaps they did, and perhaps no. Nevertheless the Light of Faith in Christ shone in the hearts of St. Paul and his loyal followers. They were willing and even glad to brave persecution and death in His name. In those humble men the light of Christian charity and brotherhood was nourished by the goodness in their hearts. Everywhere they traveled, they set an example that endeared them to God and man. It was not the light of destructiveness, of breaking things. It was the light of faith, of gentleness, of human brotherhood. You see what I mean, son?"

"Yes, Father."

"Good. Fine. More cake?"

"No thanks, Father."

He pushed back his chair and stood up.

"You may go now."

He put his hand on my shoulder and walked to the door with me. "I'll check with the Bureau of Power and Light, and see about the damage. But promise me you won't do it again."

"I promise."

He shook hands with me just like I was a man. "Good night, Jim."

"Good night, Father. Thanks for the cake."

It was almost six o'clock. The nuns lived in the west wing of the school building. I still had to see Sister Agnes, so I decided to go to the back door. At that hour it was most unusual to be seen knocking at the front door of the convent. It could only mean that a fellow was in some kind of mess. Besides, Sister Mary Thomas was in the convent kitchen. She did the cooking for the nuns. She was always good for a cooky or a piece of pie.

After I knocked, Sister Thomas opened the back door. She was the oldest nun in the convent. Some people said she was almost seventy. Her face was red and shining from the hot stove and her hands were covered with flour. The kitchen smelled like heaven, of apples and cinnamon.

"I have to see Sister Agnes," I said.

"You always have to see Sister Mary Agnes. Little man, what now?"

"Nothing much."

"Of course not. Just some trifle like bank robbery or something. And you probably wouldn't like a piece of apple pie, either."

"Just a very small piece."

"I know," she said, "just a very small piece."

I sat down at the end of the long table that ran the length of the room. On the table were six hot steaming French apple pies. Sister Thomas cut me almost half a pie.

"We have some strawberry ice cream," she said, "but I don't suppose you want any; not very much, at any rate."

"Just a bit."

She laid three scoops of strawberry ice cream on the pie.

"That's plenty," I said.

"You sure?"

"Positive."

The pie was so hot that the ice cream melted and the pink cream filtered through the cinnamon and apples. It was wonderful. It was even better than Father Cooney's cake. Sister Mary Thomas waited until I was almost finished before she called Sister Agnes on the house telephone. All the nuns were plenty scared of Sister Agnes. Being Sister Superior, she gave the orders around there.

I put the last bite of pie in my mouth just as Sister Agnes came into the kitchen.

"What's the meaning of this?" she said.

"He looked hungry," Sister Thomas said.

"Hungry? He always looks hungry — the scoundrel."

I stood up and wiped my mouth with the back of my hand. Sister Agnes was so angry she stamped her foot. She walked to my empty dish and banged it with a fork.

"Sister Mary Thomas," she said, "I've forbidden you to feed these boys. I've told you repeatedly: Stop — feeding — the boys. How in heaven's name can I hope to have any discipline in this school if they're rewarded instead of punished? I repeat it for the last, the very last time: Stop — feeding — the boys!"

Poor old Sister Mary Thomas shriveled up her shoulders, looked down at the floor and wiped her flour-covered hands on her apron. Sister Agnes swung around and faced me. She took off her glasses and scowled.

"You," she said. "You scoundrel. You reprobate. After all the disgrace you've heaped upon your immortal soul—after all the humiliation you've brought down upon your church and your city—you have the sheer unmitigated audacity to stand there facing me, gorged with chocolate cake and apple pie." She looked down at my plate. "And strawberry ice cream."

I moved my feet a little but I didn't talk.

"Well—what have you to say for yourself?"

"Nothing, I guess." I figured I'd better do something quick. So I hung my head and began to sob.

"What did Father Cooney say to you?" she asked.

I didn't say anything. I just stood there looking down at my shoes and crying softly. Old Sister Mary Thomas' face began to pucker up and I knew she felt terribly sorry for me. But Sister Agnes was hard as stone.

"So now you're crying," she said.

I threw myself into a chair and buried my face and sobbed. I could hear my own big sobs filling the kitchen. For some time nothing was said.

Then Sister Agnes spoke. "At least there appears to be some scrap of human decency left in him."

I howled.

"You'd better go home now," she said.

I kept my face covered and dragged myself toward the door. "Good night, Sister Thomas," I said.

"Good night, James."

"Thanks for the pie," I choked.

As I opened the door Sister Agnes came toward me. "One moment," she said. She put her hand on my shoulder and she was smiling—a sweet beautiful smile. "I really believe you're sorry for what happened today."

"I feel terrible," I said keeping my head down. "All those street lights. All that pie and cake. I feel awful."

She lifted my face with the tip of her finger. "I'm sorry it happened too," she said. "But since you've shown such sincere sorrow, we'll all try to forget it." She smiled again. "About your father, you won't have to worry. I won't telephone him."

I said, "Gee, Sister. Thanks!"

208

"And now, go home as fast as you can. And don't throw any rocks — at anything."

I hurried away and cut across the lawn. Except that I had eaten too much, I felt pretty good. The long cool shadows from the maple trees fell across the lawn. The rim of the big gold sun was sagging behind the mountains and the mountains were a dark blue. I walked very fast for a couple of blocks and when I thought of what would have happened if my father had found out, it made me stop and take a deep breath.

Then I remembered my little prayer to God, asking Him not to let my father know. It filled me up. I leaned against one of the maple trees on Tenth Street and started to cry. Not the same kind of a cry I had in Sister Thomas' kitchen. This was a real cry that shook me all over, until I thought I would break into pieces. I couldn't stop. I peeled some bark from the tree and cried for a long time. Then I started for home again.

In the Spring

WE WERE EATING dessert when Burton whistled. The old man gave me one of his looks.

"There's your no-good friend," he said.

"No good?" I stopped eating. "Look, mister. You don't know what you're talking about. Ralph Burton happens to be the finest first baseman this town ever developed."

"Excuse me, but I still say he's no good."

"That's because you don't know what's going on in the world."

Burton whistled again. I left the table and hurried outside. The old man just sat there, staring at his apple cobbler. He was almost forty-three, getting on in years, and out of touch with important things.

It was nearly seven o'clock, but not dark. Burton was hiding behind the elm tree in the front yard.

"Want to toss a few?"

"Nah," he said. "Let's talk."

We walked two blocks to the creek that ran through Boulder. Burton pulled out a new pack of cigarettes, and we sat on the bank. Burton was very lucky: his old man bought them by the carton. Mine smoked cigars.

"I sure hate this town," Burton said.

"It's strictly for hicks," I said. "Not even big enough for Class C baseball."

Burton looked up at the sky. "Why did I have to be born here?" he asked. "Why couldn't I have been born in some major-league city? Even Kansas City, or some other American Association town? Even some town in the East Texas League? Even Terre

211

Haute, in the Three-Eye League? Why did I have to be born in Boulder, Colorado?"

It was good to dream. I took a drag and let the smoke come sighing out. "If I had it to do over again," I said, "I'd be born in a house right across the street from the Yankee Stadium. It could be just a plain old shack with a leaky roof and no paint. What's money? I wouldn't care."

"Money don't count," Burton said. "And it don't matter what the place looks like. What counts is have you got the stuff? Can you hit that ball?"

We listened to the trickle of water through the rocks in the creek.

"Jake," Burton said, "I want to ask you a question. A very personal question. But don't pull your punches. Tell me the truth."

"Let's have it, Burt. You know me."

"What I want to know is this: Am I good enough, right now, for the big time?"

You don't just rattle off an answer to that kind of a question. I thought about it for a long time. Then I said: "Burton, in my honest opinion, you're good enough right now to hold down first base for any major-league club in the country. I seen you in action, kid. You're like a snake around that bag. As for hitting, you got the sharpest pair of eyes I ever seen."

"Aw. I wouldn't go that far."

"You're just too modest, Burt. I say you're ready for major-league ball. Right now."

"Thanks, Jake. I appreciate you being so honest."

Now it was dark and cold. To the west, the mountains began to disappear behind thick white clouds. There was a feeling of spring snow in the air. Our breaths came out in small white puffs. We built a fire between two stones and fed it pieces of drifwood from a muskrat dam. We watched the fire. It scorched our faces and left our backs cold. The heat cracked the stones and they popped open. With warm eyes we stared at the flames.

"Burt," I said, "it's my turn to ask you a question."

"Shoot."

"The truth, Burt. I can take it."

"I never lie, Jake."

"Am I good enough for major-league ball?"

"Absolutely. You're the greatest pitching prospect I ever saw."

"No, Burt. Think about it carefully. Don't just flatter me. Give it some thought."

"Okay."

He didn't speak for five minutes. Then he said: "In my opinion, you have the greatest knuckle ball in the United States of America. I never been up against Vic Raschi or Allie Reynolds, but I faced you many times, Jake. I know pitching. It's my business, because I'm a hitter. I say you're as good as anything up there, and maybe better."

All the time he talked, I watched his face. He wasn't lying. I felt it in my bones.

"Burt," I said, "thanks for your honest opinion."

"Trouble is," he said, "we're too young for the big time."

"Too young? Ye gods, Burt! In ten years we'll be twenty-four. Think of it — twenty-four! Old men. They're crying for young blood up there. Mickey Mantle, look at him. What is he — six years older than us?"

The wind came up, and we huddled closer to the fire. Beyond the creek the street lights went on. I warmed my hands and thought about a headline in the Denver Post: *Colorado Boy Pitches No-Hit Game In Majors.*

Then I thought about myself in another way — the way my father wanted it. The years had passed and I was a structural engineer, working in an office, studying blueprints. I paced the office floor restlessly. I stood at the window in misery because now I was too old to play baseball. I was married now, with a potbelly, tied down to a wife and a lot of kids. And as I looked out that window I cursed my father for ruining my natural-born talent as a pitcher who might have been a major-league immortal, with his name in the Hall of Fame. But I had been an obedient son. I had gone to college like the old man wanted. I had forgotten baseball. Now I was old and it was too late. Brokenhearted, I opened the window and jumped — a suicide.

"Burt," I said, "my father gives me a pain in the neck. He don't understand me at all."

"He's like my old man."

213

"He wants me to be an engineer, Burt."

"You kidding?" Burton laughed. "You — the sweetest knuckle-ball artist in the Rocky Mountains? You can't let him do that, Jake. It's criminal."

"Tell that to my father."

Burton dropped his chin and was silent.

"What's wrong?"

"My folks want me to be a preacher."

It was my turn to laugh.

"You — a preacher? They must be nuts. Ain't any of your family ever see you run down a bunt? Or throw to third base? You got the makings of another Lou Gehrig. Don't let 'em do it to you, Burt. Fight back!"

"They don't understand me, Jake."

"Me neither."

Now it was very cold. Tonight the water would freeze in little puddles and spring would never be here.

"Another thing about this town is the weather," I said. "It stinks."

"You said it."

"Nice and warm down South, down in Arizona. The Giants are training there this year, in Phoenix."

"Ah, the hot sun, the blue sky, green grass, batting practice, pitchers limbering up."

"After practice, a nice warm shower, then supper in a ritzy hotel, and gabbing with guys like Bobby Thomson and Leo Durocher . . ."

"And tomorrow, a nice big breakfast, more sunshine, and nothing to do all day but play ball."

It was so sweet to think about that it hurt. We put out the fire and walked back to the street. Burton lived six blocks away. He went ambling down the sidewalk, a big kid, six feet tall, with long fingers and feet. He was a southpaw, and he walked like a southpaw, favoring his left shoulder. He could really slam that ball around the infield. Nothing got through him, ever. He covered first base like a lanky gorilla.

Now he was going home to a little white house in Boulder, Colorado, where he lived with his folks and his two brothers. He would go to bed beside his brother Eddie. Tomorrow he would get up and go to school. The next day would be the same, and the next, and the next, day after day, the same monotony in the same jerkwater town.

I was just like Burton. I slept with a brother too. Tomorrow I'd wake up and eat breakfast and go to school, and just sit there, listening, dreaming, and this would go on, day after day, month after month, clear through high school, clear through college, years and years of the same grind. And for what? To be an engineer, trapped in an office. The more I thought about it, the more I hated my father for crushing my life and wrecking my best years.

I walked into the house. The old man was sitting under the lamp, reading the paper. I slammed the front door.

"What's the big idea?" he said.

"That's my business."

He shrugged and went back to his paper. I looked at the place, the same old walls, the same old ceiling, the same old floor. Here was the place I lived. This was the cage where they fed me and let me sleep.

"Trapped," I said, "like an animal. Trapped in this dump."

The old man sniffed the air and put down his paper.

"You. Come here."

"Go jump in the lake."

He swept the paper aside and put his hands on the arms of the chair.

"You've been smoking cigarettes."

"The old boy's pretty clever. Figured it all out by himself."

"I told you before. No smoking."

"So you told me. So what?"

He sprang out of the chair and grabbed my shoulders with his big hands. But I braced myself. I wasn't backing down. From now on it was a fight for life, before he crushed my spirit, before it was too late and I was old and fat and working in an office. He shook me up quite a bit, and I kept glaring at him.

"Sir," I said, "I advise you to take your mitts off of me. Either that, or you'll never see your son again."

He let go and folded his arms.

"What's ailing you, kid?"

"Don't 'kid' me," I said. "I don't think I care for it."

215

"Why, you miserable little worm!"

He whirled me around and booted me in the seat of the pants. It wasn't painful but it was plenty insulting, the very last straw. We had come to the parting of the ways.

"That did it, sir," I said. "You'll regret this as long as you live."

"I may have regrets, kid, but this isn't one. Matter of fact, this is the best I've felt in two weeks."

He went back to his chair, lit a cigar, and picked up the paper.

I went outside and sat on the porch. So it had come at last — the great decision. It had been on my mind since last August, when I mastered the knuckle ball and realized my true vocation. Of all the people in the world, only Burton understood this. Burton would go along, for now I had it all figured out, and there was only one thing to do: run away from home, run away to Arizona and try out with the New York Giants.

I didn't have to whistle for Burton. He was sitting on the front porch of his house, feeling low, chewing his nails.

"I'm through," he said. "I've had all a man can stand."

"What's wrong?"

"See that garden? Fifty feet long, twenty-five feet wide. And I got to spade it tomorrow."

"The whole thing?"

"That's what he says, the jerk."

"Why can't your brother Eddie do it?"

"Because he's the favorite around here. He takes piano lessons. He's a genius."

"What about you? Suppose you get hurt like Cecil Beame?"

"Cecil Beame?"

"Ruptured. Shoveling snow off the sidewalk."

"Is that bad?"

"He'll never play ball again."

The thought burned a hole in Burton's brain. He gritted his teeth. "They won't rupture me," he said. "They can *try*, but they'll never get away with it."

"Listen, Burt."

I told him about hitchhiking down to Arizona and joining the New York Giants.

"Okay. I'll go."

We made plans to leave next morning.

My last night at home. I cried in bed, remembering things: my brothers and sisters, Christmas Eve, my dog Rex, my rabbits, my mother, my school days, the smell of hot bread. It was good-by to all those things, to Mom and Dad and Colorado.

They would find me gone in the morning. I was probably ruining my mother's life, but it didn't matter so much with my father. He would have regrets, of course. I could see him there, as the years passed, holding my picture, tears in his eyes, saying: "Come back, son; all is forgiven. Play ball if you like."

I watched the clock on the dresser. Burton and I had agreed to meet at six. At two in the morning I was still awake, listening to the old man's snores from the next room.

Now was the time. I slipped out of bed and crawled on my stomach across the floor to the chair where my father's pants were folded. My hand found his wallet in the back pocket, and I examined it in the moonlight. There were two bills — a five and a ten. It was ten more than I'd expected. I put the wallet back, crawled out of the room, and waited for the new day.

Burton was waiting in front of the First National Bank. It was six o'clock and very cold. White clouds smothered the mountains, and the wind came from the north. It meant snow.

"We sure picked a great day," Burton said.

He hadn't had much luck. There was nothing at all in his father's pockets, so he had been forced to steal seven dollars from under his grandma's mattress. "We got twenty-two bucks," I said. "We'll make it easy."

We were on the highway. Traffic was so scarce that it was fifteen minutes before we even saw a car. Then a milk truck passed. Burton's teeth chattered, and he said his feet were cold.

"We'll never make it to Phoenix, Jake. We won't get out of Boulder, even."

It began to snow — light and fluffy at first. By six thirty it was roaring down as if the sky had caved in. A few more cars passed, none going our way. We weren't dressed for snow. We wore our red baseball sweaters with the white block B woven on the chest.

"Well, here we are," Burton said. "Still in Boulder, Colorado. Let's go down to the school and sit in the furnace room. We'll never make Arizona in this blizzard."

"So you're yellow," I said.

"I ain't yellow."

"Then what are you?"

"Just cold."

We heard a truck coming. It was barely visible in the storm. I ran out and waved. The truck stopped. Two men were in the cab. They were driving to Fort Collins, twenty-five miles away.

"Lots of room in back," the driver said.

We got aboard. The bed of the truck was piled with boxes of canned goods. A canvas protected the load from the snow. We crawled under the canvas and lay on our stomachs and listened to the crunch of the grinding tires. It was fine for a while, but gradually the cold got worse. We raised the canvas and looked out. We were in the foothills, in a raging storm. The truck crawled in low gear. Air rushed through the truck bed, pricking us like iced needles. At eight o'clock we pulled into a filling station in Fort Collins. The driver lifted the canvas.

"This is it, boys."

We were so stiff from the cold that he had to lift us out. We stumbled inside the filling station and crowded a small oil heater. An old man in a sheepskin coat operated the station. We told him we were on our way to Phoenix, Arizona.

"When I was your age, I was very proud," he said, chewing tobacco and smoking a pipe at the same time. "I never begged for rides. Always traveled first class."

"We only got twenty-two bucks," Burton said.

"A fortune," the old man said. "Enough to take you around the world."

"But how?"

"Don't cost nothing to hop a freight. One pulls outa here tonight for Salt Lake at six o'clock. Takes about eight hours. Then you grab another going south to Arizona. Travel right, that's what I say."

"And freeze to death," Burton said.

The old man puffed on his pipe and inspected us. "In them

clothes, yes. Get yourself a coupla Army blankets, a few cans of beans and a coupla sacks of Bull Durham, and you're riding like a king, clear to the baseball country."

"No freights," Burton said. "I'm a first baseman, not a bum."

"It's against our principles," I said.

The old man shook his head and spat a sizzler against the oil stove. "You won't make the Giants. Not you kids. Too soft. No guts."

"We didn't come here to get insulted," Burton said. "Come on, Jake."

Across the street was a cafe. We hadn't eaten breakfast, and we were very hungry. The old man called to us from the filling station.

"Be proud, lads. Grab that six-o'clock freight."

We ate a big breakfast and bought some candy bars. Now that I was warm and not hungry, I wanted to catch the freight. We left the cafe and walked down the street. It had stopped snowing. The sky was blue, with clouds tumbling over themselves as they dashed south. We stopped before an Army-Navy store and stared at piles of blankets and boots and knapsacks. We kept walking, but we didn't talk about the freight.

At the end of the street was the railroad yard. Two engines were pushing boxcars around. We stood watching. We were thinking of what the old man had said, but we didn't speak of it. About noon we moved back to the middle of town and decided to go to a movie.

The newsreel did it. There was a whole section showing the New York Giants in spring training at Phoenix. We sat on the edge of our seats and watched big-league ballplayers romping around the Giant training camp. When it was over, we rushed outside like new men.

"We gotta get out of here," Burton panted. "We gotta get to Arizona."

Across the street was the Army-Navy store. We bought blankets, knapsacks, gloves and woolen caps. We found a grocery store and loaded our knapsacks with cans of pork and beans, tamales, sardines and Bull Durham. It all happened very fast.

219

When we were through, we checked our finances. We were down to $3.50. It didn't worry Burton.

"Take us halfway around the world," he said.

We walked up and down the street with knapsacks on our backs and blankets under our arms. At four o'clock, it got cold again. The sky turned gray and it felt like more snow.

"I'd like to see that newsreel once more," Burton said.

Inside the theater, the main love picture was half over. Except for us, the place was deserted. We kept our eyes on the clock over one of the exits. The newsreel went on at 5:25. The baseball stuff took exactly two minutes. At 5:28 we were outside again. It was almost dark and snowing hard. But we could still feel the sunshine off the newsreel.

We walked down to the freight yard. A long train was made up, the panting engine facing southwest. We picked an open boxcar near the end of the train and climbed aboard. It wasn't our first time in a boxcar, but it was very strange now. We closed the door and went forward in the darkness. The boxcar had a stale, nasty smell. Wrapping ourselves in blankets, we sat down. For some reason, we found ourselves whispering instead of speaking out.

"I forgot my first baseman's mitt," Burton whispered.

"The Giant management furnishes all equipment," I told him.

For a long time we said nothing.

Then I put it to Burton this way: "Burt, now that we're on our way, I want to ask you a question. Tell me the truth, the real truth. Do you think we're good enough to break into the New York Giants' line-up?"

"I doubt it," Burton said. "But we'll hook up someplace. They'll farm us out. Probably the Pacific Coast League."

"That won't be so bad."

"Want to know the truth?" Burton asked. "The straight, honest-to-God truth?"

"Shoot."

"There's a chance we won't make the grade with the Coast League, either. But one thing is certain: we'll hook on someplace — the Texas League, or the Southern Association."

"Or the Three-Eye League."

"Or the Southeastern League."

"Or the Arizona State League."

"I'll play for nothing," Burton said. "Just board and room."

We couldn't roll Bull Durham in the darkness. Burton pulled out a pack of tailor-mades, and we lit up.

"Once we hit camp, no smoking."

"Right."

"Let's shake on it."

In the darkness we found one another's hands.

A tremendous crash sent us sprawling. The train was moving. We heard the faraway whistle of the engine. The train moved slowly, the engine puffing like crazy, its wheels slipping on the icy tracks. It was a rough ride. We crawled to the door and peeked out at the early darkness and the snow sweeping down.

"Might as well sleep," Burton yelled, because it was noisy now, the boxcar chattering and squealing. We stretched out, warm and very tired.

I don't know how long we slept. Suddenly there was a crash that nearly tore the blankets from us.

"Maybe it's a wreck," Burton said.

Everything was quiet and motionless. We sat up. The train began to move again. Back and forth our car moved. Then the whistle sounded, the engine chugged, and our car did not move. We jumped to our feet and listened. Far away in the night, we heard the engine, but our car did not move.

We slid open the door. The snow came down in heavy silence. Our boxcar stood alone in the white night. We were somewhere in low hills. Our car had been backed into a spur of track and uncoupled beside a cattle ramp.

We were scared. It was like being the last two people on earth. We went back into the darkness and wrapped ourselves in blankets. Burton offered me a cigarette, but I didn't feel like smoking.

"Don't fall asleep," Burton said. "You know what happens to people who sleep in blizzards."

I knew, but I asked anyway.

"They don't wake up."

I sat there thinking about my life, my wasted life, and all the trouble I'd caused my parents. I remembered all the money I'd stolen from my father's pants, and my mother's purse, and my sister's piggy bank. I remembered the chickens I'd slaughtered at close range with my father's shotgun. It all came back to me in a rush, the mess I'd made of my life — flunking algebra three years straight, cheating in examinations, listening to dirty stories and telling some of my own.

Thinking about it, I wanted to live my life over again; I wanted another chance. I wanted to live through that blizzard so I could go back home to Boulder, Colorado, and study to be an engineer.

Then I heard Burton sobbing. "I'm a rat, Jake," he said. "A no-good rat."

"No, you're not. You're okay by me."

But he insisted that he was a wrong guy, and he told me some of the things he had done in his life — punched his mother in the stomach, stolen library books, broken street lamps, sold a brand-new pair of his father's shoes, stripped hubcaps off cars, and so forth. One thing he mentioned that was really bad; and that was burning down his own house. It had happened when he was ten years old, and to that day nobody knew he'd done it — nobody but me.

We tried to keep awake, but we were too tired and slept anyhow, and when we woke up, sunlight poured through the cracks in the boxcar. We opened the door and looked out. It was bright daylight with a blue sky. A hundred yards away, state highway bulldozers were clearing the road of last night's drifts. Moving slowly behind the bulldozers were a dozen cars. We grabbed one another and jumped for joy.

"We're saved!" Burton yelled. "Saved!"

We left our stuff in the boxcar and waded through the snow to the highway. The first car behind the bulldozers picked us up. The driver was a farmer, and what he said made us silent. We had taken the wrong freight out of Fort Collins. Now we were just a mile out of Thatcher and four miles from home. But I'd had enough. It seemed years since I'd left home. I wanted to be with my folks, with my brothers and sisters.

"Well," Burton said. "Here we go again — slow but sure."

"Yeah."

"Still want to go to Arizona?"

"Sure, Burt," I lied. "How about you?"

"We can't stop now."

"That's right."

The farmer stopped his car in front of the sheriff's substation in Thatcher. The town had only one street, a block long. We just stood there. I wanted to call the whole thing off. Burt did too, but it was hard to show weakness.

Then a sheriff's patrol drove up. Two officers sat in the front seat.

"Your name Jake Crane?" one of them asked.

"Yes, sir."

The officer opened the back door. "Hop in, boys."

"We didn't do anything," Burt said.

"Just hop in, boys."

The driver made a U-turn and swung down the highway toward Boulder. We sat with folded arms.

"Arizona!" Burt sneered. "This was your idea."

"Anyway, I ain't yellow," I said.

"Who's yellow?"

"You were scared from the first. Your feet were cold. You wanted to quit."

"I shoulda quit," he said. "You and your screwball plans. Now look at us. Under arrest."

"Are we under arrest, Officer?" I asked.

"Where do you live?" he said.

"959 Arapahoe."

He glanced back at Burton. "How about you?"

"529 Walnut."

That was all the officers said. Burton made a nasty little laugh. "You and your knuckle ball," he sneered.

"It's good enough to strike *you* out," I said, "the way *you* step in the bucket."

"We're through," Burton said. "My old man was right. You're bad company."

"I won't even repeat what *my* old man says about you."

"Pooh! A bricklayer. What does he know?"

223

"A lot more than a dumb plasterer like your old man."

The car drove up in front of my house. The officer turned and opened the door. I stepped out. Burton sat like an Indian, his arms folded.

"Burt," I said. "No hard feelings."

For a moment he wouldn't even look at me.

Then he grinned. "So long, Jake. Good luck."

I turned from the car. There on the porch was my father. I walked slowly toward him, studying his face. There was no anger in his face. He stood with his hands in his pockets, erect and smiling a little.

"Hi, Pop."

"Hello, boy."

All at once it crashed down on me — the terrible thing I'd done to my pop, and I stood there crying and choking and not able to say anything. He put his arm around me.

"Come on, boy. Breakfast's ready."

"Oh, Pop!"

"Forget it."

Together we went into the house.

One-Play Oscar

THE NEW KID was sitting on the front porch across the street. I waved. "Hey, come over." The new kid got up and walked over. He had a long nose and there was a hole in his faded sweat shirt.

"Hi. What's your name?"

"Rabinowitz. Jake Rabinowitz. What's yours?"

"Anthony Campiglia," I said. "Tony for short. Rabinowitz — that's a screwy name."

"So's Campiglia."

"Yeah, kinda. You play football, Jake? We got a football team on this side of town."

"Yeah?"

"You wanna try out for the team? Cost you two bits."

"Two bits — how come?"

I told him, to buy balls and stuff.

"When you guys practice?"

"After school. Up the street a ways. You wanna try out for the team, Jake?"

"I'll see."

"Okay. So long."

Everybody was late for practice. Then it started getting dark. Me and Blucher practiced laterals. He's our left half. Al Whitehill was centering. Pretty soon Wang came. Chink kid, swell end. Pretty soon, here comes Joe Nunez, our regular center. He was with Sukalian, our other end. Pretty soon, here comes this new kid, Jake Rabinowitz. He hung around like he wasn't watching.

I said, "Hey, you guys. See that new kid? He wants to play on our team. Let's show him what we got."

225

Blucher threw five passes to Wang, who caught the first four over his shoulder and the last one in his right hand, running sideways. While this was going on, Tasi Morimoto walked out on the field.

I said, "Tasi, see that new kid? Show him what you got."

"I'll punt some," he said.

Tasi got off three spirals. One went for fifty.

Real loud I said, "Only fair, Tasi. Only fair."

The new kid walked over.

I said, "Hiya, fella."

"Hi, Tony. You guys practicing?"

"Nah. Just cutting up."

While he stood there, Smitty and Mike Miecislaus came. Now the whole team was there except Swede Olson and Rube Novikov, our guards. I went over to the guys. "See that new kid? He wants to join the squad. Let's show him what we got."

"Give him some razzle-dazzle," Smitty said.

That was okay with me, the quarterback. We got into a huddle. I called the Rattlesnake Twist, No. 23. We broke huddle and the backs lined up in a T. I called some numbers, and on 23 Nunez centered the ball. I pivoted, slipped it to Smitty, our right half, and he shoveled it to Blucher, our left half. Blucher faked through guard, pivoted, and shoved it into Tasi's belly as he came up from tailback. Tasi stopped dead, backed up three yards, and faked to pass. I came around, took it off Tasi's fingers on the Statue-of-Liberty setup, and shoveled it to Wang, our left end. Wang pivoted, lateraled to Tasi, and Tasi shoveled to Blucher. Then Blucher hit guard. It was a terrific play. The new kid was plenty impressed. He came over with his hands in his pockets and the hole in his sweat shirt.

I said, "You wanna try out, kid? Got two bits?"

He dug a quarter out of his pocket and Smitty took it, because he was treasurer. All at once we could see this new kid was no football player. He had a fat butt and little hands.

I said, "Okay, Jake. Go out for a pass. Tasi'll throw you one."

Tasi dropped back ten yards. Jake was behind him, looking at the ground, drawing figures with his toe. Tasi cocked his arm. Jake just stood there.

I yelled, "Run, Jake! Go out ten and cut!"

Jake started running, but he was all butt, and we thought he was going to fall down. After ten yards he kept right on running. I yelled, "Hey, cut!" He threw himself on the ground, like he was blocking somebody out. Tasi passed anyway. The ball hit Jake in the chest and bounded into the street. Everybody turned away, disgusted.

"We don't want that punk," Wang said. "He stinks."

I said maybe we could make a guard out of him.

Rube and Swede, our guards, just laughed.

Nunez said, "Hey, Jakie, or Julie, or Jennie! Where'd you learn to play football?"

"I guess I'm not so hot," Jake said.

"Give the lad his money back," Nunez said.

But Jake wouldn't take the money.

"Maybe you guys can use a good manager."

"You don't know enough football to manage an outfit like this," Nunez said.

"Is that so?" Jake said. "Maybe I can't play, but I know more football than any of you guys."

"Okay, Brains," Nunez said. "Who's quarterback for Army?"

"Arnold Galiffa," Jake said.

"Who's right guard for Pitt?" Smitty said.

"Bernie Barkouskie."

Tasi said, "Who's left end for North Carolina?"

"That's easy," Jake said. "Art Weiner."

"I got one for this punk," Rube Novikov said. "Where was Leon Hart born?"

"Turtle Creek, Pennsylvania. He is twenty years old, stands six feet four, and weighs 245. Anything else?"

Everybody tried, but we couldn't catch him.

"Now I got one," he said. "Who's second-string quarter for the South New Mexico Mining Tech?"

It stopped us cold.

Jake smiled. "No such guy. No such school either."

"Okay," Nunez said. "Let him be manager."

Jake was there the next day. He took down our names and weights. He brought a whistle and refereed the scrimmage. He knew plenty. Saturday we had a long practice. About four o'clock we knocked off for pop. While we were lying around under the palm tree Jake went away. In a half hour he was back with a newspaper, the San Pedro Progress.

"Here it is, boys."

He spread the sports page on the ground. It said:

Powerful All-Americans Meet Hooligans

The powerful San Pedro All-Americans, undefeated in 15 successive games, will meet the Wilmington Hooligans Sunday afternoon at two o'clock at Cabrillo Playgrounds. The Pedro lads possess speed, power and deception unlike anything seen in the South Bay area in years. Tasi Morimoto, hard-driving fullback, and Joe Nunez, slashing center, have pulverized all opposition to face them. From end to end, the All-Americans boast an impregnable line—

"Oh, boy!" Nunez said. "Slashing center. Wow!"

"Who wrote that?" Wang said.

"Me," Jake said. "Someday I'm gonna be a sports writer."

"But our team's called Wildcats," Smitty said.

"Wildcats, applesauce," Jake said. "You're Americans, ain't you? So you're All-Americans."

"He's right," Nunez said. "Slashing center—wow!" He jumped to his feet. "Come on, you creeps! Let's get out there and dig! Slashing center—wow!"

Next day we played the Hooligans. A big crowd watched, people sitting in cars around the field. At half time we were ahead 24 to 0, but that was on account of the crooked referee. Jake passed a helmet through the crowd. It got almost six bucks. One guy put in a whole buck. Jake refereed the second half. We went out there and banged their brains out. The game ended 87 to 6, when the Hooligans intercepted one of our passes. It was in Monday's paper, with all our names.

It was like that all season: San Pedro Cannery 6, All-Americans 76; St. Patrick's 17, All-Americans 88; Beach House 0, All-Americans 58; Epworth League 0, All-Americans 105; Eight-Balls 69, All-Americans 70.

Our last game was with Japanese Settlement. They were tough cannery kids from Terminal Island, across the bay from San Pedro. They were so tough they smashed Eight-Balls 75 to 0. They had a fullback named Irish Hagaromo, who was so big and powerful that he averaged seven touchdowns a game. Irish weighed 225. He was first mate on a tuna boat, and he was thirty-five years old. It was his team. He bought all equipment and coached the team. They only had one offensive play: the center got over the ball and flipped it to Irish.

We practiced hard for the Japanese Settlement game. The only way to beat them was to score a touchdown every time we got the ball; we knew Irish would do the same for his team. If we won the toss, we could keep one touchdown ahead throughout the game.

The second night of practice Frank Adamic didn't show up. He was there the next night, but he wouldn't practice.

"On account of the war," he said.

"What war?"

"The cold war."

"The what?"

"I'm a Yugoslav, you're an Italian. My old man says I can't play until the Italians get out of Trieste."

"Trieste? Who's he?"

"It ain't a he. It's a place, a country or something."

"What league they in?"

He didn't know. We practiced without him. The next night Frenchy Dorais resigned. "If Adamic quit because of the war, I got to quit too. Blucher's a German. My old man says they killed a lot of Frenchmen. I resign."

Then Mike Miecislaus quit. He said his old man was a Polack. He couldn't play with Rube Novikov because Rube was a Russian. "Not till the Russians clear out of Poland. Sorry, men. Papa's orders."

After that, Wang quit. His father said, "China will never forget, my son. You must resign." He meant the Japanese. Wang told us about it, and was very sad. But it made Tasi Morimoto mad.

"Is that so?" he said. "Well, I don't play with no Chink neither."
He quit too.

"But this is America!" Jake said.

We never thought of it any other way. Russians. Japs. Chinese.
Poles. Italians. This was a hell of a way to figure people.
Then Blucher told his old man about it, and Herman had to quit
too.

"Jake is Jewish. My old man says no soap."

"I'm an American," Jake said.

"My old man hates Jews."

"But I don't hate you, Herman."

"I like you, too, Jake. But you don't know my old man."

"I know your old man," Frenchy Dorais said. "My old man
knows him, too — a lard-bellied German square-head. That's what
your old man is!"

Blucher hit him, and Frenchy hit back. They fought all over
the field, punching each other and rolling on the ground. Then
Mike hit Rube Novikov. I tried to separate them. All of a sudden
Frank Adamic yelled, "Trieste!" and banged me in the stomach.
Wang punched Frank, and Morimoto jumped on Wang's back
and started slugging. Jake tried to break it up. Somebody
whanged him in the puss and somebody else kicked him in the
stomach. He staggered away with blood streaming from his nose.
Whitehill and Smitty pitched in too. Everybody was fighting
except Joe Nunez and Swede Olson.

Pretty soon a car drove up and two cops jumped out. One
was Oscar Lewis, of the Harbor Detail. They roughed us up and
broke up the fighting. Oscar grabbed Blucher and shook him.

"So what's this all about? So let's have the truth, or in you go,
charged with a riot."

He butted Blucher all over the place with the thick cartridge
belt strapped around his potbelly. Then he let him go and grabbed
Joe Nunez and started butting him around.

"I wasn't fighting," Joe said. "I'm a Portegee."

"Me neither," Swede said. "I'm Swedish."

Jake stepped up with a bloody handkerchief to his nose. "Officer
Lewis, I can explain everything."

Oscar lunged at him. "So you're the guy!"

He butted Jake all over the field, Jake talking fast. They were in the middle of the street before Jake got the story out.

"We're Americans," Jake said. "We got a right to play."

"So you got rights," Oscar said. "So what?"

"You're a smart man, Mr. Lewis. Maybe you could talk to the fathers of these kids," Jake said.

"So now I'm a smart man . . . Hey, Harvey. Will you get a load of this punk?"

"Let's go, Oscar," the other cop said.

Jake grabbed Oscar's arm. "Wait. You know what Japanese Settlement said, Mr. Lewis? They said everybody in the harbor precinct was yellow. Cowards — that's what they called us — all of us, you, and me, and everybody."

It worked. Oscar's face puffed up. He pulled out his notebook. "Okay, you punks. Where do you live, and what's the names of your fathers?"

We called them out and he wrote them down.

"Now get in there and practice. And no fighting."

Oscar Lewis talked to every father, and the beef was squared all around. Now we were a better team than ever.

Sunday noon the team went over to Terminal Island on the nickel ferry. We had dressed at home and were ready to play as soon as we walked two blocks from the ferry landing to the Japanese Settlement Playground. Irish Hagaromo and the rest of the Settlement team were warming up. Irish punted and passed in a gold helmet and a gold nylon suit. The rest of the Settlement team wore plain khaki suits.

Mr. Slade, the playground supervisor, was referee. He appointed Jake head linesman and one of the Settlement boys was made umpire. At game time Mr. Slade flipped a coin. Irish Hagaromo won the toss for Japanese Settlement. He waved his victory to the crowd, mostly girls, cannery workers on Terminal Island.

We got into a huddle and Smitty said, "Kick it anywhere, but don't kick it near Hagaromo."

The whistle blew and we moved upfield as Nunez's foot sank into the ball. It sailed to the right, at about their fifteen, as far

231

away from Irish as he could kick it. The left half should have taken the ball, but he stepped aside and let it roll past him, and so did the other backs. They wanted Irish to have it. He came over twenty-five yards to pick it up. We rushed down on him, and he stood there smiling as the whole team closed in on him. Then he let out a yipe, waved at the girls, tucked the ball under his arm, lowered his head and came roaring through the thickest of us.

We splattered like a pie hit by a baseball. When we got up and shook our heads, Hagaromo stood behind the goal line, bowing to everybody.

He went through center for the point after touchdown. The score was 7 to 0. Irish laughed and waved to the girls.

"We can't beat them," Wang said. "That guy's too old. He's got a wife and four kids."

We lined up to receive. Irish kicked off. The ball sailed end over end, seventy-five yards in the air, over our goal posts, out of the end zone and past the cars parked beyond the end zone. The girls screamed with joy. Irish bowed from the waist like an actor.

With the ball on our twenty, we went into a huddle.

I called, "Rattlesnake Twister. Number Twenty-three."

Irish was playing defensive center, spitting on his hands and standing there poised like a wrestler. On 82 Nunez let me have the ball. Before I could pivot and shovel it to Smitty in the flat, Irish crashed through the line, picked me up and threw me ten yards in the air. Then he dumped down our entire backfield. I landed on my back. We had lost twelve yards on the play. In the huddle again, we were bruised and plenty scared.

"Let's punt it," I said. "Let's play it safe and try to keep the score down."

We went into punt formation. As soon as Irish saw it, he rushed back to safety position. Smitty kicked. The ball went over Hagaromo's head and rolled to their forty-yard line. Irish picked it up on a dead run, stopped, waved to the girls, tucked his head down and charged into us. We were smashed right and left and he went all the way for a touchdown. Standing between the goal posts, he did a jig for the girls. They loved it, shrieking and laughing.

After that we didn't care much. He had us scared and it made us tire fast. The first quarter ended 28 to 0. Five minutes before the end of the half, with the score 49 to 0, Irish took himself out of the game. He was so tired he tossed himself on the ground and didn't bother to wave at the applause.

With Irish out, our tricks worked. It was our chance to score, and we made the most of it. In five minutes we piled up three touchdowns and kicked goal twice. The half ended 49 to 20. At half time we felt better. We knew we could win if Irish was out of it.

Lying on our stomachs in the end zone, we listened to Jake, "You're a great team. This half you'll stop that big stiff. You'll stop him so hard he'll be carried off the field."

"That's nice to know," Nunez said, holding his head. "What'll we use, a truck?"

Oscar Lewis crossed the field from a line of parked cars. We didn't know he had come to watch the game. We were ashamed as he stood looking down at us.

"I guess that Hagaromo's too heavy for you punks," he said. "You ought to complain to the referee. It ain't right."

We didn't say anything.

"He must weigh as much as me," Oscar said.

"How much do you weigh?" Jake asked.

"Me? About 250."

"Then you got to play for us. Irish weighs 225."

"I'm no football player. I'm an old man of fifty."

"Mr. Lewis, the team needs you. This is your game too. You can't just sit on the side lines — big fellow like you, all that weight. You got to get in there and use it on Hagaromo."

"Sorry, kid. I'm an old man."

Jake shook his head. "It's amazing. I can't believe it." He turned to us. "Hey, team. We got a traitor. Yes, sir. Great big powerful traitor. It's hard to believe."

Oscar turned white, but he didn't say a word. He looked hard at Jake, bit his lower lip, and walked back to the cars. The starting whistle blew and we got to our feet.

It was our turn to receive. We spread ourselves out and watched Irish come forward on the kickoff. His foot punched the ball and

233

it soared lazily toward our goal line. Tasi Morimoto took it and started upfield. We blocked all opposition except Irish Hagaromo. He and Tasi met head-on at the twenty-yard line.

Irish got up, grinning. But Tasi didn't get up. He was knocked cold. We carried him off the field and laid him on a patch of side-line grass. He moaned when we sponged his greenish face. It was warm in the sun. Suddenly a big shadow covered us. It was Oscar Lewis.

"How is he?"

"Wind knocked out. He'll be okay in a minute."

Oscar unbuckled his gun. "Gimme a helmet," he said. "Traitor, am I? Ain't nobody can point the finger of scorn at Oscar Lewis."

He reported to Mr. Slade and came back to our huddle about the fifteen-yard line. He was so mad he kept working his fists open and shut.

"Let me call this one, boys," he said. "Just gimme that ball and get the hell out of the way."

We broke huddle, Oscar in the tailback spot. Swinging his arms and spitting on his hands, Irish Hagaromo was grinning and ready for anything. Nunez centered gently. Oscar took the ball, fumbled a moment, clutched it to his belly and boomed through center, his head down, keys and coins jingling in his pockets. There was an awful thud. He and Irish Hagaromo met head on. Both went down. Both lay still. We had not gained a yard. But it was Oscar Lewis who got to his feet, reeling and staggering. Irish Hagaromo did not get up. They poured a bucket of water on his face, but even that didn't wash away the grin, and he slept cheerfully.

They stretched him out on the side lines before all the sad girls, and a substitute took his place. Oscar staggered around, holding his head in his hands. He was sick, his face bluish, his mouth open. He called for time, pulled off his helmet and left the game. He had lasted one play, but it was enough. Tasi Morimoto had got his wind back and was ready to play again.

After that, it was murder. On two plays we scored a touchdown and kicked goal. Two minutes later Wang recovered a fumble. We worked our Rattlesnake Twister and scored again. At the end of the third period we were one point behind, 49 to 48. Irish Hagaromo had regained consciousness, but he was still groggy and lying on the grass. In the fourth quarter we pulled all our fancy stuff and scored two more touchdowns in five minutes.

With seven minutes to play, we were ahead 62 to 49. Then Irish Hagaromo got to his feet and began warming up along the side lines. The girls screamed with new hope. But Irish was too mad to bow and clown around. He looked dangerous as we watched him trot up and down, his knees going high.

Five minutes before the end of the game he reported for action. It was a time-out period, and we looked to the side lines for Oscar Lewis. He was standing with Jake, and we waved for him to hurry back into the game. But Oscar made no move. Jake shook his head.

"Get in there and fight!" he yelled. "Show 'em that All-American spirit!"

With the ball on Japanese Settlement thirty, we took our defensive positions. Irish wasn't smiling any more. All at once, seeing him standing there so serious, ready to take that ball and bash our line, we weren't afraid of him. This man could be stopped. We had seen it done. It could be done again. Something had happened to us. We weren't afraid. We all felt it, because we seemed to look at one another and say it with our eyes.

The ball was snapped. Irish drove through tackle. Wang hit him low and Rube hit him high; they were both knocked down, but Irish had lost his balance. When he got to the line of scrimmage, Blucher socked him at the knees and Tasi Morimoto dived at his neck. Smitty and I just rolled in front of him. Down he went, the whole team smothering him. The gain was three yards. We got up and looked at one another. He had been stopped again. Now we knew we had him.

And we did. With tears in his eyes, Hagaromo went back to the tailback spot. He looked at us with murder jumping out of his eyes. But we weren't afraid, and on the next play he only gained one yard. And we kept dropping him. Sometimes he went ten yards, sometimes fifteen, with all of us riding on his back and hugging his legs, and though Japanese Settlement kept the ball most of the time, with Irish piling our whole team to the one-yard line, the final whistle blew and he didn't score.

We took an awful beating. When we staggered off the field Hagaromo threw himself on the grass and beat it with his fists and tore up the turf with his teeth, crying and groaning. We gathered our stuff and looked around for Oscar Lewis. But he was gone. For a winning team, we were a pretty sad bunch.

"He had to go to work," Jake said.

"He won the game for us," Tasi said.

"No, you all won it," Jake said.

"Yeah," Blucher said. "But it took outside help. Oscar wasn't a member of the team."

"Is that so?" Jake smiled.

He opened his notebook to a page with writing on it. And this is what we read:

From this day forward, having paid my dues in the amount of 25 cents, I hereby serve notice that I am a member of the All-American Team, and said team may call upon me at any time in the performance of my duties.

(signed) Oscar Lewis.
(Witnessed by) Jacob Rabinowitz.

That made all the difference in the world. We got aboard the ferry and sang songs all the way home.

The Dreamer

A POLICEMAN TOLD me about the room. He said it was up on Bunker Hill, a big gray stucco place. I went up there. Thirty-five years ago Bunker Hill used to be a fashionable neighborhood, but not today. Those twenty-room mansions are shabby now.

A big gray stucco place. There it was. I rang the doorbell. A Mexican woman opened the door. She was strong and erect.

Her hair had the shining black glitter of baked enamel. So dark, so shiny it gave her face an orange tint. This was Mrs. Flores.

The rent was ten a week. I gave her forty.

"Better see the room first," she said.

But I was tired of looking for rooms. I wanted anything, merely four walls. I wanted to be alone with my typewriter. There was work to do. I didn't care what the room was like. Mrs. Flores led me upstairs to the second floor. A very old house. Thick high doors. Brass fittings.

Seeing the room, I hesitated. It was so stark. Only four pieces of furniture: bed, dresser, chair and table. No rug. No curtains. No pictures on the wall.

"It's a lot for this place, Mrs. Flores."

"I told you to look at it first."

She wasn't angry. She merely didn't care. When she spoke I saw her white teeth. They were exquisitely flawless. She dressed in the fashion of her people — a peasant skirt and blouse, silver earrings, a matching silver trinket at her throat. Her small feet were shod in huaraches. They looked strong, comfortable.

She went after soap and towels. I opened my grip and took out the few things I owned. A few shirts, shorts, neckties, socks.

237

A whole ream of clear white paper. It was a lean time for me. But I had much to write. It fairly ached inside me.

I opened my portable and put it on the table under the window. I saw myself writing furiously, pounding night and day here in this room, the great sprawling city down below. Outside the window was the tip of an aged palm tree. It would inspire me, break the monotony of four walls.

Mrs. Flores was back with soap and towels. Her dark eyes widened when she saw the typewriter. I explained how it was with me — this was how I made my living, writing stuff.

"You'll have to leave," she said.

"Leave? Why?"

She took the forty dollars from her skirt pocket and laid it on the dresser. "It's the noise of the typewriter," she said. "The man next door needs his sleep."

The door separating my room and the next was thick walnut. The walls were thick. And my machine was quiet. I showed her, rattling a few keys. I promised there would be no noise. But her mind was firm. She shook her head slowly, persistently. I began to throw things back into my grip. I thought how unreasonable she was. And I hated the man next door, whoever he was; I cursed him.

There were footsteps in the hall. He appeared, this man who lived next door.

"Cristo!" the woman said.

He stood there looking at me and I saw the peculiar animation of love come into the face of Mrs. Flores, the dark eyes adoring him.

"Hallo," he said.

It was mechanical, cold. He could feel her animation. He did not want it. He was guarding himself from it. He was tall, intense, handsome, a Filipino of probably thirty-five. He was beautifully dressed, specially his yellow necktie shining like a little sun from his neck.

"Something wrong?" he asked.

"He writes with the typewriter," Mrs. Flores said. "You won't sleep if he stays. You need your rest. You don't sleep well."

"I sleep good," he said. "How you know this — how I sleep? You peek?"

He wanted an answer. His eyes opened in indignation. Mrs. Flores lowered her face.

"Is bad for woman to look at sleeping man," he admonished. "I do not like this."

She took it quietly, stoically. Cristo smiled at me. "Please to stay, my friend," he said. "Is good to have educated man for neighbor, with typewriter."

I thanked him and we shook hands.

"Name of Sierra. Cristo Sierra."

"John Lane," I told him.

But I watched Mrs. Flores. She showed no emotion. I wanted to hear her say, in so many words, that the room was mine. As she backed out, Cristo holding the door, she gave me a quick inscrutable look. Then I was alone in my room. I sat down and tried to work. Through my mind flashed that passion in the eyes of Mrs. Flores, the way she looked at Cristo, but it would not go down on paper.

No, it wouldn't go down. After three days, all I had to show for the ferment of my brain was wads of crushed paper. I walked the creaking floor. I pounded my head, rolled on the bed, stared at the ceiling. Alert, I listened to the sounds coming from the house. Every morning I heard Cristo leave. He was gone until late at night, sometimes after midnight. Two other roomers lived on the second floor. Old Mr. Ashley had heart trouble and was seldom heard. I never knew or saw the other man. But now I found myself forever listening for the feline swish of Mrs. Flores' huaraches. Her name disturbed me. I told myself that with her youth and beauty she should be known as Dolores or Maria, or some such name to fit the dark loveliness of her face.

Every morning after he was gone I heard her in Cristo's room. She would be in there dusting and making his bed. Her sobs would emerge like the fluttering of a trapped dove.

I learned a few things about her from old Ashley. He had lived in this house for twenty years. He remembered when Mrs. Flores had bought it three years before. She was a war widow. Her husband had left her enough to buy this house. If Ashley suspected that she loved Cristo, he didn't say it. But it was significant that he began immediately to talk of the Filipino. Cristo worked for a fruit company, where he was foreman of the warehouse.

I talked to Cristo a week later. That was the first time I saw his room. It was after dark of another sterile day, with nothing on paper. He knocked on the door separating our rooms. When I answered, the key turned and he opened the door.

"Hallo," he said. "You like little drink?" He frowned at the condition of my room.

"Mrs. Flores promised me a wastebasket," I said.

"Is hard work, yes?" he asked, nodding at the typewriter.

I liked this Cristo. Here was at least one person who understood my problems. He stepped aside and bowed toward his room. "Welcome."

His room was breath-taking. I had almost forgotten such places existed. There were the lamps: three soft-glowing floor lamps spilling light on a room so richly furnished I stared in unbelief. In one corner was a fireplace. Before it stood two luxurious red leather chairs, a low table between them, and on the table in elegant simplicity were decanters of liquor, a bowl of ice cubes and a tray of glasses.

I spun around in awe. On the walls were Currier and Ives reprints mounted in expensive frames. It was a corner room, two sides redecorated in knotty pine and stained with bright shellac. I touched the draperies hanging from the double windows. They were gold-figured chintz against a blue background. And all the time Cristo watched me, pleased. Standing before the fireplace, he fixed highballs, his lips turned in a quiet smile. He seemed to invite me to browse around. I prowled everywhere, opening doors. Here was his clothes closet. It was as one might expect, his suits hanging neatly, like headless figures of himself. And there were his ties — not as many as I imagined, a dozen or so — but each a stunning eye-catcher. I closed the door and paused before the one next to it.

"Do you mind?" I asked. "I might as well see it all."

"Halp youself."

It was the bathroom. The absolutely private bathroom of Cristo

240

Sierra. When I saw the stall shower behind panels of opaque glass I envied Cristo for the first time.

"You're lucky," I told him.

His dismissal was a shrug. He handed me a highball. I crossed the room to a bowl of fruit and a display of flowers on the table beside his studio couch.

"So you like flowers too," I said.

"No."

"You like Mrs. Flores?"

"Is fine woman," he said, taking in the room with a wave of his hand. "She give me all this. Rent, five a week. I wish to pay more. She will not take."

"She has good taste."

"Fine woman. But not for Cristo Sierra."

"I hear her in here every day. She cries."

"I know. Cannot halp. Is not my type."

I wondered about his type but I didn't ask.

We sprawled in the leather chairs, smoking and sipping our drinks. We seemed to know there was serious talk ahead. We drained our glasses and he filled them again.

"Mr. Lane," he said. "I have big dream. Big. You are writer. You will understand."

His dream was a return in triumph to his native village of Villazon, seventy miles north of Manila. Twenty years ago, when he was fifteen, Cristo had come to the United States. Somehow he had escaped the poverty and desolation of Villazon only to find himself trapped by the glittering poverty of California. But that was in the past. Somehow he had survived. He had picked grapes in Modesto, cotton in Bakersfield, asparagus in Sacramento, celery in Venice, cantaloupes in the Imperial Valley. He had canned tuna at San Pedro. He had been hungry in Oxnard, Lompoc and San Diego. Once he had nearly died of pneumonia in the Sutter County Hospital. Once he lived a whole month in the Union Station at Berkeley.

But not once in all those years had he fallen in love, nor met the dream of his soul. Now he was glad he had not found her during that bitter time. He might have lost her out of his inability

to keep her gowned and fed. But good times finally came to
Cristo. He had saved his money for years. Because he had learned
the ways of workmen, he was well paid for his knowledge. Now
he was a foreman, a boss.

"Look. I show you."

He drew out a small book that recorded his bank deposits. I
read the figure. It was nearly seven thousand.

"Soon I go back to Villazon," he said. "I buy tobacco
plantation."

For he knew exactly what he wanted. A hundred acres in the
hills above his native village. As a boy he had played in those
hills with his dog. Soon he would return like a hero and bring
prosperity to his family.

"Soon?"

"Soon as I find wife. That is my dream."

"Maybe you won't find her. It may take years."

He shook his head. Now he was ready to find her. He had
money now. That was the difference.

"Mrs. Flores would make a wonderful wife."

"Is not my type."

"What is your type?"

"Is not the type of Mrs. Flores. Is different."

"Where do you look for her?"

"All over Los Angeles. Every night. All day Saturday and
Sunday. I walk in the street, in the stores, I keep looking. In the
show, in the cafe. On Sunday in the church. All over Southern
California I look. Sometimes I go to Long Beach, San Bernardino.
Pretty soon I find her."

"And you want an American girl."

"Must be American. Typical American girl. Was time was
prejudice for Filipino. Is no more. Must be American, for children.
To get pioneers, for plantation."

"Mrs. Flores is American."

"Is not my type," he snapped.

After that, conditions improved for me in the Bunker Hill
house. Cristo left his door open and I was free to use his shower.
He insisted I help myself to the fruit bowl. Usually he returned
from work around six in the evening. Every night he came to

the door and glanced at the new wastebasket Mrs. Flores had supplied. It was usually full of crumpled paper, crushed evidence of another futile day. After a while, showered and dressed, a gala necktie at his throat, Cristo left and I knew he was off to prowl the streets and cafes, searching for his dream woman.

One day he stayed in his room because of a cold. He wasn't seriously ill, merely fretful. Mrs. Flores tried to come in to make his bed but I heard him chase her away crossly.

"You're sick," she said. "Can I help you?"

"No. Is only cold. I wish to be alone."

In a moment Mrs. Flores came to my room. Her face was worried, her eyes gleamed with concern. She held a hot-water bottle and a small package.

"Please," she said. "Will you give him these?"

The package contained mustard plasters and nose drops. I took the stuff to Cristo. He examined everything with a look of horror, sneezed and turned his face away.

"Is crazy, that woman. Here is best thing for cold."

He poured himself a jigger of whisky and swallowed it laboriously.

The next morning he was on his feet again. I heard him bounce out of bed and leave for work. On my way to breakfast I met Mrs. Flores. She couldn't hide her concern.

"How is he?" she asked.

"Cured," I said. "He went to work."

"Then the medicine helped?"

"Just the thing."

She smiled with vast satisfaction. She was happy.

When I came back from breakfast there were some pleasant improvements in my room. The window was hung with fresh white curtains, there was a small hooked rug before my bed, and another chair—a rocking chair.

Cristo Sierra found his dream girl four weeks after I arrived at Mrs. Flores' rooming house. I am sure of the date because my rent was due and I didn't have it.

Somewhere around midnight Saturday Cristo came to my room. I sat in the rocker, reading a stack of futile manuscripts, trying to salvage a few sentences. Cristo was not jubilant over his discovery. He was rather like the buyer of a car who had finally found what he wanted.

"I see her tonight," he said. "Is wonderful. Just what I want."

"What's she like?"

"Is typical American girl."

"Did you talk to her?"

No, he hadn't even met her. He had only seen her at a night club.

"I wish your opinion," he said. "Tomorrow I take you to look at her."

We left the house Sunday night and walked down Angel's Flight to downtown Los Angeles. Cristo was magnificent in a blue gabardine double-breasted suit over a black shirt, and a purple necktie. I felt lowly and threadbare beside him, my shapeless slacks drooping miserably. But I was glad to be away from the house. I couldn't write there. I was thinking of moving.

We took a taxi and drove out to the Sunset Strip. It was a long fare, nearly ten miles. Somewhere along Wilshire Cristo ordered the driver to come to a stop before a flower shop.

"What is good flower for beautiful woman?"

I told him they all like orchids.

He went inside and after five minutes emerged carrying a big box.

"So you got roses," I said.

"Orchids. Is very expensive flower."

"One orchid is plenty."

"For her I buy dozen."

The price would have paid my rent for six weeks. We moved along the Strip now, gaudy neon tubes lighting up the boulevard. Cristo was calm, puffing a cigar as he watched the heavy traffic. He neither looked nor acted romantic. This was business to him.

The place was called The Tampico. We got out and Cristo paid an enormous cabfare. There was a pompous simplicity about The Tampico, even to the snobbish doorman who was plainly annoyed by my formless suit. Cristo entered the place with suave jauntiness. He gave the flowers to the headwaiter, tipped him five dollars and immediately we were seated at a ringside table.

After my little room it was good to be in a place like this — the

244

soothing lights, the music, the perfumed and beautiful women.

"Does she work here?" I said.

He smiled without answering. The dance floor cleared and the floor show began. Then I saw her. She was a torch singer, tall, blonde, marvelously curved beneath silver lamé and with orchids pinned to her hair. She went by the name of Charleen Sharron and she sang in a husky voice of tortured love, the agony of love, and a man named Bill who sometimes beat her but she loved him anyhow. She sang rather well and she was very lovely, but she simply didn't fit as mistress of a tobacco plantation in the Philippine hinterland. I watched Cristo as she sang. His cold appraisal was a little frightening. Nor did he applaud when Charleen Sharron finished her third encore and bowed out. He was more interested in the ovation she received.

"You see," he said, realizing I was still unconvinced. "They like her."

It wasn't any of my business. I was merely the man next door, trying hard to put something on paper. But suddenly I'd had enough of The Tampico, and I stood up.

"Let's get out of here."

We went outside and got into a cab. He leaned back and seemed to wait for me to say something about the singer. But I tricked him. I deliberately said nothing.

Finally he asked, "How you like my woman?"

I shrugged. Already in spirit he possessed her — a girl he had seen but never met. It was hopeless, a small tragedy. Cristo was going to get hurt. Again. I remembered the story of his youth in America, the loneliness, the injury he had suffered because he was of another race, and the hard shell he had nourished to protect himself. Twenty years ago he had come to California from across the Pacific to make his fortune. In toil and in desperation he had survived and made it. The same despair now moved him toward a woman like Charleen Sharron. Cristo's America was a picture-book land. His ideal American woman was a picture-book heroine. She would become his bride, she had to become his bride, because his symbols were mixed. Because, to his way of thinking, she was America. And he wanted to return to Villazon a conqueror with America at his side.

The events of that night left me sleepless and tossing until daybreak. But I wasn't the only one who couldn't sleep. Before dawn I heard it outside in the corridor, the soft padding sound of Mrs. Flores' huaraches. The sound traveled as far as Cristo's door. Then it returned and moved down the stairs.

Then came the love letters. Here is what happened: A couple of nights after we visited The Tampico Cristo showed me a gold cigarette case he had bought for Charleen Sharron. He wanted to send a love note along with it. Would I write it for him?

"I pay you," he said. "Ten dollars."

The rent was overdue. I accepted. I rolled a sheet of paper into my typewriter and wrote that I loved her endlessly, that I worshiped her from afar, that she sang like the wind on a summer night. Cristo was very pleased. He paid me ten dollars immediately. Then he handed me another five.

"Good job," he said. "I give you bonus."

He wrapped the cigarette case for mailing and, signing the letter with his first name only, attached it to the package. I pointed out that he hadn't written his return address. He smiled mysteriously.

"Not yet," he said. "She must not know for few days."

So that was it. I began to understand his plan. In the following two weeks I wrote six love letters to the girl at The Tampico. It was the only writing I did during that time. By now the spark of creation had burned out inside me. A cloying sense of guilt enveloped me. I knew I was a charlatan, selling my meager talent to deceive an innocent person. The very sight of my typewriter made me shudder and, though I ate better than I had in weeks, my spirit slowly expired from hunger. Every letter to Charleen Sharron accompanied some expensive gift—perfume, jewelry, a dozen pairs of nylons.

Finally Cristo came to my room with the most exciting gift of all for his dream girl. It was in a large box and even as he ripped it open I dreaded the sight of its beauty. Somehow I knew this would surpass everything. It was a silver fox cape. I touched it and I was without words.

"Good, yes?"

"This is it," I said. "You can't do more."

"Right. Tonight I tell her who I am. You write big love letter."

It took me two hours to write a one-page note. I was drained out. But it was finally done — the last of Cristo's love letters. It was flat and full of clichés he didn't notice. He signed it with his full name and he wrote his address after it.

"Now we wait for answer."

It came the next afternoon. It was brought by a boy from the telegraph office who was looking for Cristo Sierra. I signed for the message. In the doorway stood Mrs. Flores, her dark eyes penetrating, fluttering in unconcealed distress.

I fingered the telegram in the light of the window. I wanted to open it, to read with my own eyes the rejection of Cristo Sierra by Charleen Sharron. She had to reject him. It couldn't be otherwise. I remembered her as I had seen her at The Tampico, beautiful, voluptuous. Suddenly I recalled something that had completely escaped me until that moment. She was cold — as cold as ice. She was like Cristo. Then I was sure this grotesque romance would be consummated. I lay on the bed and stared at the ceiling. I blamed myself, yet I couldn't understand why I should be miserable at Cristo's happiness.

He came home around seven. I heard him in the next room. I felt his expectancy. He opened the door and peeked inside, grinning.

"Over by the typewriter," I said.

He stood before the telegram rubbing his hands together. He tore open the envelope and read the message, a smile seeping into his face. He handed the message to me and walked out. The telegram was signed by Charleen Sharron. It read: "Please come and see me."

He dressed: the full treatment — tuxedo, black bow tie, patent leather shoes, black topcoat. I watched him take a last look at himself in the mirror. He radiated conquest.

"Let me know how it works out," I said.

"You, I tell first. My friend John Lane," he said. "Good friend."

He meant the letters, I didn't answer. After he was gone I poured myself a drink from his supply of bourbon. It was eight-thirty. This was going to be a long night.

At a quarter to nine I heard the swish of Mrs. Flores' huaraches. She knocked at my door. Until then I had tried to keep her from knowing that I used Cristo's room. I didn't care any more now. After I shouted for her to come in, she opened the door and came through to Cristo's room.

"Good evening," I said.

"Why did you write those letters to that woman?" she asked.

"You've been rummaging through my wastebasket, Mrs. Flores. That's not nice."

"Nice? And you?"

"He paid me to write them."

"And you took the job."

It was impossible to tell her emotion. She didn't appear angry, but she left me uncertain. She moved closer.

"What's she like, this Charleen?"

"Very attractive."

"And I?"

Startled, I looked up at her.

"You're much more than that," I answered.

It pleased her. She sat in the red chair opposite me and crossed her legs. They were firm and smooth and brown.

"I suppose Cristo thinks her a typical American girl."

"His exact words," I said.

"Poor Cristo."

She rose to leave.

"Don't let the rent worry you," she smiled. "I won't throw you out."

I was still thinking of her an hour later, when Cristo's steps sounded in the hall. They were the steps of doom, of defeat, echoing bitter failure. He entered with the gray face of a man who had weathered an ordeal. His arms were loaded with packages. He dumped them into a chair and stood over the mass and I saw again the silver fox cape, the bottles of perfume, the jewelry. He faced me, the hurt deep inside him tightening the muscles around his mouth, his eyes dry and bright and wanting darkness. I got up and walked out of the room. Closing the door, I heard a little gasp of pain. Then he began to cry.

Three days later he was still in his room. I wasn't worried for him; he need the loneliness, the friendship with himself. What disturbed me more was the sudden disappearance of Mrs. Flores. Mr. Ashley was worried about it too. He wanted to call the police.

"I know this town," he said. "Something's happened to her. She's too pretty."

On the fourth night of Cristo's self-imposed exile I began to think Ashley was right.

I knocked on Cristo's door. He opened the door. He looked agitated, restless.

"Mrs. Flores has disappeared," I told him.

"Is bad. Look."

His room was in chaos. The carpets needed sweeping, his studio couch wasn't made up, glasses were scattered on chair arms and ash trays were glutted. The fruit bowl was empty save for apple cores and peach stones. The flowers in the vase were wilted.

"Where she go?"

"Nobody seems to know."

"Bad," he repeated. "Is fine woman."

Back in my room I heard footsteps in the hall — the click of high heels. They stopped before my door. A knock. I opened the door.

A woman stood there, straight and blonde, her yellow hair wind-blown. The dress she wore — it was gold satin, tight and daring — the quick gust of perfume took my breath away. I could only stare.

"Good evening." She smiled.

"Mrs. Flores!"

She stepped inside and I took my time examining her from the toes of her high pumps to the little banner of ribbon in her yellow hair. It was unbelievable, yet there she was. It was a little pathetic too.

"Now what?" I said.

She nodded toward Cristo's door.

I knocked and opened the door. She stood beside me in a kind of gaudy elegance, but I sensed her nervousness as Cristo turned in his chair to look at us.

"I want you to meet a friend," I said.

At first he didn't recognize her. His breath filled his body as he arose. His brown eyes widened. His mouth opened. Bravely she crossed to him, her eyes fixed upon him.

"Hello, Cristo," she said.

"Mrs. Flores! Mrs. Flores!"

He said it over and over, looking at her in unbelief. "Mrs. Flores — why you do this?"

It was an innocent but a brutal question. She put her hand to her mouth as if to hold back her words.

"I'm a fool," she gasped. "Such a fool."

Then she was gone, running out of the room and down the hall. We heard her rushing down the stairs and the click of the lock in her door. Cristo stared after her.

"She is so beautiful," he said. "More beautiful than my Charleen."

"She loves you."

"For me she do this. Change to blonde. Is wonderful. I am big fool. Twenty years in America, I look for wrong thing. Is not clothes. Is not yellow hair. Is love. Is here." He tapped his heart.

"Tell her that, Cristo."

"Make good pioneer."

"Wonderful."

I watched him square his shoulders and stride down the hall. From the top of the stairs I saw him below, knocking at Mrs. Flores' door. It opened and she stood there.

"I wish to make big apology," he said.

"Oh, Cristo!"

She threw her arms around him. I watched them a moment. Then everything cleared in my mind. All those weeks, the things I had to say, the things I wanted to write — I could write them now, the feelings in my blood; they would mix with ink and stretch themselves across fields of white paper. I rushed back to my room and sat down before my typewriter and it flowed like magic.

Helen, Thy Beauty Is to Me —

WHEN LOVE CAME to Julio Sal, he was not prepared. Julio Sal, Filipino boy, forty cents an hour, Tokyo Fish Company, Wilmington. Her name was Helen, she wore a smooth red dress and she worked at the Angels' Ballroom, in Los Angeles. Five feet, four inches was the height of Julio Sal, but when that Helen's golden head lay on his shoulder, strength and grandeur filled his body. A dream shaped itself in his Malay brain. She sensed it too. She always sensed that sort of thing in the Filipino customers. A gallant flame possessed them, and they bought more tickets. The dances were ten cents apiece; she got half of it.

Towering over the golden hair, Julio Sal saw half a hundred of his countrymen gazing after him, watching the serpentine undulations beneath the red dress, watching the fast-diminishing roll of tickets in Helen's left hand. The dances were one minute long. Somewhere behind the four-piece colored band, a bell clanged the end of each number. Since ten o'clock Julio Sal had danced continuously.

Now it was almost midnight. Already he had spent twelve dollars. Forty cents remained in his pocket. It meant four more minutes with the golden hair, and it meant his fare back to the canneries.

The bell clanged, the dance ended, another dance began. In the best alligator style, Julio jittered the dream toward the glass ticket box. Her hand over his shoulder tore a stub from the string and dropped it into the slot.

"Only one left," the girl panted as Julio bounced her in the corner. It was her first word in an hour. Sweat oozed from the dark face of Julio Sal. Again he gazed across the floor at the group of his countrymen.

251

Ten of them strained against the railing, each clutching a fat roll of tickets, ready to rush upon the golden girl the moment Julio's last ticket disappeared inside the glass box. Despair clutched the heart of Julio Sal. Resolution showed in his brown eyes.

"I get some more," he said.

The bell clanged, the dance ended, another dance began. There was a smile on the girl's white, hot face as she dropped the last ticket into the slot. This time it was a waltz, a breathing spell. Julio Sal nodded to the ticket man, who made his way through the couples, coins jingling in his money apron. Dismay seeped into the faces of the Penoys pressed against the rail. Julio's fingers dug into his watch pocket. Surprise widened the blue eyes of Helen when she saw forty cents — nickel, dime and quarter — pinched between Julio Sal's thumb and forefinger.

"Four tickets," said Julio Sal.

The ticket vender rolled a cigar through his teeth. "Only four?"

"Please."

The bell clanged, the dance ended, another dance began. Out of the corner of his eye Julio Sal saw the dismay leave the faces of his little brown brothers. Their smiles mocked him. They had waited so long; they would gladly wait another four dances. The bell clanged, the dance ended, another dance began; again the bell clanged.

"Helen," said Julio Sal. "Helen, I love you, Helen."

"That's nice," she said, because all the Filipinos loved Helen, because all the Filipinos managed to say it when they got down to their last two or three.

"I write you letter," said Julio Sal.

"Please do." Because she always said that; because letters meant that they would be coming back on payday. "Please write."

"You write me too?"

But the bell clanged, the dance ended and he had no more tickets. She slipped from his arms. The wicker gate opened and he was lost in an avalanche of little brown men fighting for the golden girl. Smiling weakly, he stood at the rail and watched her settle her child's face against the chest of Johnny Dellarosa, label machine, Van Camp's, San Pedro. A wave of tenderness suffocated Julio Sal. A small white doll — that was his Helen. The blissful future revealed itself in a reverie that shut out the boogy-woogy and the clanging bell—she was frying his bacon and eggs in a blue-tinted kitchen like in the movie pitch, and he came grinning from the bedroom in a green robe with a yellow sash, like in the move pitch. "Ah, Helen," he was saying to her, "you are most wonderful cook in whole California. Pretty soon we take boat back to Luzon to meet my mamma and papa."

The reverie endured through twenty-five clangs of the bell before he remembered that his pockets were empty and that it was eighteen miles to Wilmington.

On his way out, buttoning his square-cut, shoulder-padded, tight overcoat, Julio Sal paused before a huge photograph of the Angels' Ballroom Staff; forty beautiful girls, forty. She was there, his Helen, her lovely face and slim-hipped figure third from the left, front row.

"Helen, Helen, I love you."

He descended the stairs to Main Street, saw the fog flowing north like a white river. Julio Sal, well-dressed Filipino boy—black serge suit, hand-tailored overcoat, black patent-leather shoes, snappy, short-brimmed hat. Breasting the white river, he walked south on Main Street. Eighteen miles to the harbor. Good. It had been worth while. He breathed fog and cigarette smoke and smiled for his love. Mamma, this is Helen; papa, this is Helen, my wife. The dream held. He couldn't marry her in California. The law said no. They would go to Reno. Or Tijuana. Or Seattle. Work a while up north. Then home to the Philippines. Mamma, this is Helen. Papa, this is Helen.

Eighteen miles to Wilmington.

II

He arrived at six o'clock, his patent-leather shoes in ruins. Behind the cannery, in the duplexes, the five Japanese families were already up, lights from their windows a dull gold in the deep fog.

He smelled the fertilizer vats, the tar, the oil, the copra, the bananas and oranges, the bilge, the old rope, the decaying anchovies, the lumber, the rubber, the salt—the vast bouquet

253

of the harbor. This, too, was part of the dream. While working here at this spot, I met my love—I, Julio Sal.

Like one barefoot, he walked down the long veranda of the flat, salt-blackened building. They were single apartments set like cell blocks—one door, one window; one door, one window. A board creaked beneath his step, a baby wakened and cried. Babies, ah, babies. A little girl, he hoped, with the face and eyes of Mamma Helen.

He lived in the last apartment; he and Silvio Lazada, Pacito Celestino, Manuel Bartolome, Delfin Denisio, Vivente Macario, Johnny Andrino and Fred Bunda—all young men who had come to America as boys in the late 20's.

They were asleep now, the cramped room reeking with the odor of fish, bodies, burned rice and salt air. Bunda, Lazada and Celestino were in the wall bed; Andrino lay on the davenport; Bartolome, Macario and Denisio on the floor. Good boys. Loyal countrymen; though he had been gone all night, none had taken his bed in the bathtub.

On tiptoe he made his way over the sleepers to the bathroom. Through the gray fog-swept light he saw that someone was in the bathtub after all. The sleeper lay deep in blankets, old linen and soiled clothing, his head under the water spouts, his feet on the tub incline. Julio Sal bent down and smiled; it was Antonio Repollo. He had not seen Antonio in two years, not since the Seattle and Alaska canneries. Julio Sal whistled with pleasure. Now his letter-writing problem was solved. Antonio Repollo was a graduate of the University of Washington; he could write beautiful letters. Antonio Repollo was not only a university graduate, he also wrote poetry for El Grafico in Manila.

Julio Sal bent over and shook him awake.

"Antonio, my friend. Welcome."

Repollo turned over, a laundry bag in his arms.

"Antonio, is me. Julio Sal. I have girl."

"Is American?" asked Repollo.

"Is blonde," said Julio Sal. "Is wonderful."

"Is bad," said Antonio.

"No," said Julio Sal. "Is good, very good."

"Is very bad," said Repollo. "Is worst thing possible."

"No," said Julio Sal. "Is best thing possible."

He slipped into his greasy dungarees, found a clean shirt behind the kitchen door, and put that on too. It was Vivente Macario's turn to cook breakfast. Since 1926, at the asparagus fields, the celery fields, the canneries from Alaska to San Diego, Vivente Macario always prepared the same breakfast when his turn came — warmed-over rice, three cans of sardines stolen from the cannery, a hunk of bread and tea. They sat around the knife-scarred breakfast nook and ate quietly over a table whose surface was a mass of initials and dates of the hundreds of Filipino cannery workers who had come and gone throughout the years.

His brown face glowing from cold water, Antonio Repollo came into the kitchen. The poet, the college man. He was here, in their house, and they were honored; had even provided him with a bathtub in which to sleep. They made a place for him at the table, watched his long beautiful fingers remove sardines from the can.

"Julio Sal," he said, "what is the name of the woman?"

"Is Helen."

"Helen? No more? No Anderson, no Smith, Brown?"

"No more. Helen, all the same. Helen."

"He has girl," explained Repollo." Name of Helen. He wish to marry this girl. American girl."

"No good," said Fred Bunda.

"Crazy," said Delfin Denisio.

"Too much trouble" — Johnny Andrino.

"Helen?" Manuel Bartolome talking. "Is not same Helen for to work Angels' Ballroom, taxi dance?"

"Ya, ya," said Julio Sal. "She is him, all the same."

Bartolome sucked his big lips tight. "Is no good, this woman. Cannot be. For to marry, I try myself. She damn liar. You give money, she take. Give you nothing."

"No, no," smiled Julio Sal. "Is another Helen. This one, she is good. This one love. She like me. She say 'write letter.' This I am do tonight."

"Gnah," said Bartolome, coughing an evil memory from his mouth. "For why you believe that? Is applesauce. I am write letter, too — six times. She take my money, give nothing. She no love you, Julio Sal. She no marry Filipino. She take his money, but she no marry. Is not love. Is business."

The strong fist of Julio Sal whacked the table. "I make her love me. You wait. You see. Pretty soon, three months, cannery close down. I have money. We go for to get married. Reno, Seattle."

"Is bad," said Pacito Celestino.

"Crazy," said Vivente Macario.

"Is terrible," said Delfin Denisio. "Is awful."

"Is love," said Julio Sal. "Is wonderful!"

III

Said Julio Sal to Antonio Repollo, "You will write letter for me tonight, yes?"

Said Antonio Repollo, "No."

It was evening. The poet, Antonio Repollo, sat before his portable typewriter, line upon line of typescript rattling across the page. The fog had cleared. The moon showed big and yellow, rising over the American-Hawaiian docks.

"I am disappoint," said Julio Sal. "I write letter myself."

He asked for paper, and Repollo gave it to him. He asked for a fountain pen, and got that too. He sat across from the poet, his tongue making a bulge against his cheek. A half hour passed. Sweat broke out upon the brow of Julio Sal; the paper before him was white and untouched. Pleading eyes observed the dancing fingers of Antonio Repollo.

Said Julio Sal, pushing the paper away, "I cannot do. Is too hard to write."

Said Repollo, "You are a fool, Julio Sal. Sixteen years ago in Hawaii I say to you: 'Go to school, Julio Sal. Learn to read English, learn to write English; it come in handy someday.' But no, you work in the pineapple, you make money, you play Chinee lottery, you shoot crap, you lose the cockfights. You have no time for American school. Me, I am different. I have big education. I am graduate, University of Washington. Maybe next year we go to Pasadena for the Rose Bowl."

"Maybe I write the Spanish."

"This Helen, she is Spanish?"

"No. She is American."

"What for you write Spanish?"

"I cannot write the English. I write the Spanish. Maybe she have Spanish friend."

"Fool, Julio Sal. Fool you are."

Julio felt tears stinging his eyes. "Is true, Antonio. I am make big mistake. You write for me letter. Next year I go for the school."

"I work hard for education. For write, I get paid. El Grafico, she pay me, for poetry, ten cents a word. For prose, one cents. First-class rates."

"I pay you, Antonio. Write beautiful letter. I pay you first-class rates. How much for this, Antonio?"

"For letter, prose composition, is one cents a word. Same rates I get, El Grafico."

Antonio rolled a clean sheet of paper under the platen and began to write. Julio Sal stood behind him and watched the letters dance across the white background.

"Good," said Julio. "Is wonderful. Write whole lots, Antonio. I pay one penny for the word."

The creative instinct in Antonio Repollo at once grew cold. He swung around and shook his hand under the fine nose of Julio Sal. "How do you know is good or bad? You cannot read the English good. How you know this?"

"She look good, Antonio. Look fine."

"I read to you," said Antonio. "I wish to give satisfaction all the time." As though harking to a distant foghorn, Julio Sal looked out the window and listened as Antonio read:

"Dear Miss Helen: The Immortal Bard has said, 'What's in a name?' I concur. And though I know not how you are yclept for a surname, it matters little. Oh, Miss Helen! Lugubrious is often the way of amour; profound its interpretations; powerful its judgments. Oh, bright Diana of the Dance! My love for you is like a muted trumpet sobbing among the brasses. Destiny has brought us together, and the aroma of devotion rises from your Humble Servant—"

Julio Sal shook his head. "Is no good, Antonio. Is terrible. Steenk."

"Is wonderful!" shouted Repollo. "Better than my stuff for El Grafico!"

Julio Sal sighed at the moon. "Antonio, you write, I talk. You put 'em down what I say."

A haughty shrug from Antonio. He lifted his palms. "As you wish, Julio. Same price for dictation. One cents a word."

Julio Sal was not listening. Both hands were cupped at his heart as the moonlight bathed his brown eyes. "Oh, lovely Helen!" He spoke in his native Tagalog. "Oh, wonderful moon girl! Thy beams have filled my soul with wild pleasure. Could I but kneel at thy feet in worship, the hem of thy red gown in these unworthy hands, I should die for joy. Many there are who are worthier than Julio Sal, but no man can say he loves you more. My wish and my hope is that you will become my bride. Back to the beloved motherland we will go, there to live forever beneath the coconut palms of beautiful Luzon. My wealthy father and mother shall welcome you to their plantation of fifteen thousand acres — rice, dates, pineapples and coconuts. Over it all you shall reign like a queen to the end of your days."

That was too much for Antonio Repollo. "You lie, Julio Sal. Your mamma and papa are peasants. They are poor people, Julio Sal. You betray them with such lies. You make them capitalist dogs. Caciques."

"You write," said Julio Sal. "I am pay one penny for the word. You write 'em down."

Repollo wrote it down, wrote three hundred and fifty-six words in all. They counted them together — three dollars and fifty-six cents. Expensive. But Antonio made no charge for punctuation marks, for "a" and "an," nor for the envelope, or for addressing it to Miss Helen, in care of the Angels' Ballroom, Los Angeles. Julio Sal was pleased with the cool, clean typescript and the boldness of his signature at the bottom, underscored three times, with a whirlwind flourish of curlicues.

"I pay," said Julio Sal, "come payday."

It came six days later, and Julio Sal paid thirteen dollars and eighty cents for that letter and three more. Even so, he managed to save another fifteen, for it had been a big week, with overtime. She did not answer his letters. But he could understand that;

the life of a taxi dancer was not an easy one — to dance by night, to sleep by day, with never a moment to herself. All that was going to be changed someday. Pretty soon — after the tuna.

He saved his money. Was Betty Grable playing at The Harbor? All the little brown men loved Betty Grable; her autographed photograph hung over the kitchen sink; en masse they went to see her picture. All but Julio Sal. Seated on a piling at Dock 158, he smoked a cheap cigar and watched the stevedores load the President Hoover, bound for Hawaii and the Philippines. Came Madeleine Carroll, Virginia Bruce, Carole Lombard, Anita Louise — big favorites with the Penoys. But Julio Sal stayed home. There was the night Sixto Escobar fought Baby Pacito at the Hollywood Legion. And the night the bolo-punching Ceferino Garcia flattened Art Gonzales to the cries of "Boola, boola!" from his countrymen in the gallery. Where was Julio Sal? At home, saving his money.

IV

In September the tuna disappeared. And where does the tuna go, when he goes? No one can say. Overnight the roaring canneries shut down. No fish, no work. If wise, the Filipino boy had saved his money. Maybe he had three hundred, maybe five.

Home now? Back to Luzon and Ilocos Norte? No, not yet. Big money up north in the crops — lettuce, prunes, hops, olives, grapes, asparagus, walnuts, melons. Take rest, few days. Go to Los Angeles, see some girls, buy some clothes, chip in together and buy big car, ride down Hollywood Boulevard, maybe see Carole Lombard, maybe Anita Louise, can't tell. Then to the great agricultural centers of the north. Merced, Stockton, Salinas, Marysville, Woodland, Watsonville. Good-by to friends and fellow workers — to Celestino, Bartolome, Bunda, Denisio, Lazada, Macario. See you up north.

Said Antonio Repollo to Julio Sal that last day, "The prunes, she is good in Santa Clara County. You come with me?"

Said Julio Sal, "No. I go to Los Angeles for to get Helen. We go to Reno, maybe. For to get married."

259

Said Repollo, "You have letter then? She say yes?"

"No letter. Just the same, we get married."

"Maybe," said Repollo, not meaning it.

"No maybe. Is truth. You wait. You see. Pretty soon Mrs. Julio Sal, with ring."

"You have money, Julio Sal? Costa plenty for to have American wife."

"Three hundred fifty, I have."

"Is very small amount."

"Is plenty. I get some more in the crops."

Repollo took out his wallet. "I loan you twenty buck. After asparagus you pay me back."

"Is plenty, three hundred fifty."

Repollo held out a five-dollar bill. "This, for the wedding present. Some chocolate. Compliments, Antonio Repollo."

Mist welled up in the eyes of Julio Sal. He folded the greenback and wet his lips. "You are good Filipino, Repollo. Smart man. I tell Helen. Maybe someday I tell her you write letter on the machine—someday, maybe. *Gracias*, my friend."

"Is nothing," said Repollo. "For that I am A. B., University of Washington. Pretty soon we play Minnesota; we win maybe."

When he left the apartment that last time, a grip in each hand, his topcoat over his shoulder, he smelled sweet and clean, did Julio Sal, and he knew that, according to the pictures in Esquire, he was sartorially correct, even to the tan golf sweater that matched his light brown tie. There was one slight imperfection in his ensemble—his brown shoes. They had been half-soled.

It was forty minutes to town by way of the big red cars. At a quarter to one Julio Sal was on Hill Street. On the corner, there in the window, a pair of shoes caught his eye. They were light brown, a pock-marked pigskin, moccasin type, light soles, box toes. Fifteen dollars was the price beneath the velvet stand. Julio Sal bit his lips and tried to hold down his Spanish-Malay passion for bright leather. But it was a losing battle. Relishing his own weakness, he walked through the glass doors and stepped into a fragrant, cool world of leather and worsteds, silks and cashmere.

At two-thirty the new Julio Sal strutted up Hill Street with the grandeur of a bantam cock. The new shoes made him taller; the new gabardine slacks gave him a sense of long, virile steps; the new sport coat, belted and pleated in back, built him into a wedge-shaped athlete; the soft wool sweater scarcely existed, it was so soft, so tender. That new hat! Dark green with a lighter band, high crown, short brim, pulled over one eye. At every window Julio Sal watched himself passing by, wished the folks back in Luzon could but see him passing by. The transformation had cost him a hundred and twenty-five. No matter.

Said Julio Sal to the handsome Filipino flashing past the shop windows, "Is better first to become engaged. Wait few months. Hops in Marysville. Asparagus in Stockton. Big money. After asparagus we get married."

The idea came to him suddenly, giving warmth to his conscience. But the coldness of guilt made him shudder. The first jewelry store in sight swallowed him up. An engagement ring. He was not happy when he walked into the hot street again, his purse thinner by seventy-five dollars. He felt himself falling to pieces with a suddenness that left him breathing through his mouth. Crossing to Pershing Square, he got no pleasure from his new clothes as he sat in the sun. A deep loneliness held him. What was the matter with Julio Sal? This Helen—not once had she answered his letter. He was a fool. Bartolome had warned him. But what was Filipino boy to do? For every Filipino girl in California there were twenty-two Filipino boys. The law made it so, and the law said Filipino boy could not marry white girl. What was Filipino boy to do? But Helen was different. Helen was taxi-dance girl. Working girl. Big difference. At once he felt better. He got up and walked toward Main Street, proud of his new clothes again.

V

First at the ticket window of the Angels' Ballroom that night was Julio Sal. It was a few minutes before seven. He bought a hundred tickets. On the stand, the four-piece colored band was tuning up. As yet, the girls had not come out of the dressing rooms. Julio Sal followed the wicker fence down to the bandstand, six feet from the dressing-room door. Then the band began to play the blatant hotcha wired down to a loud-speaker that spewed it in all directions out on the street.

By seven-fifteen the noise had lured five Filipinos, three Mexicans, two sailors and an Army private. The dressing-room door opened and the girls began to appear. Among the first was Helen.

Said Julio Sal, waving his tickets, "Hello."

"Be right with you," she said.

He watched her walk to the bandstand and say something to the trumpet player. She had changed in three months — changed a great deal. The memory he retained was of a girl in red. Tonight she wore a blue pleated chiffon that spilled lightly to her shoes. Something else — her hair. It had been a golden blond; now it was platinum. He had no time to decide whether or not he liked the changes, for now she was coming toward him.

"Hi. Wanna dance?"

"Helen, is me. Julio Sal."

The bell clanged and she did not hear him. Hurrying to the gate, he felt his legs trembling. She met him there, flowed into his arms professionally, yet like a warm wind. It was a waltz. She danced easily, methodically, with a freshness that made him feel she enjoyed it. But she did not remember him — he was sure of it. He was about to speak his own name when she looked up and smiled. It was friendly, but there was some peculiarity about it, an iciness in her blue eyes that made him suddenly conscious of his race, and he was glad she did not remember Julio Sal.

"You been here before?"

"First time," he said.

"Seems like I seen you someplace."

"No, no. First time here."

Gradually the place filled. They were mostly Filipinos. For an hour they danced, until he began to tire. Beyond the wicker fence were a bar and tables. He felt the pinch of his new shoes and longed to sit down. It made no difference. Dancing or sitting with her, the price was the same — ten cents a minute.

"I buy you a drink," he said.

They walked off the floor to the tables. Each was marked with a Reserved card. The waiter standing at the end of the bar dashed forward and yanked the card from the table where they sat. The bell clanged. The girl tore a ticket from the roll and stuffed it into a blue purse that matched her dress. Her small fingers tightened at his wrist.

"What's your name?"

"Tony," he said. "Is Tony Garcia."

"I like Tony. It's a swell name."

The waiter was tall, Kansas-like, tough, impersonal.

"Something to drink?" said Julio Sal. "What you like?"

She lowered her face, then looked up with blue, clean eyes. "Could I have something nice, Tony? Champagne?" She took his head in her hands, pulled it against her lips and whispered into his ear, "I get a percentage." He already knew that, but the touch of her lips, the warmth of her breath at his neck, the scent of her perfume, left him deliriously weak. The bell clanged and she tore away another ticket.

"Champagne," said Julio Sal.

"It's seven bucks," the waiter said.

"Seven?" Julio rubbed his jaw, felt soft, cool fingers under the table, squeezing his knee. He looked at the girl. Her face and eyes were downcast, her lips smiling impishly.

"Champagne."

They waited in silence. Four times the bell sounded and four times Helen's crimson nails tore at the thinning roll of tickets. The waiter came back with two glasses and a bottle on a tray. He gave Julio Sal a slip of paper.

"Nine?" said Julio Sal. "But you say seven."

"Cover charge."

"Is too much for to pay, only little bottle wine."

The waiter picked up the tray and started back to the bar. Julio called to him. "I pay," he said.

After he paid, the cork popped. Julio lifted his glass, touched hers. "For you, for prettiest girl in whole California."

"You're sweet," she said, drinking.

Julio tested the wine with his teeth and tongue. Only fair. He had tasted better in San Jose, and for a third of the price. The bell clanged, the red nails nibbled, a new dance began. It was a waltz, Blue Hawaii.

Helen's eyes closed; she sighed and swayed to the music. "My favorite number. Dance with me, Tony."

They walked to the floor and she pressed herself hard against his body. The bell clanged as they reached the orchestra. She tore away another ticket and spoke to the trumpet player. The next three numbers were repeats of Blue Hawaii. Julio Sal was very pleased. She liked the music of the islands. She would like the music of the Philippines better.

She clung to his arm as they walked back to the table. The wine glasses were gone, the bottle of champagne was gone. Once more the table was marked Reserved. Julio Sal called the waiter.

"I thought you beat it," the waiter said.

"No, no. Only to dance a little bit."

"That's tough."

"But she was whole bottle. Only little bit, we drink."

"Sorry."

"Bring 'nother bottle," demanded Julio Sal.

They sat down, Helen holding the few remaining tickets like beads. "It's a shame," she said. "We hardly tasted it."

"No shame. We get more."

The waiter brought another bottle and two glasses. He handed Julio Sal another piece of paper, but Julio wouldn't accept it; he pushed it away, he shook his head. "I already pay. This one for nothing."

"Gotta pay."

"No. You cheat me. Nine dollars, not one drink."

The waiter leaned across the table and the waiter's thick hand clutched the throat of Julio Sal, pushed back his head. "I don't have to take that kind of talk from a Filipino. Take it or leave it."

Nausea flowed up and down the bones of Julio Sal—shame and helplessness. He smoothed back his ruffled hair and kept his wild eyes away from Helen, and when the bell clanged he was glad she busied herself tearing off another ticket.

The waiter cursed and walked away. Julio Sal panted and stared into his calloused hands. It wasn't the waiter and it wasn't the nine dollars, but why had she tricked him with three encores of Blue Hawaii? Julio Sal wanted to cry. Then there were cool fingers on the back of his hand, and he saw her sweet face.

264

"Forget it," she said. "I can do without, if I have to."

But Julio Sal no longer cared, not even for himself.

"Waiter," he said.

That night Julio Sal drank five bottles of champagne, drank most of it himself, yet the bitterness within him remained dry and aching, and drunkenness did not come. There was only thirst and desire, and a salty satisfaction in playing the fool. At midnight he stared in fascination as the red nails clawed the three hundredth ticket. Sometimes she said, "Wanna dance?" and sometimes he asked, "Drink?" Sometimes she squeezed his hand and asked, "Having a good time?" And always he answered, "Very good time."

Searching for a match, his fingers touched something hard and square in his pocket.

He brought out the jewel box that held the engagement ring. It was a single diamond set in white gold. He held it under her eyes.

"You like?"

"Beautiful."

"I buy for girl. She die."

"Automobile accident?"

"Just die. Sick. You want ring, you keep."

"I couldn't."

He slipped it on her finger. She tilted it to and from the light, laughing as it sparkled.

Three times the bell clanged, but she forgot the roll of tickets. Then she looked at him again, studied his delicate nose, his fine lips. She lifted his hand and pressed a kiss into the calloused palm.

"You can take me home. That is, if you want to."

He stared into his empty glass, twirled it around and smiled at the memory of the little speech he had prepared that afternoon, the words he planned to say when he slipped the ring on her finger.

"Don't you want to?"

"I like, very much."

"Do you have a car?"

"We take taxi."

265

She pushed her chair closer to him, so that they sat crowded side by side. She held his hand in both of hers, pressed it, played absently with his fingers.

When he suggested one more bottle of champagne, she frowned. "It's for suckers."

"I am sucker."

"You're not either. You're nice," she said.

"I have friend," he said. "Name Julio Sal. He know you."

"The guy that writes all them crazy letters? He must be nuts."

"Ya. He nuts."

He looked at the clock over the bar and wanted to sigh; instead a sob shook itself from his throat. It was twelve-thirty. The dream was dead.

"I wait for you at door downstairs," he said.

He got up and left her sitting there. It was warm in the street. He walked a few doors north to a small, hole-in-the-wall, all-night grocery store. Boxes of figs and grapes were tilted toward the street. The sight of them increased the acrid, cigarette-and-champagne dryness of his mouth. He bought a bunch of grapes for a nickel, waved the clerk aside about a paper sack. The grapes were Black Princes, big and meaty.

He put one of them into his mouth, felt it burst between his teeth, tasted the sweet juice that filled his mouth. A grape from Sonoma County, from the vineyards around Santa Rosa. He had picked grapes in Sonoma—who could say, perhaps from the very vine upon which this bunch had grown.

Eating grapes, Julio Sal walked a block to the Terminal Building, took his overcoat and grips from the ten-cent lockers, went down the stairs to Los Angeles Street and the bus depot. The ticket agent nodded.

"One-way ticket Santa Rosa," said Julio Sal.

266

Printed January 1985 in Santa Barbara &
Ann Arbor for the Black Sparrow Press by
Graham Mackintosh & Edwards Brothers Inc.
Design by Barbara Martin. This edition is
published in paper wrappers; there are 500
cloth trade copies; & 50 copies handbound in
boards by Earle Gray have been numbered
& signed by the author.

JOHN FANTE was born in Colorado in 1909. He attended parochial shool in Boulder and Regis High School, a Jesuit boarding school. He also attended the University of Colorado and Long Beach City College.

Fante began writing in 1929 and published his first short story in *The American Mercury* in 1932. He had no difficulty in getting into print and published numerous short stories in *The Atlantic Monthly*, *The American Mercury*, *The Saturday Evening Post*, *Collier's*, *Esquire*, and *Harper's Bazaar*. His first novel, *Wait Until Spring, Bandini*, was published in 1938. The following year *Ask the Dust* appeared. (Both novels have been reprinted by Black Sparrow Press.) In 1940 a collection of his short stories, *Dago Red*, was brought out by Viking Press. *Full of Life* appeared in 1952, and *The Brotherhood of the Grape* in 1977.

Meanwhile Fante had been occupied extensively in screenwriting. Some of his credits include *Full of Life*, *Jeanne Eagles*, *My Man and I*, *The Reluctant Saint*, *Something for a Lonely Man*, *My Six Loves*, and *Walk on the Wild Side*.

John Fante was stricken with diabetes in 1955 and its complications brought about blindness in 1978, but he continued to write by dictation to his wife, Joyce, and the result was *Dreams from Bunker Hill* (Black Sparrow, 1982). He died at the age of 74 on May 8, 1983.